A TASTE OF DECEIT

VALERIE KEOGH

BLOODHOUND
— BOOKS —

www.bloodhoundbooks.com

Print ISBN 978-1-914614-72-9

ALSO BY VALERIE KEOGH
BOOKS PUBLISHED BY BLOODHOUND BOOKS

THE DUBLIN MURDER MYSTERIES

No Simple Death

No Obvious Cause

No Past Forgiven

No Memory Lost

No Crime Forgotten

No Easy Answer

PSYCHOLOGICAL THRILLERS

The Three Women

The Perfect Life

The Deadly Truth

The Little Lies

The Lies He Told

The Couple in the Photograph

For my niece, Eilis Hudson, with love.

CHAPTER ONE

Perhaps sex shouldn't be on my mind, I was certain it wasn't on Kasper's. Our earlier row had left me tingling with sexual frustration, deprived of our usual great make-up sex not only by the hundreds of miles I had put between us, but because of all that had happened before.

Buying the ridiculously expensive cottage in the Cotswolds had been my idea so it was only right I should use it as an escape. I fled there and left my husband, Kasper, in London.

I had lusted after a place in the country since friends had bought one in the Cotswolds town of Broadway. They had invited us for a weekend to indulge ourselves in far-reaching views, babbling brooks, tall leafy trees, peace and quiet. I had opened one of the mullioned windows, leaned out, and taken a deep breath of air filled with the scent of a nearby magnolia tree in full bloom. It was all so perfectly idyllic I'd immediately wanted a similar retreat.

It took a month before I was able to persuade Kasper it would be a good idea, painting a picture of weekends away from London noise and pollution, of afternoon tea parties on the lawn, the women in floaty floral dresses, the men wearing straw boaters. Kasper, raising an eyebrow at the idea of wearing a hat, had finally agreed it would be a pleasant diversion. He gave the go-ahead to spend almost three hundred grand of what he always referred to as his hard-earned dosh on a house only half a mile from the centre of Broadway.

The traditional nineteenth century terraced cottage – rather smaller than I'd wanted, with its cosy living room and separate compact dining room – was as much as the paltry sum of money Kasper would commit to would buy. The extended kitchen was the best part of the cottage. It opened onto a patio overlooking an impressively long garden planted with a profusion of fruit trees. Upstairs, there was a main bedroom with an en suite, one smaller bedroom and a tiny bathroom.

Kasper, who didn't see it until after we'd signed the contracts, was horrified at the size of the property. 'It's miniscule! I thought my buck would have a lot more bang than this outside the capital.'

'This is the Cotswolds, darling. Premium properties come with premium prices.' I had been too busy with a measuring tape to worry about his reservations. Too engrossed in my dreams and plans to admit he was right. A month later, the cottage was furnished to my taste. 'Luxury country,' I'd explained to friends. 'We'll have you all down for a visit.'

But that was before Covid and its restrictions changed our lives.

'Soon,' I'd said to our friends.

When the first lockdown eased, I drove to Broadway for the day to check the cottage was okay, walked around the small, beautifully furnished rooms, then shut the door and motored back to London.

It was another month before Kasper and I headed to the Cotswolds for a weekend, desperate for a change of scenery even if that meant swapping our spacious apartment for the smaller confines of the cottage. Unfortunately, our timing was off. It had been raining for days, the windscreen wipers swishing to and fro as they battled the driving rain on the slow Friday afternoon exit from London. It wasn't a good start and it was destined to get worse.

Kasper's fingers tapped impatiently on the steering wheel as the car crawled along. 'Did you talk to Hazel about meeting up while we're there?'

Unfortunately, Hazel, and her husband Lewis, these friends whose house purchase in the town had spurred me to follow suit, had packed themselves off to their villa in Portugal at the first hint of the virus and had been holed up there ever since. 'They're in Portugal.'

'Portugal!' He flicked me a look. 'Lucky them.'

The rain didn't let up the entire journey. We parked on the road outside the cottage and dashed through a deluge to the front door where water was dripping from the gutter overhead. Large dollops landed with a plop on the step beside me as I slid the key into the lock and pushed. As an interior designer, I had appreciated the beautiful original oak door when I first saw the cottage. Its age, its fabulous patina. But as a wet irate owner wrestling with rain-swollen wood, I yearned for uPVC. While I struggled, Kasper stood behind me muttering.

It wasn't a good start to the weekend.

Thanks to Covid, there were no restaurants open in the town and I hadn't thought to bring food with us. A five-minute internet search later, I discovered some of the restaurants were doing takeaways. Unfortunately, the first ones I tried were too busy to accept another order. Kasper was perched on the edge of a sofa that was too small for his six-foot-two height. He glowered at me as I hung up and peered at my iPad for the number of the next restaurant. Luckily, this one, my last hope, resulted in success.

'Collect only, I'm afraid,' I was informed when I asked for our order to be delivered.

The restaurant was almost a mile away. Rain was hammering on the front window, a wind whistling down the chimney. It wasn't a night for going outside for any reason apart from hunger, but I wasn't planning on needing to. 'They want us to collect it.' I lifted my dainty sandal-shod foot. 'I suppose I could go...'

Kasper stood with a grunt of exasperation. 'Right, what's the name of this damn place then?'

I gave him a grateful kiss on the cheek. 'I'll have a glass of red waiting for you when you get back.' I'd brought down several bottles on my previous visit. There was no need to tell Kasper I'd also brought heavier walking shoes which were tucked away in the bottom of the wardrobe. I listened to him muttering as he pulled on the coat he'd left hanging in the porch and I smiled.

It was only seven, but ominous clouds and heavy rain made it feel later. It was chilly, too, and I regretted not bringing coal or wood. It would have been nice to light the fire. Hindsight, it was a useless tool.

Heavier rain pelted the window. Kasper would be soaked. And understandably grumpy. It was time to do some damage limitation. Hurrying upstairs, I grabbed a couple of fluffy bath towels and a heavy cotton bathrobe. Back in the living room, I laid them over the arm of the sofa, then switched on the lamps to lend a warm atmosphere to the chilly room. There were candles in a kitchen drawer, I fetched a handful and set them into the empty fireplace.

With them lit, and more positioned around the room where their flames reflected in the windows and made the raindrops glisten, it looked so much better. Perhaps the weekend wouldn't be a complete disaster.

CHAPTER TWO

It was almost an hour before I heard Kasper's hand slap wetly against the front door and I hurried to open it. The sight of him, hair plastered to his head, a drip wobbling on the end of his nose, his pale-grey jacket, now steel-grey wet, almost dragged a laugh from me but it seemed unnecessarily cruel so I swallowed it down.

Kasper's large cold-reddened hands were clutching a brown paper bag to his chest. Not designed to cope with the rain, it was already disintegrating, the sides of it turned to brown mush.

'There was no parking outside the blasted restaurant.' He wiped rain from his face. Water dripped from his jacket onto the tiled floor of the porch.

'Give me the food.' I took it through to the kitchen and dropped it on the table then hurried back to make sure Kasper removed his shoes before stepping onto the cream carpet.

He'd hung up his coat and kicked his shoes off, but in the living room he flicked a hand through his wet hair, droplets of water peppering the Farrow and Ball school-house-white walls. I wanted to yell at him to be careful, to be more considerate. Biting my tongue, I handed him the towel I'd left ready. 'Poor darling, dry yourself off, and here–' I handed him the robe. '– why don't you change into this, you'll be nice and cosy then.'

Too cold to argue, he did what I suggested and took the towel. A minute later he was rubbing it over his naked body, his wet clothes in a pile on the floor behind him.

Even wet, cold and looking more than a little grumpy, I still thought he was the most handsome man I'd ever seen... and I'd seen my share. Tall and muscular, tight dark curling hair covered his chest, the same dark hair slicked back from a high forehead. Blue eyes and ridiculously long eyelashes completed what I, and any woman with a beating heart, would classify as drop-dead gorgeous. I'd always been considered tall but against his six-two, my five-ten felt petite. We looked good together, his darkness a striking contrast to my blonde hair and pale skin.

We'd been married a year. A second marriage for us both, my first ending in an acrimonious divorce three years before, his when his wife was killed in a hit and run. Neither of our marriages had resulted in children, theirs despite trying, mine because children didn't appeal.

Kasper and I had a good relationship, made better by periods of time apart. His role as legal consultant to an international property company frequently took him away on business. I'd gone with him a few times but the novelty of days on my own in a strange city soon wore thin. Now I rarely went with him unless I wanted to shop in New York or Milan.

My role as partner in an interior design business ended with my divorce when my ex bought me out. I used the money to visit far-flung friends while I considered my options and returned to London after almost a year away with a half-hearted idea of setting up on my own. But then I'd met Kasper, and everything changed.

I'd travelled the world, met all sorts and knew a good 'un when I saw him.

He was still grieving for his wife when we met, but I knew he was destined to be my happy ever after.

I knew it the first time I saw him.

———

That weekend was the only one Kasper and I had spent together in the cottage in Broadway. It wasn't a colossal success; in fact it was what my friend Tracy Robinson called an "unmitigated disaster" when I told her it had rained solidly for the two days we were there.

'Rain like you've never seen, Tracy. Heavy, relentless. And the cloud was so low and dark that we needed the lights on the whole time. Then, as if things weren't bad enough, the newsagent's in the town had to shut when one of its staff tested positive for Covid. Poor Kasper had to drive for miles to get a Saturday paper. I think he drank a bottle of wine when he got back.'

'Not your best idea then.'

My friend was the mistress of the understatement. 'No. And now we're stuck in London for the foreseeable.'

Locked in. Together. I hadn't realised how much I relished my solitude, my freedom, until Covid kept Kasper in London. He had a home office, of course, and stayed in it most of the time, but apart from the occasional business meeting in the city, he was there, hampering my freedom. Plus, for Zoom calls to the US and Japan he was working crazy hours, staying up late or getting up early. Disturbing me.

I could have been nice, made allowances for the strange times we lived in, compromised more. But nice had been slapped out of my vocabulary years before. Literally. To this day, when I heard the word, I winced. My mother was a proponent of her own particular theory that lessons instilled with the accompaniment of pain were more likely to be remembered. 'Nice girls get left behind,' she'd say, raising her hand to lay the flat of it against my face with a force that almost knocked me off my feet. The sting of it would last as her words wormed their way into my brain. *Nice doesn't get you happy ever after. Whack. Nice is for fools. Whack.*

Only once in all those years of her *lessons* did I try to duck out of the reach of her swinging hand. Once, but never again... she caught me by my hair and pulled me closer so that we were nose to nose. Then she pushed me away... held me there by my hair while she slapped and slapped and slapped...

So it probably isn't surprising that I wasn't keen on being *nice*.

Many people's relationships flourished under lockdown conditions. Ours struggled. We'd have got back on track eventually. I knew where my future lay... with Kasper in our fabulous penthouse apartment... and I'd have worked hard on it once we returned to some semblance of normality, and by that I meant his spending days abroad again.

It wasn't the struggle to keep going that sent me fleeing to Broadway.

It was that final row.

CHAPTER THREE

B roadway with Kasper's company was one thing but being there on my own was something else altogether. Dull, boring, lonely. On the fourth day, when I found myself watching a mindless quiz show on TV, I knew I had to find something to entertain me. Something to keep my mind from drifting back to the last few hours with Kasper.

The sun was shining as I walked the length of the high street. Broadway was an exceptionally pretty town with some strikingly attractive Cotswold stone buildings. I slowed as I passed the stunning house I'd admired on previous wanderings, its honey-coloured stone enhanced by the bright sunshine. According to a worn wooden sign attached to the front gate pillar, it was called Broadway Manor. A dull name for such a fine house.

I stared in fascination at the tall leaded windows, the oak door set back in an arched stone entrance, the chimneys that soared from multiple points on the high gabled roof. A small garden to the front was planted with box hedge, a standard bay tree stood in a pot to each side of the entrance. All well-maintained if a little predictable. I imagined there would be an impressive garden to the rear. The house was set only a few feet back from the road but, try as I could, my curious eyes were prevented even a glimpse thanks to those leaded windows.

A little further along, however, the stunning Lygon Arms Hotel was somewhere I could enter. Masked, of course. It was as lovely inside as out, and I'd have liked to have sat and had a drink, lunch maybe, or dinner. But not on my own. Instead, as I had on a previous visit, I strolled around admiring the décor and left again.

Opposite the hotel there was a row of surprisingly upmarket shops few of which were open and I gazed at their displays feeling like a child looking into a sweet-shop window.

It showed the level of my boredom that I stopped at the newsagent's and read each of the many notices and adverts that were affixed to the inside of the window with tape. It was the usual bizarre collection. Cottages to let, kittens free to a good home, free-range eggs for sale, cleaner wanted – some of the notices so old the tape was brown and curling at the edges. The one that made me stop, stare, and reread looked relatively recent.

Craft your way to sanity!
Bring your craftwork along and join like-minded folk.
Whether your thing is knitting, crochet, sewing, art or anything else, all are welcome.
A maximum of 6 people.
Contact details below.

As an interior designer, I certainly appreciated craftwork but the thought of sitting around in a circle of women with needles click-clicking and mouths blab-blabbing didn't appeal to me. Bored as I was, had the world been normal I'd never have considered joining such a group. Two things persuaded me.

The first was the world was a long way from normal and I couldn't survive many more days living in a small town without someone to talk to. The second was the address on the bottom of the notice. *Broadway Manor*. The house I'd admired. The outside was tantalising, I yearned to see the inside. Was this my opportunity?

I pulled out my mobile and snapped a photo of the notice. It was worth considering.

At the war memorial I turned for the walk home, slowing almost to a stop as I passed the manor house again. It was such a fantastic building, a night of clicking and blabbing seemed a fair trade for the opportunity to explore the interior.

Back in my cosy cottage... cosy, that wonderful interior design euphemism for small... I sat at the kitchen table and looked around. I couldn't attend the craft group without something *crafty*. My gaze landed on the bookshelf. In between the cookery books I'd brought down when I'd planned dinner parties and tea parties sat an artist's pad from my interior design days. I pulled it out and flicked the pages, quickly realising it had belonged to my ex. There were a few finished sketches, a couple of half-completed drawings, a page or two when he'd started but gave up after scrawling lines across the page.

A smile flickered. Could I pull it off? A skilled interior designer, my mood boards had made clients gasp with pleasure but if drawing was required I left that to my ex because apart from straight lines to delineate the size and shape of a room, I couldn't draw to save my life. But the arty-crafty group didn't have to know that, did they?

I put the pad down and searched for a pencil in the kitchen drawer. There wasn't one nor was there one in the tiny pseudo writing desk that fitted into the alcove beside the fireplace in the living room.

The lack of a pencil wasn't going to ruin my plan. No doubt

the newsagent's would be able to supply me with one. First, I needed to see if I could join. Six people. It might be that they'd already reached that number. The notice hadn't looked old, but it may have been there for months.

My mobile was on the table. The picture of the notice was clear. Repeating the number to myself, I brought up the keyboard and dialled.

It rang several times. I was about to hang up when it was answered with a breathless *hello*.

'Hi.' I put my free hand on the artist's pad as if in support of the lie I intended to tell. 'I'm ringing to enquire about the notice I saw in the newsagent's. In Broadway. About the craft group.'

'Okay. Great, I'm Claire Brandon, the group was my brainchild, so what would you like to know?'

'I moved here recently, and I thought it would be a nice way to meet people who shared similar interests.' *Moved here recently*. It wasn't quite the truth, not exactly a lie. 'But I don't do knitting or anything, sketching is my thing.' *Definitely a lie.* 'I wasn't sure if that would be acceptable.'

'Oh, don't worry, we're not a bit prescriptive, it's more a support group, you understand. And it's a great way to get to know local people. We've been going a few months now, stopping and starting as Covid regulations allow. It would be lovely to have a new face join us, and you're in luck, we have room for one more. I'm sticking with a maximum of six despite the relaxation of restrictions.'

A support group? I tried to inject enthusiasm into my voice. 'That sounds great. How often do you meet?'

'Once a week, on a Wednesday. Tomorrow night, so good timing. We meet in my house where there's loads of space, especially when we had to follow the two-metre rule for Covid precautions, you understand.'

I raised my eyes to the ceiling and wondered if this was a big mistake. Grand and all as the manor was, it was simply a house. 'I understand.' I hoped she didn't hear the sarcasm that coloured my words.

'You'll join us then?'

It would make a good story to tell when I returned to London. My friends would howl with laughter at the thought of me getting involved with a craft group. It would also, I hoped, beat sitting and staring at the four walls. 'I'd love to, thank you so much. My name is Jocelyn Dexter.'

'Great! You said you moved to Broadway recently. Is that to the town itself?'

'Yes, 265 High Street.'

'Oh, that's the little cottage not far from us, I saw the *for sale* sign a few months ago, how lovely to be able to meet you.'

I bristled at the *little cottage*. 'Yes, it'll be lovely to meet you too.' Pretending ignorance of the venue, I asked, 'I jotted the phone number down but I've forgotten the address.'

'Broadway Manor. You pass by our house on the way to the shops. It's on the left. The name is on the gate, you can't miss it.'

'Oh yes, I think I noticed it.'

'Such great timing! We'll see you tomorrow night. The meeting starts at 6pm and we generally finish about nine. You just need to bring whatever it is you're working on.'

Whatever I was working on? I imagined them at the end of the night doing a big show and tell of all they'd achieved, picturing crocheted squares and embroidered daisies on the corner of table napkins. 'I'm not really comfortable about showing my work so I hope that won't be an issue. Simply being among artistic types will be a great motivator and inspiration for me.' *What drivel I could spout on demand.*

'Oh yes, that's how we feel as a group, we encourage one another. Don't feel intimidated, you don't need to show your work unless you wish. No pressure. Some of the group like to share, but there's no obligation of any sort. We're very easy-going.'

The last was said with such emphasis that my antennae immediately twitched. I assured Claire that I'd be at the meeting the following night, hung up and tapped the mobile against my chin.

Five women I didn't know. There were bound to be interesting stories... and secrets. And if there was one thing I loved more than old houses, it was hidden secrets. If they were there, I'd find them.

For the first time in days, I wasn't bored.

CHAPTER FOUR

It was only a couple of minutes' walk from the cottage to Broadway Manor. I spent longer trying to decide whether to be enthusiastically early or dramatically late and longer again trying to decide what to wear. Going for arty, I opted for an ankle-length patterned skirt and a matching wrap-around cashmere top that accentuated my waist. I tied my long, expensively sun-kissed blonde hair in a ponytail with a scarf in a clashing colour. It was tempting to gild the lily and add chandelier earrings but, after trying them on, I decided it was a step too far and settled for the diamond studs Kasper had bought for my last birthday.

I'd managed to get a pencil in the newsagent's that morning and spent several minutes scribbling with it to file the point to a more used rounded shape. I put it and the sketch pad into a big holdall and at exactly two minutes to six, left the cottage.

It was a minute after the hour when I walked up the short garden path between the rows of neatly pruned box hedge. The front door was set back in the stone porch. Close up, I could tell the door was oak, unlikely to be original but it was certainly old with a patina that made me instinctively reach out and lay a hand on it, feeling the passage of years on the smooth worn surface.

There was no doorbell. A large knocker sat dead centre. Not brass. I ran my fingers over the silvery grey metal ring. It was rough and heavy. Iron, I guessed, raising it to hit the metal plate underneath. The sound was loud, echoing.

It was answered almost immediately, the heavy door pulled inward with a series of ominous creaks and rattles that wouldn't have been out of place in a horror movie, and despite my complete disbelief in all things otherworldly, I shivered.

'Hello!' Not Morticia Addams or even Bela Lugosi but a very ordinary-looking woman with a welcoming smile. Assuming this was Claire Brandon, she was older than I'd expected. On the phone, her light bubbly voice made her sound younger, but fine lines fanned each side of smiling pale-blue eyes, her jawline was soft, and a discernible white line along the parting in her shoulder-length brown hair was evidence that a hair appointment was overdue.

Maybe my age, or a year or two either side of my forty-nine years, but she'd let herself go a little. 'Claire?'

'Yes, yes, that's me. And you must be Jocelyn. Do come in. We're all here.'

The door opened directly into a large square hall. A dramatic cantilevered staircase rose from the centre and vanished upward to darkness. I'd have liked to follow it, see what lay beyond the shadows. So much to take in, I brought my attention back to what I could see – the drama of the entrance hall. Underfoot, the floor was uneven flagstones. Bare stone walls were either draped with tapestries or hung with huge oil paintings.

Although still daylight, it was dark inside and wall lamps

had been switched on. They added a theatricality to the space, and suddenly I was filled with unaccustomed nervousness as if I'd wandered into the middle of a play and didn't know the words.

'We're in here,' Claire said, pointing towards a door with a long slim hand. She led the way and pushed open a panelled door.

After the dark hall, it took a few seconds for my eyes to adjust to the bright room, light flooding through large windows on two sides. My first impression was that everything was over-large. A trio of sofas, each looking to be capable of comfortably seating five people, were positioned around a fireplace as big as my cottage's en-suite bathroom. Behind the sofas, a circular mahogany table was surrounded by six ornate carved chairs, four of which were occupied.

'Right,' Claire said cheerfully, 'you sit here.' She tapped the back of one of the two empty chairs.

I sat on command, feeling like a well-behaved Afghan hound. It was tempting to swing my ponytail back and forth to emulate a dog's happy disposition but I didn't think the lady of the manor would have found it amusing.

Claire, still standing, looked around the table. 'Everyone, I'm sure you'll join me in making our newest member, Jocelyn Dexter, welcome. Perhaps you could all introduce yourselves.'

I dropped my bag on the floor and waited to be entertained.

'Right, who wants to start?' Claire took her seat.

A pale, pretty woman sitting on my right raised a hand. 'Might as well be me.'

I looked at her and smiled, trying not to make it obvious I was staring at her hair – I'd heard that people had taken to cutting their own hair during the closures necessitated by Covid but it was the first time I'd seen the evidence, and it wasn't good.

I imagined her standing in front of a mirror, perhaps with dress-making shears in her hand, cutting one side, then attempting to get the other side to match, trimming again and again until she'd nowhere else to go, leaving her with an appalling too-short crop.

'My name is Sarah Hodgson.' The chopped-hair woman spoke with a breathy excitement more suited to a girl of eighteen, not a woman of, being kind to her, maybe sixty. 'I'm married, with two children who've thankfully flown the nest. I live about two miles from Broadway, in Laverton.' She held up the garment she'd been working on. 'My eldest girl had a baby recently so I'm making her a christening dress. Mostly, I knit jumpers for a shop in the town.'

'Beautiful jumpers that are snapped up as soon as they go for sale,' Claire added.

A flush of pleasure coloured Sarah's pale cheeks. 'I love knitting.'

The next woman in the circle raised a hand. 'I'm Aileen Davis, I live in Chipping Campden and come here to escape from my two darling sons, Freddie and Elliot.' She looked apologetic as she added, 'I love them more than life itself, but I need a break from them now and then.'

'Aileen was home schooling for a few months,' Claire explained.

'Not toddlers then,' I said, pretending an interest I didn't feel.

'No, thank goodness.' Aileen's round face creased in amusement. 'Elliot is thirteen and Freddie eleven. They're really bright boys, and super well-behaved, but exhausting too, so it's great to leave them with their dad and escape for a few hours.' She lifted a big ball of blue wool and a crochet hook. 'I mostly make things for the house, decorations and such. I find it relaxing.'

'I'm Ruth Matheson.'

The voice had cut in abruptly and I looked from Aileen's cheerful face to the severe, almost forbidding countenance of the woman who sat next to her, obviously impatient that these extended introductions were cutting into their crafting time. 'I live the other end of Broadway, on Station Road. I sew.' Small piles of material in different patterns sat in a semicircle on the table in front of her. She picked up a piece from each, pulled a needle and thread from a box and proceeded to sew without another word.

There was an uncomfortable silence before Claire waved a hand to draw attention back to her, then nodded to the next member of the group. 'Your turn.'

A petite woman with wild curly hair, overlarge spectacles and a high colour in her cheeks, she nodded obediently. 'Hannah Woods–'

'Woods, not Wood,' Ruth interrupted. 'A very important distinction.'

Hannah laughed, a full-on belly laugh that brought a smile to other faces – not all though, I saw Claire's face tighten. 'Very important,' Hannah said when she'd stopped laughing. 'She's referring to a problem we had last year when we had flyers made. For our stall at the monthly farmers' market. We had a local firm make them and when they arrived we saw that instead of Woods Farm, no apostrophe, they'd changed it to Wood apostrophe *s*. Possessive,' she added, as if I was stupid.

Hilarious. 'So they remade them, I suppose.'

Hannah looked surprised. 'Remade them? I wouldn't have asked that of them. It's a small local company, profit margins are tight enough. No, I armed one of my boys with a bottle of corrector fluid and he removed every errant apostrophe.'

Claire coughed loudly, drawing attention. 'Sorry.' She reached for a glass of water. 'It's this dry air.' One small sip and she put the glass down. 'Why don't you tell Jocelyn about your craftwork, Hannah.'

Hannah stared at her without a word, the colour fading from her cheeks. Then with a shake of her head, she looked at me. 'I live about two miles away, in Willersey, with my husband Doug, four children and a collection of cats, dogs and rabbits. And I like to embroider.'

She picked up a frame and turned it to show me and I nodded in what I hoped was appreciation of the mass of colourful flowers she'd sewn.

'And now, my turn.' Claire inclined her head. 'Like Ruth, I sew. I'm making bunting for the various festivals we have here in Broadway. Many have been delayed by Covid restrictions but soon they'll start happening again. The committees are always looking for something to make them colourful so it's rewarding to be able to do my part.'

Rewarding... how very lady of the manor that sounded... I'd bet she was on every committee there was to be had in the town. 'How lovely,' I said, wondering what had possessed me to join this group. I could feel their eyes on me, waiting for my two-pennyworth. It was tempting to come up with a tall tale to see how much I could get them to swallow.

'My name is Jocelyn Dexter, I've moved here only recently. I used to draw but haven't done much for a while and thought it would be a good time to pick it up again.' I reached down into my bag for the sketch pad and put it on the table. An offering on the altar of belonging.

Five sets of eyes settled on it as Claire looked from the pad to me with an almost possessive pride. 'How wonderful to have an artist in our little group.'

I wanted to disabuse her of this wildly inaccurate notion and perhaps would have done and explained I was a scribbler rather than an artist, a trier rather than an achiever. I might have done if I hadn't looked around the table and seen such a mix of emotions cross the faces of the other women: anger, frustration, despair.

It seemed to me then, there was more fun to be had in keeping quiet.

CHAPTER FIVE

To my surprise, apart from a collective moan about the weather and the forecast of a storm to break the heatwave, there was little in the way of chat as everyone concentrated on their craft. I kept the sketch pad in my hand rather than placing it flat on the table so nobody could see I was simply moving the tip of the pencil gently over the image on the page drawn by my ex-husband sometime in the past. By the end of an hour, boredom was driving the lead through the page.

Movement at the end of the table dragged my eyes up. Claire was on her feet and without a word, she disappeared. A toilet break perhaps. I wondered when I could make a request for the same. Seeing more of the house might compensate for a wearisome evening.

Toilet break or not, when Claire returned she was carrying a loaded tray and wearing a smug smile. She put the tray on the sideboard and I could see it held a bottle of wine and six glasses. A glance around the other faces told me this wasn't out of the ordinary. Perhaps they took it in turns to provide refreshments. No, on second thoughts, maybe not. The expression on Claire's face was one of a benefactor bestowing her largesse on the underlings of the estate. She'd not want to share the pleasure of dispensing.

The others finished what they were doing and pushed the sundry items of their craft to one side in expectation of the glass that was placed in front of them.

'We always have white,' Claire explained, looking at me as she poured the wine. 'Less worry about staining our work should there be an accident.'

Since they'd all carefully pushed their various pieces out of the way, this felt like overkill. Perhaps the desire for safety also accounted for the quarter-filled glass. Short of dropping it... and I was ever so tempted... there was no chance of slopping the contents over the brim.

Claire put the still-half-full bottle back on the tray and sat. 'Cheers!' Holding the glass raised she looked to each of us, her gaze lingering finally on Ruth, her mouth tightening. Sitting almost directly opposite, I saw a shadow pass over Ruth's face as she became aware of Claire's regard.

Ooh, what's going on between the lady of the manor and Ms Impatience.

Nobody else appeared to notice, or if they did it was lost in the echoing cheers that ran around the table, ending in silence as we all sipped the nectar Claire had bestowed upon us.

I waited, hoping something exciting was going to unfold to make up for the previous hour, but if I'd hoped alcohol would loosen tongues I was destined for disappointment. Instead, Aileen kept up a running monologue about what her two boys had done or said during the week. She had an amusing way of speaking about her offspring that didn't prevent me from wondering if I could drink up and escape.

The others looked interested in what she was saying, their laughter sounded genuine. Or maybe they were simply better actors than I was.

A few mouthfuls emptied my glass. The others had paced themselves better... or perhaps they were aware that no top-up would be offered. Because it wasn't. Despite my lifting the glass to my lips and giving a slight laugh of surprise to find it empty before putting it down heavily on the wooden table, neither my laugh, nor the clop of glass on wood, got Claire's attention. Or perhaps it did and she was simply ignoring me.

Finally, Aileen's anecdotes about her two boys ended. I wanted to whoop in relief but instead smiled and nodded along with the others, hoping my expression, like theirs, would be read as, *gosh, that was so interesting*, and not, *thank goodness you've stopped droning on and on about your stupid brats.*

'I do love to hear about Freddie and Elliot,' Claire said, getting to her feet. Perhaps her words were sincere. Perhaps the group was genuinely enthralled by the exploits of two prepubescent boys. Their lives so devoid of interest, of fun, of anything remotely entertaining that the craft group and the tales of two boys was the highlight.

I looked with longing at the wine bottle. Another drink might have made the rest of the evening bearable. But that wasn't happening. Claire put her glass on the tray. It was the signal for those who had a few drops of wine left to finish and hand the glass over in response to her smile.

The only relief offered by the end of the decadent bacchanal orgy of drinking was it put an end to the dull conversation. I opened my sketch pad again and picked up the pencil. Now and then, as if looking for inspiration, I stared ahead, my eyes flicking right and left to examine their faces. Claire's pleasant but forgettable; Aileen's round almost-pretty face with her cow eyes fixed sycophantically on Claire; Hannah's button nose barely supporting the large heavy glasses she wore; Sarah with her pale skin and bad haircut, and finally, and most interesting of them, the sallow-skinned Ruth, her short dark hair heavily flecked with grey, her default expression appearing to be grim.

Of the five women, she struck me as the most interesting, and the dynamics between her and Claire intrigued me. More than once, I caught Ruth looking at her with narrowed eyes that seemed to impale but although Claire had to be aware of the scrutiny she didn't squirm. She simply ignored it, much as she had my less-than-subtle hints about a refill.

It was only when Ruth looked away that Claire stared at her unblinkingly, her mouth twisting in dislike... or was it simple hatred? I quickly returned my gaze to the sketch pad when Claire looked my way.

There were secrets here. Well-hidden ones. Whether they were sufficient to alleviate three hours of boredom, I wasn't yet sure.

I ran the pencil over the lines on the pad several more times, then, hoping the small amount of alcohol might loosen the tongues of these lightweight drinkers, I asked, 'Did you all go to the same school?'

It was Aileen who answered. 'I'm new to the area but I think the others did.'

Nobody elaborated.

'So, apart from Aileen, you must all know each other well?'

Sarah gave an uncertain laugh and looked around the room but when nobody else looked up from their work, she answered, 'Ruth, Hannah and I went to the same school and have stayed friendly since. It's a small town.'

'But you don't live here, do you, you live out in...?' I smiled and shook my head. 'I'm sorry, where did you say?'

'Laverton.'

'I haven't been there – is it as nice as Broadway?'

Sarah opened her mouth to answer but before she'd time to

utter a word, Ruth's harsh voice rang out. 'You ask a lot of questions, Jocelyn.'

Her glare would probably have wilted lesser people; it made me smile. 'Didn't you know? I'm a private investigator, it comes with the territory.'

I thought my flippant remark might lessen the tension, make them all laugh. Instead, they gaped at me. I was going to comment when I saw Claire raise a hand.

'Perhaps we should concentrate on getting what we're doing finished, the evening is nearly over.'

The lady of the manor had spoken. Sarah and Aileen immediately got on with their work. After sending a rancorous glare towards Claire and a sharp one to Hannah, even Ruth got her head down, sticking the sewing needle into the fabric she was holding with what I thought was unnecessary force. I watched as Sarah flicked a look between all three women then concentrated on her knitting. It was almost amusing.

But I didn't like being silenced and stared at Claire with dislike. Perhaps it would be worth my while to find out their secrets after all.

CHAPTER SIX

My request to use the ladies a short while later was met with a raised eyebrow. Claire even went so far as to check her watch, a subtle criticism of my inability to wait a mere twenty minutes and pee in the comfort of my own home.

'I'm sorry, it was the wine.' *Because the tiny drop she'd given us would have had that effect.*

What could she say? With a condescending nod, she got to her feet. 'I'll show you where it is.'

I'd hoped she'd take me up that stunning staircase, instead she led the way down a short corridor where she stopped and pushed open a door into a tiny cloakroom. 'Here you go. I'll wait for you. In case you get disorientated when you come out.'

After all that alcohol maybe?

There was nothing to keep my attention in the small utilitarian room. I waited a few seconds, flushed the toilet, ran the tap, fluffed the towel. In the small mirror, I stuck my tongue out at my reflection. *Stymied!*

When I opened the door, Claire was leaning against the wall opposite. 'Thank you,' I said. 'Such a relief.'

'Good, let's get back.'

When we returned to the living room there was a tenseness in the air that floated above a strange unsettling undercurrent. The other women stared at us, guilt written on their faces, their eyes slinking away as we retook our seats. I thought Claire hadn't noticed, but when I sat and picked up my sketch pad, I glanced her way and saw something flicker on her face. I frowned. It appeared remarkably like sadness. Then it was gone but when she looked around, I saw the same emotion linger in her eyes.

The gathering ended when the big mantlepiece clock chimed the first of nine sonorous bongs. I was both fascinated and appalled when, like clockwork toys that had wound down, everyone – even the haughty Ruth – immediately stopped what they were doing. By the time the echo of the final toll had faded everyone was packed up, ready to leave.

I envied the power Claire had to make the group jump on command. It was tempting to hold the pencil to the page and plead for one more second but that would draw unwanted notice to what I was doing. The dark lines I had scrawled across the page, the scored paper where frustration had pressed the pencil down. It might give them the wrong idea about my talent. I made a point of shutting my pad only when everyone else was on their feet. My reluctance to finish drew a sympathetic smile from Aileen.

'It's awful having to stop when you're in the zone, isn't it?'

In the zone? She crocheted, for pity's sake, she wasn't painting the Sistine Chapel. I smothered the snort of laughter in a cough that made her rear back in alarm. I raised a hand. 'Oh, don't worry, it's not Covid, I think some of the fibres from the mohair wool you were using caught in my throat.'

Aileen held onto her genial expression for a second before it fell away, replaced by a whipped puppy look that almost made me regret my remark.

'Perhaps if you're so sensitive, this isn't the place for you,' Ruth said, reaching to lay a hand on Aileen's arm as if to join ranks with her against me. There was a hint of anger in Ruth's eyes when she looked at me, more than was warranted for my mistake in upsetting Aileen.

It seemed to be directed toward me for a different reason and I wondered why. She didn't know me after all, didn't know what I was capable of, what I had done.

If she had... she wouldn't be looking at me in anger, she'd be looking at me in fear.

CHAPTER SEVEN

We left the meeting together, playing follow the leader behind Claire to the front door. Covid, thank goodness, had put paid to hugs and air-kissing, and so far elbow-bashing, despite Boris' best attempts, hadn't really caught on. A chorus of awkward goodbyes and smiles of varying degrees of sincerity and we were out the door with a speed that would have delighted most hosts.

I'd had a vague idea to separate one of the women from the herd and pump her for information on the relationship between Claire and Ruth. But before I could make my play and draw any of the other three aside with the idea of inviting her to meet up for a chat over coffee, they all quickly dispersed and climbed into cars parked on the road outside.

Dust rose as they took off, mini tornadoes that swirled towards the path where I stood indecisively. Hannah's car was last to leave. She must have seen me standing there and raised her hand in a friendly wave as she pulled away. To my surprise, because friendliness really wasn't my thing, I lifted my hand and waved back.

My plan frustrated, I looked at the house wondering if

perhaps staying to chat to Claire might be a better option. Here too, I was out of luck; she'd already disappeared, the door shut and probably locked.

There seemed to be no choice left for me but to head home.

———

The night was chillier than I'd expected and darker than a late July night should be thanks to the heavy storm cloud that hung over the town like a bad omen. I guessed many people would be praying for rain but selfishly I hoped it would hold off for another couple of weeks, unable to think of anything worse than another wet day in Broadway.

It seemed sensible to get home quickly, just in case, and by the time I reached the cottage my black flat shoes were dull from the dirt kicked up as my feet sped along the path. The cottage was in darkness. It hadn't mattered up to now. I'd never been out this late in Broadway without Kasper and had no reason to venture out alone since my arrival. Perhaps I should get a timer for a couple of the lamps to make returning home more welcoming.

My keys, as always, had drifted to the bottom of the paraphernalia that accumulated in my handbag despite my best intentions. The search took on a desperate panic as I assumed the keys had either fallen from my bag or had been stolen by some ne'er-do-well who was that minute rifling through my home looking for anything of value. It was always at that last edge of panic when my fingers would close over the cold metal. The combination of relief and anger for being so stupid was allied with the promise to clear out my bag at the first opportunity and to put my keys into one of the zipped pockets within the bag for both safety and ease of locating.

Once inside, I immediately forgot about the panic, till the next time.

The cottage had no alarm. It was one of the things I'd planned to organise when we purchased it but so far I'd not bothered. In London, I'd never have contemplated doing without, but here in sleepy Broadway it didn't seem a major consideration.

I slammed the front door shut, checking the Yale lock had engaged. It was faulty and didn't always. It was yet another of those things I planned to get changed but hadn't got around to doing. The door opened into a porch so small that a pair of Kasper's casual shoes took up almost a quarter of the floor space. I'd have liked to have kept my shoes on and would have if they hadn't been covered in grey dust, and the living-room carpet I'd insisted on buying wasn't a cream wool that was completely unforgiving of the merest smidgeon of dirt. 'It will make the room appear bigger,' I'd insisted when Kasper had queried my choice. Cream carpet, white walls, pops of colour in cushions on the white sofa and in the artwork on the walls.

It looked fabulous on paper, took great photos for Instagram but it was proving hell to live with. The stupidest decision I'd made recently. Or one of them anyway.

Leaving my shoes beside Kasper's, I pushed the door open into the room. Even with the white walls and cream carpet, the room could only be described as small. Cosy, I had described it to my friends. The *little cottage*, Claire had said. Now after spending time in her home, I had to agree with her. Little... small... miniscule. The living room, the completely inadequate kitchen, the whole damn cottage. What had I been thinking to have spent so much money on such a tiny place?

I'd have liked to have boasted to the group about my lavish London home, but I'd shot myself in the foot there with my intimation that I'd moved to Broadway. Not precisely a lie, not really the truth.

It hit me they hadn't asked about my husband. Did they think I'd moved to Broadway alone, perhaps following a break-up? Too polite to ask. Too damn *nice*. I pulled my jacket off and dropped it on the sofa before taking my mobile from my pocket.

Not surprising, there were no messages from Kasper, and he'd not answered any of several I'd sent. I contemplated tapping out yet another message asking for forgiveness but tossed the mobile onto the sofa without. I'd plan what to say and send a message later.

I rested my head back, the argument with Kasper rico-cheting painfully around my brain. I'd no time for regrets, but it didn't mean I wasn't willing to face my mistakes. Especially great big life-changing ones.

I'd leave it another week, or at least a few more days, then I'd go home. Sort everything out. Get on with my life.

CHAPTER EIGHT

The other participants of the craft group probably had their evening meal before the meeting but that had been too early for me. Nine, on the other hand, was too late. Peckish rather than hungry, I settled for a slice of toast with hummus I'd bought from a delicatessen in the town.

I took it through to the living room, switched on some music and ate to the accompaniment of Adele singing something moody and sad.

It was almost eleven before I turned the volume down and reached for my mobile. No point in putting it off any longer. I'd ring, and when he didn't answer I'd leave a voicemail, adding a hint of pleading for effect. I pressed the phone icon, held the mobile to my ear and waited.

Had it been answered it would have caught me by surprise, and my practised words would have been swallowed to leave me silent and helpless. But it wasn't. I waited for the invitation to leave a voicemail before starting on my rehearsed spiel.

'Kasper, hi, it's me. You're not answering which means you're still annoyed with me. Perhaps it's good to spend time apart. You can concentrate on all your Zoom calls, and I can keep myself occupied here. I've joined a craft group. I know you'll laugh when you hear that, but it's interesting. Small-town women have secrets too. Okay, that's it for now. I'll keep ringing until you forgive me and answer.'

I dropped the phone on the sofa and rested my head in my hand. Kasper was such a gorgeous man; I did miss him.

To distract myself, I thought about the five women I'd met earlier. The daft crafty quintet. *The DCQ*. The acronym made me smile. It would be my own private joke. Tomorrow, to keep my mind from drifting back to Kasper and the mess I'd made of things, I'd start to dig and see what secrets the women were hiding. That they were hiding something was a given. The signs were obvious: the sharp glances, reluctance to answer questions and the funny looks they gave each other when they thought nobody was watching. Most of all was that strange undercurrent when Claire and I had returned to the living room.

Claire... such a polite woman... so lady-of-the-manor gracious. Wouldn't it be courteous to call on her in the morning and tell her how much I enjoyed the night? With her impeccable good manners, she'd no doubt invite me in for a cup of tea which I'd accept with gratitude. Tongues hadn't been loosened over a drink, maybe they would be during a tête-à-tête over coffee.

Curiosity was part of my make-up; I liked to know what made people tick, why they did what they did. People's pasts fascinated me. I liked to dig for the secrets that were hidden behind polite facades. Unfortunately, most people turned out to be dismally dull and I was constantly disillusioned.

My friends, some of whom I'd known for years, accepted my inquisitiveness without complaint and even teased me about my almost pathological desire to know everything that was going on with everybody. Since my social group was small, and we'd all known each other for so long, there was nothing new to learn about them in any case.

Kasper had few friends and the ones he had were mostly work colleagues and invariably tight-lipped. The friends from his past had also been friends of his late wife. A boring bunch of do-gooders, there wasn't an interesting one among them. Perhaps it was my imagination, but I felt they eyed me with distrust. Maybe they thought Kasper had moved on too soon... maybe they thought I'd taken advantage of the grieving widower... of the extremely wealthy grieving widower.

If only they knew.

'You were born nosy,' my friend Tracy Robinson had said more than once. 'You should have been a detective not an interior designer.'

It wasn't appropriate to tell my friend how much snooping I did in customers' homes. I justified my actions by telling myself I was able to meet their needs more effectively as a result... which wasn't precisely a lie. It had allowed me to push the boundaries when I discovered that an outwardly conservative couple kept an eye-watering collection of sex toys and bondage items in their bedside lockers.

I'd added spice to the dull colour palette they'd requested, dramatic wallpaper on certain walls, a certain phallic suggestiveness to some of the light fittings, an element of dark overtones to some of the paintings. The couples' initial shocked expression when they saw it turned to pleasure that gave me such satisfaction and convinced me that my intrusion into their privacy was warranted.

Mostly though, when I poked around, I found the usual detritus that everyone lived with. Old, faded photographs, concert tickets, programmes, flyers, bus/train tickets. Trash that had at one time held such happy memories and been kept for so many years that it felt a form of treachery to throw any of it out. All of it was boring and lacked any mental stimulation.

It was the minimalists that fascinated me the most. Those who kept nothing from their past, happy to survive in the here and now.

Kasper was such a man.

CHAPTER NINE

I was worried when I'd first visited Kasper's home that I'd see trappings of the life he had led with his late wife – photographs, feminine doodahs, a female vibe to certain areas of the house, maybe even a certain tweeness. I'd met her, she'd struck me as the twee type so I'd expected holiday souvenirs, maybe nothing as tacky as a gondola that lit up to remind them of their honeymoon in Venice, but maybe, with the money they had, a colossal Murano glass chandelier.

But there'd been nothing.

I'd walked into the spacious living room of the penthouse apartment with the stunning view over London rooftops and searched for anything that would indicate he'd been married before. Had shared his home with another woman. But apart from a huge sofa, two armchairs, and a strangely ugly lamp, there was only a beautiful vase sitting off-centre on the oak mantelpiece. Nothing else.

I'd fought with my ex-husband for ownership of various bits and pieces we'd acquired over our years together and couldn't imagine living such a minimalistic lifestyle as Kasper and his wife had done.

It wasn't until I'd moved in with him I'd ventured to ask why there was nothing of hers about, regretting the question immediately when his face distorted with grief, feeling not guilt for asking the question but a twinge of anger that he should still be upset about her death.

'I'm sorry,' I lied, reaching for him, holding him tightly while he drew ragged breaths. I tried to control my impatience and bit my tongue on the words I wanted to say – *get over it, she's gone, I'm here*.

It was a few minutes before he pulled away and wiped a hand over his face. 'Laurie liked clean lines, empty spaces. And she hated photographs, especially ones of herself.' He crossed the room to the vase that was the only, lonely occupant of the mantelpiece. 'This is my memory of her. We bought it in an antique shop when we stayed in the Lake District for a long weekend a few years ago. When I look at it, I see her laughing face, can almost hear her voice. It's all I need.' He picked it up and ran his hands over the curves. 'Everything else of hers, clothes and jewellery, I gave away to charity after her death.'

Remembering some of the jewellery I'd seen Laurie wear, I had a dart of annoyance at this action but then shrugged. It wasn't exactly to my taste anyway, too ornate, I preferred the simplicity of diamonds.

I'd known the details of the hit and run that had resulted in Laurie Dexter's death and the subsequent search for the driver who'd callously left her lying on the side of the road to die. It had been on the news. There'd been hushed whispers in the gym. And there were comments on Facebook, Instagram and Twitter accompanied with sad-faced tearful emojis. I'd been glued to it all for days, consumed by it, even when it disappeared from social media, when the whispers stopped, and people started saying *Laurie who* when I asked if they'd heard any news.

Kasper had told me about it shortly after we'd met. The bare details, not the horrendous truth that his wife had been found by a man walking his dog in the early morning, the whining animal dragging him to the crushed, broken body. Those details I'd read in the newspaper reports and the social media expressions of disgust aimed at the driver of the car who had never been traced.

I still checked out social media for details, but Laurie had had her sixty minutes of fame.

She'd had her time in the apartment too. I gradually introduced colour and some personal items: a photograph of me and Kasper taken at the Ritz; some items I'd managed to acquire following my divorce, including a painting my ex didn't know I'd taken. He'd moved so often since our divorce, he'd think he mislaid it somewhere.

The vase that reminded Kasper so much of Laurie was moved from the mantelpiece to a side table. I was devastated when I knocked into it, and it fell to the floor smashing into a million shards of glass.

Impossible to mend.

Like Laurie had been.

CHAPTER TEN

The morning after the Daft Crafty night, I waited until 11am before venturing down the street to knock on the door of Broadway Manor. I'd practised saying *thank you for a lovely evening* a few times to ensure I'd captured the correct level of sincerity in my voice.

The promised storm hadn't materialised. The dark clouds had vanished as quickly as they'd arrived and it was yet another blisteringly hot blue-sky day. Gardens on the short walk between the cottage and the manor sported lawns that were a decidedly unattractive umber rather than lush green. Sensible gardeners had stuck to planting drought-resistant pelargoniums in borders, pots and hanging baskets. Mostly bright red, they gave the town a jaunty continental feel.

There was no indication of activity in the manor house as I approached the front door, the leaded windows on either side effectively deterring my prying eyes.

I lifted the heavy knocker, the metal pleasantly cold, and rapped it a couple of times. Too gently perhaps. When there was no answer, I reached for the knocker again and lifted it to strike harder. Three times. The door opened before the reverberating echo of the third blow had faded.

The woman who answered the door wasn't familiar. Nor was she friendly. A dark-haired slim woman, with thin colourless lips and large eyes, she held fast to the door with one hand as she looked down her long nose at me. I half-expected to be told the tradesman's entrance was around the back.

She didn't say it, but her curt *yes* implied the same thing. As if I'd been assessed and found wanting. I swallowed my annoyance with difficulty. 'Hi, I'm Jocelyn Dexter, is Ms Brandon home?'

'Is Miss Brandon expecting you?'

The heavy emphasis on the *Miss* wasn't lost on me and it immediately flushed my irritation away. I let my smile of amusement show and saw a tightening in the expression of the grim-faced woman who continued to guard the entrance. A personal assistant, or perhaps a housekeeper who saw protecting the family as part of her role. I felt as if I'd stepped back in time by at least a century, or perhaps onto the set of Downton Abbey. 'No, she isn't. Is it possible to speak to her?'

I hoped I'd be invited to wait inside. The stone porch gave little shelter from the blistering heat of the sun that was slanting to hit my back.

The unsmiling protector of the house would probably have preferred to leave me where I was. Instead, with a reluctance she made no attempt to hide, she huffed and sighed as she pulled the door open. 'You'd best come in while I go and enquire.' She stayed behind the door as if to protect herself. Perhaps it was a hangover from Covid, or perhaps the woman was always wary of strangers.

I stepped into the hallway I'd admired the night before.

'Wait there.' The woman pointed to the spot where I stood.

I looked down, half expecting to see an X drawn on the flag-stone. There wasn't, of course, but I made an issue of shuffling into the middle of the one she'd indicated as if there were.

Once she'd left, her flat shoes clomping across the hall, the sound fading as she vanished into the deeper regions of the house, I ignored the command to stay where I was and crossed the broad expanse of space to examine the paintings I'd noticed the night before. Stern-faced men and simpering women, posed with horses and dogs, the paintings good without being exceptional. I moved from one to the other and was admiring the hanging tapestries on the opposite wall by the time a sharp clip-clip of heels on stone alerted me to someone returning.

Being perceived as well-behaved was in my best interest so I hurried back to X marks the spot.

'Hello,' Claire said, crossing to stand before me with an expression that was more confused than welcoming, two frown marks between her eyes, her lips a straight dash of red in a pale face. 'Forgive me, but had we arranged something?' She shot a harried look behind her before putting a hand on my elbow and leading me into the room we'd sat in the previous night. Shutting the door behind us, she waved to the sofa. 'Please, have a seat. Would you like a coffee, or tea?' Her face relaxed into a smile. 'To be honest, I could do with a cup myself.'

It was what I'd hoped for. 'Coffee would be lovely, thank you.'

Claire left without a word and returned a minute later. She dropped heavily onto the sofa opposite and looked at me with a vague smile as if wondering why I was there and what she was going to do with me. 'Teagan will bring the tray in when it's ready.'

Teagan? The grim-faced woman who had opened the front door perhaps. Or maybe the manor, like Downton Abbey, had a whole host of staff for Claire to rule over with lady-of-the-manor condescension.

It might have explained the slight haughtiness, but it didn't explain the sadness I'd seen flit across her face the previous evening, a sadness that still lurked in her eyes.

CHAPTER ELEVEN

Typically British, we chatted about the weather for several minutes as we waited for the mysterious Teagan to bring the coffee. When we'd worn out the topic – it was hot, how many ways was there to say it, and no, that storm hadn't amounted to much – I brought the conversation around to the previous night and my reason for arriving unexpectedly. 'I wanted to thank you for allowing me to join your group, I had a really good time.' I wondered if I sounded too enthusiastic when I saw Claire blink in surprise.

'I wasn't sure if it was your thing. Small-town living can be a little–' She tilted her head side to side. '–dull, I suppose.'

Since I'd thought the meeting was dull beyond belief, I struggled to swallow my words of agreement. Luckily, the door opened and the woman who'd answered my knock came through with a tray balanced on the flat of one hand. She didn't look any friendlier than she had earlier so perhaps grump was a default setting.

Rather than placing the tray on the coffee table, she unloaded it, placing a delicate cup and saucer in front of both of us. The pot of coffee, jug of milk – hot, of course – and bowl of brown sugar was placed in the middle. The final addition was a small plate of what looked like handmade biscuits. She added teaspoons before straightening and turning to Claire with no change to her expression. 'Will that be all, madam?'

'Yes, thanks, Teagan.' Claire waited till the woman had left before reaching for the cafetière and filling the two cups.

'Has she been with you a long time?' It was the only reason why such an appalling attitude could be accepted.

Claire added milk and sugar to her coffee before sitting back with the cup and saucer in her hand. 'She joined the staff when I was a child, so it feels like she's been here forever.' Claire reached for a biscuit, dipped it into her coffee and popped it into her mouth. 'You should have one, I'm gluten intolerant so Teagan makes them for me and they're exceptionally good.'

'No, thank you, I'm not long since breakfast.' I sipped my black coffee. 'She makes good coffee too.' It was only average, but in my experience compliments brought more information than criticism.

'I'll tell her, she'll be pleased.'

I couldn't imagine anything pleasing the sour-faced Teagan. She probably had stories to tell but would hold onto her secrets like a vice. I didn't often give up on anyone, but I wasn't wasting my time on impossibilities. It was time to turn the conversation to more interesting topics. 'Getting back to last night, I enjoyed myself, it was nice to meet some local people too. I suppose you've known them all for years.'

Claire reached for another biscuit, dunked, and popped it into her mouth before answering. 'Ruth, Hannah and Sarah, yes. Aileen, like you, is new to the area.'

'It hasn't been an easy time for people, it was a great idea to organise the group.'

'I wasn't exactly being selfless.' Claire waved a hand around the room. 'I have all this space; it seemed the ideal time to make the most of it.'

'I'm sure your friends were grateful.' I smiled encouragingly and didn't rush to fill the silence that followed. Most people were uncomfortable with it and hurried to say something. Often the very things I wanted to hear. I almost smiled when Claire shuffled on the seat.

'They're not friends, precisely. I went to boarding school whereas they stayed local.' She reached for the coffee pot and held it out in a silent question.

I didn't want more coffee but the social niceties of drinking it oiled conversation so I accepted. 'And after school?'

Claire dunked another biscuit before she answered. 'I went to Cambridge to read art history, then spent a few years working for the Uffizi. In Florence,' she added as if I might not know where this world-famous gallery was. As if Claire, the lady of the manor, was more sophisticated, intelligent, and worldly wise than I. Yet another curl of dislike for the woman unwound from my tightly guarded store of negative emotions.

I pinned a smile in place and kept it there while Claire went on and on about her time in Florence, the paintings she'd worked on, the famous artists she'd met. Behind the smile, I waited for a chink I could explore, use, exploit. That there'd be one I didn't doubt... everyone had a weakness.

It was simply a matter of finding it.

CHAPTER TWELVE

Annoyingly, Claire had a lot to say about her time in Florence and wasn't embarrassed about monopolising the conversation, until she glanced at her watch and gasped. 'Goodness, where has the time gone?'

'Vanished in good conversation, as it often does.' I hoped I sounded sincere. If I never heard another word about art, I'd die happy.

Claire pushed to her feet. 'This has been nice; I don't get many visitors.'

If she bored those who did visit to death, I wasn't surprised. Left with no choice, I grabbed my bag and stood. 'Covid has made visiting difficult until recently, hasn't it?'

'It's not just that, you probably don't know, but I only returned to Broadway a few months ago so I don't really have friends here. It was partly the reason I decided to start the group but...' Her voice faded as if she realised she was saying too much.

Some of the pieces were clicking into place. 'But you ended up with people you knew, who'd never been friends, and you're not sure that's going to change?'

For a few seconds, I wondered if I'd said the wrong thing as Claire's eyes widened, but then she laughed, a sound filled with genuine amusement. 'I seem to be very transparent,' she said, with a shake of her head.

I was curious. 'You wanted a maximum of six people. When they rang, couldn't you have said it was full?'

'Sarah and Aileen rang. Ruth and Hannah simply turned up the first night. I couldn't have turned them away without making huge waves.' She walked to the door and opened it. 'Now, I really must go.'

A hundred questions were balanced precariously on the tip of my tongue. For an inherently nosy person it was an uncomfortable sensation. But I'd managed to discover an interesting piece of information. Claire had no issues with Sarah and Aileen, but she did with Ruth and Hannah.

Now all I needed to do was dig a bit to uncover the story.

Outside again, I looked up and down the street. If fate was my friend, I'd see one of the other women heading in my direction, but life rarely worked that way. Unwilling to give up that easily, I wandered through the town, peered in a few shop windows, bought a litre of milk I didn't need. I'd taken a few steps towards home when I changed my mind and turned to walk the opposite direction. A quick check on my phone told me Station Road wasn't far.

———

The afternoon was hot and sticky, the sky a clear blue. A beer garden outside The Swan was busy, a couple of free tables almost enticing me to stop. *Almost.* The temptation to see if I could find where Ruth Matheson lived was stronger. According to the map, Station Road was a little over half a mile long. I was wearing flat shoes, it was a nice day, and I'd nothing else to do.

It would have been perfect to have bumped accidentally into Ruth, but on the walk between the town and the railway station that gave its name to the road I didn't see anyone. Failure wasn't a word I entertained and when I turned for the walk home, the litre of milk bumping against my thigh, I considered my options.

Almost back on High Street, I saw an elderly man in his front garden deadheading pots of petunias and gave myself a mental kick. Ruth Matheson struck me as a woman who made an impression – favourable or otherwise. She'd lived in Broadway all her life. She'd be known.

I slowed as I approached the man. 'That's a beautiful display.' To a series of audible creaks, the man straightened and twisted around to look at me. 'Fabulous colours,' I added, pointing to the flowers. I was being sincere. By accident or design scarlet petunias had been combined with cerise pelargoniums in a clash of shades that appealed to my interior designer brain.

'Thank you.' A weathered hand tipped the brim of a battered hat back the better to see me. 'Visiting, are you?'

'No, actually, I've moved here.' I waved a hand towards the town. 'I bought a cottage on the other end of High Street.' It was easier to stick to the same not-quite-lies I'd given to Claire: I'd moved there, not bought the cottage as a weekend retreat, a bolt-hole. I wasn't one of those irritating people who pushed house prices out of the range of locals and who only used the home for a week or two in the summer, leaving it vacant and lonely the rest of the year.

The type of person this man, this local, would automatically dislike.

He needn't have worried. I was already regretting the

purchase of the blasted cottage in this dull, provincial hole. Kasper had been right. The only consolation was that house prices, especially in rural areas like this, had increased thanks to the pandemic as people rushed from the cities, so we should get more money for it. Not from a local, obviously, but from another Londoner who thought it was a good idea. I'd look at buying a place in Portugal or Italy instead.

For now, the lie was more useful to me. 'It's such a lovely place to live. I'm just getting to know people.' I stuck out my hand. 'Jocelyn Dexter.'

He brushed his hand against his corduroy-clad thigh before enveloping my smooth pale hand in his garden-rough fingers. 'Stephen Melville Evans. Pleased to meet you.' He shook my hand gently, bowing slightly as he did so with an old-world courtesy that half amused, half charmed me. Handsome even now when he must be in his seventies, I guessed he'd been knock-dead gorgeous in his youth. There was still a very sexy twinkle in the blue eyes that were assessing me as much as I was him.

'Very pleased to meet you too, Stephen Melville Evans.' For the first time that day, my smile was sincere. Curious, I pointed to the plants behind him. 'I hope you don't mind me asking, but the colour choice, was it accidental or planned?'

'You like it?'

'I'm an interior designer, colour clashes fascinate me.'

'Me too.' He smiled. 'My wife and I used to have a holiday home in Spain. Colours always seemed more vibrant there, I wanted to try and replicate it.'

'You did a good job.'

'Thank you.' He looked like he was going to say more but a call from within the house had him tilt his head that direction. 'That's my wife calling, I'd better head in. It's been nice to meet you.'

It was now or never. 'I'd better get back to my search anyway.'

'Search?' A bushy eyebrow arched in question.

I hunched up my shoulders. 'I promised to call around to a woman I recently met. I know she lives on Station Road, but I've stupidly forgotten the exact address. Even more foolishly, I didn't think to get Ruth's phone number.' I gave the self-deprecatory laugh I knew would appeal to this old-world gentleman. Here I was, a damsel in distress waiting to be saved.

'Ruth... do you mean Ruth Matheson?'

'Yes!' I widened my eyes, an expert in feigned surprise. 'Do you know her?'

'Everyone knows Ruth.' The three words were said with that carefully neutral tone of voice that said more than the speaker wanted to give away. He leaned forward to point a finger back the direction I'd come. 'It's about ten minutes' walk, I can't remember what number the house is, but it's called Station Cottage.'

'That's great, thank you so much.' I'd liked to have stayed chatting and tried to winkle out details of his relationship with Ruth but there was something in the man's demeanour that warned me against it. Old-school decency – it was hard to get his type to gossip.

I lifted my hand in farewell and headed towards Ruth's lair.

CHAPTER THIRTEEN

A mere eight minutes after speaking to the charming man, I was staring at a wooden sign engraved with Station Cottage. It was affixed to a gate pillar, the wrought-iron gate opening into a pretty garden planted with a profusion of flowers in various hues and a shrub with attractive leaves and pink blossoms. The cottage, in honey-gold Cotswold stone, was bigger than mine and detached. Envy darted. This was what I should have bought. A bright-red wooden front door separated two bay windows on the ground floor, and there were two sash windows on the floor above.

I lingered at the gate before deciding there was nothing to lose by knocking on the door. I'd make it up as I went along.

The gate opened smoothly without the merest creak or squeak. No surprise there, Ruth had struck me as a woman who liked everything to run as it should. The stony path to the door crunched underfoot, a sound that always took me back to my grandparents' house with its long gravel driveway. The house my mother left, the life she regretted losing, regret she never successfully hid. It was a loss she passed on to me, imprinting on me as a young child the love of status, the desire for money, the awful sensation of believing what you had wasn't quite as good as whatever was in the distant field.

Imprinting... such a good word. So much better than saying she coped with her regrets by beating me onto the correct path, the one she hadn't taken, sure that this time she was making the right choice... even if this time it was my life, and they weren't the choices I'd wanted. *Whack, whack, whack.* After years, I couldn't tell the difference... her choices were mine.

I batted the memories away, stepped up to the door and reached a hand towards the bell set into the wall on the right. I pressed it firmly and took a step back.

Although I kept my attention resolutely on the door, I saw the net curtains in the bay window to the right twitch and felt eyes sweep over me. Would Ruth refuse to answer or would curiosity overcome her reluctance?

It seemed curiosity won when a short while later, as I was about to give up, the door opened and she stood in the gap staring at me.

'Hi.' I held my smile in place despite the unwelcoming glare. 'I hope you don't mind me calling like this, but I was visiting with Stephen and his wife and when he said you lived nearby, I thought it was fate and you'd not mind my calling around.'

'Stephen?' The glare had softened, replaced with a puzzled grimace.

I waved down the road. 'Stephen Melville Evans. Such a sweetheart, isn't he? We met in Spain a few years ago at an expats club.' It was a calculated risk that Ruth and Stephen weren't on friendly terms, and she'd never know the lie. It didn't matter anyway, there was no future for me in Broadway so any fallout from my lies would be immaterial.

But my knowing Stephen seemed to have elevated me slightly in Ruth's eye. Only slightly and there was obvious reluctance in her voice when she said, 'No, I don't mind you calling.' She stood back. 'Please, come in.' In the hallway, she hesitated before reaching for the handle of a door behind. 'We can sit in here.'

The formal sitting room looked as if it was rarely used. A dull-brown velvet three-piece suite was draped with cream anti-macassars I hadn't seen used in decades. A dried flower arrangement filled the grate of the fireplace, lacy spider's webs adding a rather macabre finishing touch I didn't think Ruth had noticed. Or maybe she had. Maybe it was her take on *will you walk into my parlour, said the spider to the fly*.

But when I turned suddenly and caught a twisted expression of dislike on the older woman's face, I wondered which of us was the spider and which the fly. It disconcerted me. I was used to being in control, of being the manipulator not the manipulated.

It made me wary. No bad thing.

Ruth hovered in the doorway. 'Would you like a cup of tea?'

It was said with such obvious reluctance and with such an expectation that the answer would be no, I almost smiled. 'Tea would be lovely, thank you.' I would have preferred coffee, would have killed for a G&T, but I decided to play the game and watched a fascinating array of emotions flit across Ruth's face as she tried to hang onto the correct one, the one that said she was a willing hostess.

Once she'd gone, the distinct if muffled sound of cupboard doors shutting in the kitchen telling me I was safe for a few minutes, I got to my feet for a quick snoop. A dresser to one side of the chimney breast held drawers. I slid the top one open carefully, tilted my head for any evidence Ruth was returning, then quickly rifled through the contents. There was the usual rubbish that accumulates in most homes: a remote without batteries, nail scissors, assorted pens. The second drawer held more interesting items: an envelope containing photographs and the previous year's diary. I cocked my head to listen once more and heard the faint hum of a kettle. Another minute perhaps.

The first few photographs were uninspiring views but near the back were some more interesting ones. A photograph of Ruth, a younger, softer version, her hair in the same style but without the grey that streaked through it now. She was with a handsome older man and even in the not-particularly-good photograph, I could see she was looking at him with affection, maybe even love. Her husband or partner perhaps?

I turned the photo over, hoping for a name but all that was written was a date that had my eyes widen in surprise: *Jan 2021*. Turning the photo over again, I peered closer. What had occurred in such a short space of time to turn this pleasant-looking woman into a grim-faced harridan?

Slipping the photograph back into the envelope, I took out the next. This time Ruth and the unknown man were sitting side by side on a sofa, in a room I immediately recognised. The sitting room of the manor.

Curious.

The distinct rattle of a tea tray came from the direction of the kitchen. I slotted the photograph back in its place, returned the envelope to the drawer and shut it quietly. Then, with a shrug, opened it again and pulled out the diary.

I was sitting with a butter-wouldn't-melt smile when Ruth appeared in the doorway holding a large laden tray.

She put it gently onto the mahogany coffee table. Her reluctance to provide refreshments didn't stop her from going all out to impress. I recognised the Sadler cube-shaped teapot and matching sugar bowl and jug, the pink rosebud-strewn porcelain with the gold trim instantly recognisable to someone for whom antique shops were a passion. At a rough estimate they were worth nearly a grand. The fine bone-china teacups and saucers in a different Sadler pattern were worth less, but still expensive items to be used on a daily basis. I guessed they weren't, and that Ruth, despite her obvious and inexplicable dislike of me, was determined I should be impressed.

'I love that Sadler set,' I said when Ruth took the seat opposite.

If she was impressed with my knowledge, she didn't comment. 'It was my mother's.' She picked up the teapot and poured, half filling each of the two cups. 'Milk?'

'Please.'

Ruth added to both cups. 'Sugar?'

I swallowed the temptation to say a trite, *I'm sweet enough.* 'No, thank you.'

Finally, Ruth handed the cup and saucer across the table, waiting until I had a firm grip before taking her fingers away as if afraid I'd drop it. She sat back with hers but made no attempt to drink. Her eyes were fixed on me with startling directness, as if trying to decide what to make of me. 'Why are you really here?'

I'd taken a mouthful of tea and her question caught me by surprise, making me choke and splutter. I covered my mouth with my free hand and held tightly to the saucer, afraid I'd disgrace myself by dropping it and smashing the fine china.

Ruth didn't budge, merely pushing down the corners of her mouth in evident distaste at this display of ill manners. She waited till my coughing had ceased before taking a sip of her tea, as if to show how it was done, and placing the cup and saucer gently down on the tray. 'Stephen Melville Evans is the perfect gentleman, but we're not on speaking terms, therefore I cannot believe he'd bring my name up in conversation without cause. So–' Her narrowed eyes seemed to be trying to look through to my soul. '–it seems to me it was you who brought it up in an endeavour to find out where I lived.' Her lips pursed. 'The puzzle is why. We barely spoke last evening, and I gave no indication I wished to further any relationship with you.'

Further any relationship. The stuffed old trout. Her attitude made me look at her in a different way. Maybe we weren't so unalike. 'I was curious.'

'About me?' Ruth laughed. 'I'm a nobody in a small town filled with nobodies. Why on earth would you be curious about me?'

'The animosity between you and Claire Brandon.' I sipped the tea and waited.

The look of dislike on Ruth's face returned. She sniffed and folded her arms across her chest. 'Nosiness is a particularly odious trait.'

I didn't take offence. 'I've always viewed people with avid curiosity, conscious of facial expressions, determined to work out what every twitch, grimace and sideways glance means. I had a lot to contend with when people wore masks allowing them to hide more easily. The relaxation of the rule was a relief to me, and I relished seeing those puzzling expressions again. Trying to figure out what people are thinking is better than a jigsaw puzzle to me.'

'So that's your excuse?'

'Excuse.' I see-sawed my hand. 'Explanation.' I put the cup and saucer down carefully and sat back, matching the older woman's posture, arms folded across my more generous breasts, my long, painted, manicured nails contrasting with the blunt bare nails opposite. 'You're not going to pretend there isn't something off between you and Claire, are you?'

'I don't feel obliged to make a comment about my relationship with anyone in Broadway.'

'It's to do with a man, I'm guessing.'

Ruth's eyes flicked to the drawer holding the photographs, then back to search her uninvited visitor's face for any evidence

I'd have crossed every boundary of etiquette as to snoop among her belongings.

I kept my expression carefully neutral. It wasn't hard. For a woman like me who'd do anything to get what I wanted, man-made masks weren't necessary. I could put one in place anytime.

CHAPTER FOURTEEN

I stayed silent and watched the struggle in the expressions flitting across Ruth's face, waiting for the very moment when she realised it didn't matter if she told me or not, I would find out somehow. In a small town, there would always be someone willing to tell, I simply had to ask the right person the correct question.

'You'd find out anyway,' Ruth said, coming to the same realisation. 'I don't know why you want to know but if it will offer you some entertainment, why not.' She slid her hands up her bare arms, pushing her fingers under the short sleeves of the pink blouse she wore and keeping them there.

Hugging herself for comfort or protection.

'I've known the Brandon family for many years. Claire's mother, Marcie, was in the same flower-arranging club as me, I often went back to the manor with her for coffee afterwards. Claire had moved away at that stage and rarely came home. I became friendly with both Marcie and her husband, Alan. When she died suddenly a little over two years ago, my friendship with him continued.' She unwrapped her arms and reached for the teacup, holding the saucer steady in one hand while she lifted the cup to her lips.

It had to have been cold, but she took three sips in quick succession before putting it down. 'Alan is a gentle, kind, intelligent man. A pleasure to spend time with.' Memories slipped over her, relaxing the stress lines on her face, softening her eyes, curving her mouth. 'He desperately missed Marcie, but he is a man who likes women's company and eventually...' Her voice faded. 'Last Christmas he asked me to marry him. I suppose I knew, really, that it was a desire for companionship that made him ask...'

'But you were in love with him?'

'I'm fifty-five. I've never been married. Love was something that happened to other people.' The corner of her lips lifted in a smile of disbelief. 'It wasn't something I expected, nor was it, if I'm honest, something I wanted to happen, but it did.

'We were planning a quiet wedding in the new year, but then five months ago, he became unwell.'

'Covid?'

Ruth nodded. 'He'd been vaccinated, so he didn't get it too badly and didn't need to be hospitalised, but he's elderly, it took its toll. Teagan contacted Claire. It was before lockdown came in March, so she was able to make it home.' Ruth sighed, a sad sound edged with despair. 'Claire didn't know about me and her father. When she found out, she was horrified.'

I bet she was. Claire, with her lady-of-the-manor demeanour, wouldn't have liked playing a secondary role to Ruth. Wouldn't have liked a woman her own age as stepmother.

'Alan was very sick for several weeks. Claire refused to allow me to see him, then lockdown made that impossible anyway.' Ruth rubbed her hands together. 'I hoped to visit him when restrictions were relaxed but Claire insisted he wasn't strong enough. I ring to speak to him but every time I do, I'm told he's asleep. Alan's a Luddite so doesn't have a mobile phone. I wrote him several letters, but I have no idea if he ever received them.' She smiled and shook her head. 'The housekeeper—'

'The delightful Teagan.'

Ruth looked at me in surprise. 'I gather from your obvious sarcasm that you've met her. And yes, she's the most difficult woman. She didn't like me visiting even when Marcie was alive, and she certainly made her feelings felt when I continued to visit afterward. I think it was her who...' She stopped suddenly, her mouth twisting. 'I don't know why I'm telling you all this. I don't even know you.'

'Sometimes it's easier to speak to a stranger.'

'Perhaps.' Ruth sighed again. 'It's good to talk. I know that. It's what I do for a living after all.'

It was my turn to show surprise.

She raised one overplucked eyebrow. 'I'm a counsellor, didn't you know?' There was a sneer in her voice. I'd claimed to be intensely curious about people, yet I didn't know a simple fact I'd probably have found on the internet if I'd bothered to look. Stupidly, I'd never checked what Ruth or the others did for a living, assuming they were stay-at-home mums, or retired. Boring women who'd achieved little.

I frowned. I was slipping. It wasn't like me, but then I'd had a lot to worry about recently. Time to get back in control. 'You've not managed to see Alan for months?'

'No, he's not been out of the house. I think Covid probably took a lot out of him, leaving him vulnerable—'

'And susceptible to his daughter's criticism when she arrived home and found out her father was seeing a woman her age.'

'He wouldn't have wanted to upset her.'

'Upset her!' I snorted. I had never allowed anyone or

anything to stop me getting what I wanted. It was my turn to sneer. 'You're going to let Claire stop you from being with a man you're in love with? That's crazy. Ridiculous even.'

'There's nothing I can do.'

Nice women get nothing, whack. 'No, I suppose there isn't.' It was time to leave. I'd got as much from Ruth as I was going to. She wasn't telling me everything though, I could see it in her eyes, in the tightening of the hand that rested in her lap. There was something else, and I desperately wanted to know what that something was. Secrets were like a drug to me, the more I found out, the more I wanted to know.

Suddenly, my day was full of possibilities.

CHAPTER FIFTEEN

I was halfway home before I realised I'd left the litre of milk sitting beside the sofa in Ruth's house. I wondered if she'd see it, or if she'd find it there, sour and tainted in a few weeks' time.

My head was spinning as I made my way home. Ruth's tale fascinated me.

Had she fallen in love with the man or the lifestyle he offered? Lady of the manor. Even in such a small town as Broadway, I could see the position carried some weight. Claire had mentioned making banners for the committee. Membership would have been something she'd have taken on by right. How galling it must be for Ruth to see it, a position she should have had, would have had if Covid hadn't tossed the world into a maelstrom.

I'd have wondered if Ruth had lied about being in love with Alan Brandon had I not seen the evidence in the photograph. No, that wasn't what she was hiding. I clutched my handbag tighter. Perhaps the previous year's diary would give me the information I needed.

Back in the cottage, I took a glass of wine with me and went into the back garden. I'd arranged a table and chairs under the spreading leafy boughs of a large tree. I sat in the shady nook, took a sip of the wine, and opened my bag for the diary.

There was nothing quite like the excitement of expectation. But so often it fizzled out in disappointment as it did now. The first few pages of the diary were annotated with times and initials. I assumed they referred to counselling sessions but they told me nothing. And after March last year, the diary was completely blank. There were no phone numbers, no addresses, no scribbled notes of assignations with anyone. I threw it aside in frustration.

I should have taken the photographs instead, there may have been other more interesting snaps in the collection. Ruth might have guessed I'd taken them, but she couldn't have proven anything. Missed opportunities. For the second time that day, I wondered if I was slipping, and my fingers tightened on the wine glass.

My self-doubt increased my determination. I'd find out what Ruth was hiding. And perhaps, in the process, I'd see if I could help her get back with Alan Brandon. Philanthropy wasn't my thing, but Claire's superior attitude had got under my skin and seeing her put in second place to Ruth appealed to me.

If I could do it without harming anyone, well and good, but I wasn't one to shirk from doing what was necessary.

When my glass was empty, I returned to the house for a refill to oil my thinking processes and sat sipping as the shadows stretched, and the heat of the day faded. Tomorrow, I'd find out where Hannah lived. Discover what her story was. Perhaps talking to her would tie up all the floating strings. Willersey. I'd no idea where that was but remembered she'd said it wasn't far.

I'd find it, then ask the first person I met if they knew where Hannah Woods lived. It had worked in finding Ruth, I might be equally lucky with Hannah.

My bag was slouched on the table. I pulled it closer and rummaged inside for my mobile. I held it for a moment before dialling and holding it to my cheek. Kasper didn't answer. He was never going to forgive me. I waited for the voicemail to kick in and left a message. *'Hi, I'd hoped you'd have forgiven me by now, Kasp. I'll wait here another week or so, give you time to miss me.'*

I put the phone down, picked up the glass and drained it. Alcohol, as I'm sure Ruth would have told me, wasn't the answer, but it took the edge off the questions.

CHAPTER SIXTEEN

Too much wine on an empty stomach resulted in a restless night. Or maybe it was the sticky heat, the rustling of leaves outside or the sick feeling in the pit of my stomach when I thought of how things seemed to be falling apart. Slipping away. Bouncing out of my reach, just enough to be tantalising. Enough to make me wonder if one more stretch of my fingers, one more action, would make everything all right.

Kasper. I'd made a mistake there.

There didn't seem to be anything else to do but to stick to my plan and hope for the best. Meanwhile, there was enough entertainment in Broadway to keep my mind from drifting to the dark shadows where scary stuff waited to pounce.

I tossed the sheets aside at seven and climbed from the bed exhausted from the twisting and turning. It was already warm, hinting at another blistering hot day. I took my coffee outside to a seat that caught the morning sun and sat sipping it, hoping the caffeine would give me energy for the day.

It didn't work so I went back to the kitchen for something to eat. There was cereal, a fruity granola I'd bought because Kasper liked it. Personally, I didn't want to be prising bits of seeds and nuts from between my teeth for the rest of the morning, but since there was nothing else I poured some into a bowl. The fridge was bare apart from an almost empty litre of milk and a few bottles of beer and wine.

I smiled as I remembered the milk I'd left in Ruth's house, wondering if she'd found it, hoping she hadn't, hoping it would be there stinking her house out for weeks to come. My smile faded when I unscrewed the cap of the Tetra Pak, the odour of sour milk a smack in the face. I poured it away in a noisy, sour, glug-glug.

With the bowl of dry granola in one hand and a fresh coffee in the other I went back to my seat in the garden. To my surprise, the cereal was more palatable in its dry state. I ate the lot washed down with the black coffee. Either the food or the second coffee did the job and I felt better. A shower would complete my transformation into a fully functioning human.

I hadn't come up with any better plan than driving to Willersey and hoping, as with Ruth, I'd get lucky and speak to someone who knew where Hannah lived. The thought of driving around in the heat of the day wasn't appealing but there didn't seem to be any point in going too early. I stayed in the garden and tried not to think. Of anything. It wasn't possible and my mind drifted to where it shouldn't.

Frustrated, I returned to the house for my mobile and dialled Kasper's number to leave yet another voicemail tinged with regret. *'Another day apart, I hope you're missing me. Forgiving me. Ring me, Kasp, I miss you.'*

To be doubly sure, I tapped out the same message and pressed send.

A gallon of coffee and a shower didn't make a lot of difference and when I looked in the mirror, I saw the truth staring back at me. I didn't like it.

Suddenly my plan seemed ridiculous.

Crazy even.

The linen dress I'd thrown on was already sticking to me as I locked the front door. I contemplated the tiny front garden. Kasper had insisted it be easy to maintain so we'd had the grass replaced with Astroturf. The pot on either side of the door held standard bay trees... good fake ones that would fool most people. I regretted listening to him. A pretty cottage garden would have looked so much nicer, suited the place far better and might have lifted my mood. Plus, caring for it would have given me something to do rather than this hare-brained scheme I'd set my sights on.

Too late. Like a lot of things.

I was still standing on my doorstep lost in thought when I heard my name called. It took a second to drag me back from what might have been, and seconds more to place the smiling face that stared my way. Sarah, her Covid haircut hidden by a wide-brimmed straw hat.

Maybe it was my lucky day after all. This stroke of good fortune was all that was needed to perk me up. Successful plans were dynamic ones ready to respond to whatever came along. And today, that was Sarah.

'Hello.' I covered the few steps to my front gate with a broad welcoming smile. 'How lovely to see you. I was saying to Claire yesterday how much I enjoyed meeting everyone the other night and how I hoped we could all become friends.'

'Claire is so lovely, isn't she?'

There was no guile in Sarah's voice, no edge to her words. She was, as I'd decided at Wednesday's meeting, exactly what you saw... honest, possibly not very bright, maybe a little dull, malleable, biddable. Perfect for manipulating.

'An absolute sweetheart,' I said. 'I was a bit lonely, if I'm honest, so it was so wonderful to be able to join the group.' I waved to the cottage. 'Do you fancy coming in for a coffee?' I held my hands up, turned the corners of my lips down. Humble was the best approach with women like Sarah. 'Sorry, you're probably on your way somewhere, I don't want to delay you.'

There was no hesitancy, her nod of acceptance enough to send her hat sailing. She gasped, as if the rays of the sun would burn her pale skin in the seconds it took me to recover the hat from where it had landed in the middle of the patch of Astroturf and hand it back to her.

'Thank you.' She pulled it down tightly. 'I burn very easily.'

The brim of her hat hid her face from me and my sneer from her. Only a desire for information encouraged me to wish for more time in her company.

She fussed with her hat for a few seconds more, tilting the brim down, the collar of her polo T-shirt up. The sun hadn't a hope of sneaking a ray near her pasty pale skin. 'I wasn't going anywhere really,' she said. 'I come into Broadway every week to do a grocery shop, but it was so hot in the car I thought I'd get a breath of fresh air before heading home.'

A breath of fresh air by walking ten minutes down a long, hot, dusty road? And she a woman with a pathological fear of the sun? Hmm, I didn't believe a word of her pathetic story. The idea that Sarah had walked along the road in the hope of meeting me... or perhaps Claire... was too obvious to ignore.

Maybe Sarah wasn't such a dullard after all.

And maybe it was my lucky day.

CHAPTER SEVENTEEN

'There's a nice shady spot in the back garden. We could sit there, have a cuppa and a natter.'

This time Sarah put a hand to her hat before nodding. 'That sounds perfect.'

The keys were still in my hand, I opened the door and waved her inside.

She took her hat off only after I'd shut the door, perhaps afraid that an errant ray of sunlight would sneak in behind her. The hat left her already ugly hair stuck unbecomingly to her head. 'So hot,' she said, pushing her fingers through it. Only running a razor over it would have made any noticeable improvement. She moved through to the living room and looked about with curious, assessing eyes. 'Very cosy.'

Cosy! She meant bloody small, and it was hard to be annoyed, she was correct, the cottage was miniscule. Hard to be annoyed... but it didn't mean I wasn't livid at the implied criticism.

I chewed and swallowed the reply I wanted to make and led onward through the kitchen to the back door. I'd left the key in the lock. It took a bit of rattling and jerking to turn it. I could feel perspiration pool in my armpits and under my breasts, and the first stirrings of dislike for this stupid woman soured my belly.

Finally, the key turned with a grinding noise I'd been ignoring since we'd moved in. Both front and back door locks needed to be replaced, but why should I bother, I wasn't going to stay there. The next owner could have that thrill.

'I think you might need a new lock.' Sarah laughed as I pushed the door open.

I wanted to use a vulgar phrase beloved of my friend, the *no shit, Sherlock* Tracy used at every opportunity. It suited Sarah's remark to a T but it might alienate the woman before I'd had a chance to pump her for the information I hoped was lurking behind that pallid, pretty face. The shaded spot under the tree should put her in a comfortable mood. 'Have a seat and I'll get us some coffee, or would you prefer tea?' I remembered I'd no milk. 'It'll have to be black I'm afraid, I was on my way to get milk.'

Her face fell, then immediately brightened. 'Any herbal tea?'

'Sure, there's mint, camomile, and ginger, I think.'

'Ginger would be lovely, thanks.'

Leaving her to duck and dive away from the odd glint of sunshine that winkled through the leaves above her head, I went back to the kitchen. With the kettle on, I opened the cupboard in search of the ginger tea. Typically, I found the other options I'd offered her but not that.

Reluctant to go back and admit we didn't have it, I opened the fridge and looked for the tube of ginger puree I'd brought from London when I was filled with the dream idea of hosting dinner parties. The tube was shoved to the back of a shelf. Taking it out, I groaned when I saw the best-before date. It had passed even before I'd brought it down. I removed the lid and held the tube to my nose. It still smelled gingery. I squirted a generous amount into a glass jug and poured boiling water on top.

When my coffee was made, I took a spoon and tasted the ginger infusion. It wasn't bad. In fact, when I had another sip, I thought it was more than okay and poured it through a strainer, pleased with my improvisational skill. Sarah would never know the difference.

Back in the garden, I handed her the mug. 'Here you go, I hope you like it. It's a brand I bought in an epicurean tea shop in London a few months ago.' Then, in case she asked for a second cup, 'You're in luck, it was the last spoonful. I must get more when I'm next in the city.' The lies rolled off my tongue with practised ease.

Sarah sniffed uncertainly before taking a tentative sip. 'Oh yes, it's very nice. You must give me the name, I might be able to get it online.'

Very unlikely. 'Sure, I'll get it for you before you leave.' We sat for a moment in silence. 'I'm really enjoying living in Broadway,' I lied. 'You've always lived around here, haven't you?'

'Yes, my parents had a house a few miles outside the town. They're both gone now.'

Gone as in *left* the area and were living elsewhere, or gone as in *dead*? I guessed by her suddenly mournful face it was the latter. Euphemisms annoyed me, why couldn't people say what they meant? 'That must have been sad for you.' It seemed the appropriate thing to say.

'Yes. They died within a few weeks of each other. The family home was left to me and my two siblings equally and had to be sold. I'd have liked to have kept it, obviously, but we didn't have the money to buy the others out. Our house in Laverton isn't worth nearly as much so selling it wouldn't have worked.'

'Shame.' I gave a moment to show sympathy for her

dilemma before swinging the conversation around to the reason I invited her in. 'I really enjoyed meeting everyone on Wednesday. I suppose you know the others well. Apart from Aileen, she's new to the area, isn't she?'

'Yes, she's not long moved here. Ebrington, I think.'

I wanted to correct her. Aileen had said she lived in Chipping Campden. I had a good memory for things that interested me. 'She seems to have her hands full with her two boys.'

'Yes.'

I was pleased to hear little interest in her voice, I didn't want to get into a conversation about child-rearing. Anyway, I'd pussyfooted around long enough, it was time to get to the nitty-gritty. If there was any. 'I don't want to speak out of turn and please stop me if you think I am but–' I put my mug down on the wooden table and settled my expression into one of serious concern. '–I sensed a certain hostility between Ruth, Claire and Hannah. I'd hate to put my foot in it by saying the wrong thing.'

One of my chief faults was to underestimate people and when I saw Sarah's eyes sharpen and her mouth twist, I knew I'd done it again. Not as much of a muttonhead as I'd thought after all. I continued as if I hadn't noticed the change in her demeanour. 'I remember I made a terrible faux pas at an interior design conference a few years ago. A man was being a nuisance, making inappropriate comments and being generally a sex pest so I went to one of the organisers and told her, not knowing the man in question was her husband. It was very awkward. I'd still have reported the man but maybe not to his wife.'

It was a good enough story. A lie, but one designed to garner sympathy for my position. But Sarah was proving to be a tougher opponent than I'd expected. Or maybe it was simply the age-old distrust of the local for the outsider. A Londoner too. Time to play the sympathy card. 'I've been a bit lonely since I came to Broadway, if I'm honest, and was hoping the group would be a way to make friends. I don't want to jeopardise that by saying the wrong thing.' I shrugged. 'Some people automatically distrust Londoners; I don't want to give anyone extra ammunition.'

This was proving to be far more difficult than I'd anticipated and, not for the first time, I wondered if I was slipping, losing my edge. The idea sent a shiver of fear racing through me. Perhaps this is what made the difference, perhaps Sarah saw the fear and interpreted it her way because instantly her eyes softened, her mouth resumed its natural friendly curve. She put the mug on the table and stretched a hand to lay it on my arm.

'Oh dear, I hadn't thought how hard it must be for you being on your own here.' Colour flushed her pale cheeks. 'I'm sorry, I'm assuming you are alone... you've not mentioned anyone... partner or children...' She stopped abruptly and smiled. 'Seems it's my turn to make one of those ghastly faux pas.'

I felt the sticky weight of her hand on my arm and wanted to shake it off. I didn't like being pawed by people even if she was trying to be kind. 'No, that's okay. You're right, I'm alone here. My marriage...' I shrugged, leaving her to fill in the details according to whatever scenario was running through her head.

'Oh, you poor thing.' Her hand squeezed my arm, I fancied I could feel rivulets of her sweat mixing with beads of mine and the idea made my stomach churn. Luckily for our growing camaraderie, she removed her hand.

When I glanced down and saw the glisten of her sweat on my arm, it was too much for me. With a hand over my mouth, I rushed away and made it to the bathroom as a spasm hit. My stomach hurled a bellyful of coffee into the bath, splattering the pristine white with splashes of dull brown. I ran the tap to wash it away, scooping handfuls of water to wash out my mouth.

Only when I had soaped my arm with water as hot as I could bear, did I feel calmer. Rinsing my mouth out a final time with some toothpaste, I ran a brush through my hair, took a deep breath and returned to the guest sitting in my garden.

Sarah's face was a picture of concern as I made my way back to the shady arbour. 'I'm so sorry,' I said, lowering myself gingerly onto the seat as if I were a delicate flower. 'It just hits me sometimes.' That *it* was the disgusting slime from her sweaty paw, she didn't need to know, let her think whatever she wanted.

'I understand.'

Silence settled over us. Sarah had moved her chair to dodge the sneaky sun's rays while I'd been inside and now sat more than an arm's length away from me. I was safe from her pawing hand. I'd never understood this need for physical touch... apart from sex, of course... but the hugging, groping, grasping that seemed to be part of social interaction made my lips curl in distaste. For me, the restrictions introduced by Covid were a blessing and I hoped they'd last.

I also hoped my act had been enough to convince Sarah to shelve her reservations and let me in on whatever secrets she was privy to. If after that morning's shatteringly hard work I didn't achieve something, I'd be pretty peeved. But with a glance in her direction, I knew that wasn't going to happen. She had that tight-faced constipated look of a woman who'd decided to martyr herself and tell the truth.

CHAPTER EIGHTEEN

'I'm telling you this in complete confidence,' Sarah said, leaning towards me.

Pleased she was out of touching distance, I hid my amusement at the words every tattletale the world over used to precede a disclosure. People, in general, were so predictable.

I leaned forward a little to mirror her movement... classic demonstration of mutual trust and understanding. 'You can trust me.' Obviously, Sarah's mother had never said to her what mine had said to me many times over the years: *never trust someone who says trust me... whack.*

'You were partially right.'

I said nothing into the silence that followed this short statement, afraid she'd change her mind if I showed too much eagerness.

'You said you sensed hostility between Claire and Hannah but you're not quite right there. It's not hostility as such, at least–' She screwed up her nose and wagged her head from side to side as if trying to shake the correct word out. '–maybe there's an element of that at this stage. It's been years after all. Maybe it's grown into hostility. You never know, do you, how things will change?'

I was almost chewing my tongue as I waited for her to tell me what the blasted story was. *Shut up and get on with it, you stupid woman.* I didn't trust myself to say anything so simply nodded as if in agreement.

It seemed to be sufficient. Sarah mirrored my nod and sat back clasping one hand in the other. 'It was maybe twenty years ago. Claire had gone to boarding school, then on to university so hadn't really spent much time in Broadway over the years. It was only then, when she was made redundant, that she came home for an extended period. Burnt out, I heard.'

Burnt out? Reluctant though I was to interrupt this long-drawn-out tale, I needed to know what she meant. 'What was it she did?'

Sarah blinked. 'Oh, you wouldn't have known. She's an art historian, very well-regarded, I believe. Back then she was working in the Uffizi. It was a very intense, high-pressure role.' Sarah gave a quick smile. 'I often wondered if she'd really been made redundant or whether it had all been too much for her.'

Strange, Claire had given me the impression she'd been very happy at the Uffizi. Rewriting her own history perhaps. Bringing my attention back to Sarah, I waited impatiently as she lost herself in her own convoluted thoughts. This better be worth it.

When she stayed silent, I ventured a question. 'If it's not hostility, what is it?'

But Sarah wasn't a woman who'd answer a simple question with a straight answer. 'Claire wasn't seen around the town for a week or so after she returned home. When we did see her, we were shocked at how thin and fragile she looked.'

'We?' Getting blood from a stone would have been child's play in comparison.

'Hannah, Ruth and me. We'd been friends at school and despite diverging careers, time away at university etc, we came back to Broadway eventually and continued our friendship, meeting regularly for coffee and a chat.' Sarah took the hat she'd hung by its brim on a spare chair and fanned her face with it. 'We were sitting in the bay window of The Broadway Café one morning – it's a jewellery shop now – and saw Claire passing outside. It was Ruth who suggested inviting her to join us for coffee.' Sarah stopped wafting the hat, holding it between her hands, looking at it as if the mystery of the universe were hidden in the sweaty band.

'But you weren't friends?'

'No, but we were all Broadway girls. That meant something. Means something.'

I didn't think she realised how offensive that sounded. I decided to forgive her – for the moment anyway. 'So what happened?' *Get on with it, for pity's sake.*

'Ruth can be quite persuasive. She went out, had a word with Claire, came back with her in tow and virtually pushed her into a chair. We never talked about anything in particular when we met. It was nattering and laughing.' She met my eyes. 'You know the way women are when they get together.'

This dragged a reluctant smile from me. 'Kasper used to ask what we'd talked about when I came home from meeting my girlfriends and was always puzzled when I said *nothing*.'

'Exactly.' The hat was dropped onto the table. 'We nattered, but Claire simply sat without saying a word, her eyes down as if pretending she wasn't there, or maybe hoping we weren't. It was uncomfortable for all and soon the conversation died. Ruth had an appointment and she left. I hoped Claire would leave with her, but she didn't move. I remember meeting Hannah's eyes and hiding my smile when she raised hers to the ceiling in frustration. Maybe we'd have both left then, but just as I was about to say goodbye, Claire looked at Hannah and asked if she was still living in Willersey and working on the family farm. Before she answered I got to my feet and said I had to go. I scarpered and left the two of them sitting there.'

I was surprised to see tears appear in Sarah's eyes. It struck me that I'd misjudged her. I wasn't used to meeting genuine women who cared, women who didn't have an agenda. I was thrown and now, more than anything, I wanted her to leave. I no longer wanted to know what secrets these small-town women were keeping. Be careful what you wish for, isn't that what they say, those sanctimonious people who sit in judgement on the likes of me, because now she'd started, it didn't look as though Sarah wanted to stop.

'Hannah later told me they'd stayed talking for about an hour and arranged to meet that evening for a drink. And that was the start of it.'

It?

Sarah obviously saw my puzzled expression and clarified. 'They fell in love.'

CHAPTER NINETEEN

I thought nothing surprised me anymore but the news that Hannah and Claire had been lovers was so unexpected that I felt my lower jaw drop. Claire? The lady of the manor was obviously not as rigidly conservative as I'd thought.

But this was the twenty-first century. It was an interesting piece of news, but it wasn't the earth-shattering secret I'd expected to discover. It was more a *so what* bit of news.

'What happened?' That it hadn't worked out was obvious since Claire had been away from Broadway for many years, and Hannah had never left. It wouldn't be the first love affair to end. Again, it was mildly interesting but hardly worthy of the work I'd put in to wheedle it out of the irritating woman sitting opposite.

'I only know part of it.'

Oh great, so now I was going to be left with half a story.

Sarah didn't appear to notice my annoyance, she continued. 'They were together for several months. Hannah was still living with her parents. They have a farm and she worked on it. Still runs it very successfully. But back then, her parents were still alive, and she wasn't sure what she wanted. Claire wanted her to move to London with her, but Hannah is an only child and there were certain expectations. The farm had been in the Woods family for generations.'

I was trying to remember whether Hannah had mentioned a partner, or family, but apart from where she lived, I couldn't remember anything about the woman bar the high colour in her cheeks and those ridiculously large glasses she wore.

'Next I knew, Claire had packed her bags and left. Hannah never mentioned her again. When I asked her what had happened, she looked at me blankly as if she'd no idea what I was talking about. I guessed Claire had dumped her and it was too painful to speak about, so I dropped it. A year or so later, Hannah married one of their farm labourers and had a string of children, one after the other. They're still together and have always seemed happy enough. He's a big, muscular, quiet man. Lives for the farm. Works all hours. Hannah leaves it to him and their eldest two boys and rarely gets involved with the day-to-day running of it anymore.

'Claire didn't come home until a few months ago. I don't know much about what she's been doing since she left. I heard she was in Paris for a while, but she was back in London when her mother suddenly collapsed and died. She didn't come home for the funeral which shocked a lot of people.'

I was trying to digest all this information, slip it into what I'd already learned from Ruth. 'It must have been a hell of a surprise when Hannah rocked up to Claire's house the first night of the craft meeting.'

Sarah sighed. 'I knew about Hannah and Claire, but Aileen didn't, and she didn't know why the atmosphere plummeted when Teagan showed them into the room. I swear every drop of blood left Claire's face.'

'I've met Teagan, I'm surprised she let them in.'

'Why? Teagan hates Claire, she's never forgiven her for not

coming home to see her mother, blames her for old Mrs Brandon's heart attack.'

I'd got it all wrong. Not an old loyal family retainer... or at least not Claire's.

'Teagan is a narrow-minded nasty woman.' Sarah gave a dramatic shiver. 'Really nasty. She doesn't approve of Claire's lifestyle and isn't slow about making it obvious.'

'Why didn't Claire get rid of her?'

'Teagan's been with the family forever. You can't simply fire someone like that. Anyway, I don't think Mr Brandon would have allowed it. She is as devoted to him as she was his wife, fawns over him in a way I find a little nauseating. Everyone knows she's half in love with him.'

It was the perfect opportunity to bring the conversation around to what hopefully would be much juicier gossip than a thwarted love affair. Romeo and Juliet never did it for me. Hamlet or Macbeth with their intrigue, destructive family dynamics and back-stabbing were more to my liking. 'Teagan, half in love with him, Ruth, completely in love with him, he must be an incredibly charming man, I hope I get to meet him.'

Sarah's blank expression told me she was either an incredibly good actor or she truly didn't know about the relationship between Ruth and Alan Brandon. 'I don't know where you got that idea.' Any camaraderie vanished, and she was back to the steely-eyed woman on the defensive. 'Ruth was a close friend of Marcie's, that's all. Small-town gossip can be vicious, you shouldn't listen to it.'

It was tempting to say I'd heard it from the horse's mouth, but I decided against. Obviously, friendship between the two had waned over the years leaving me in the envious position of knowing secrets that Sarah didn't. 'Oh, I'm sorry, I must have misunderstood. Stevie is lovely but he does tend to get the wrong end of the stick sometimes.' I'd no compunction about sacrificing the charming Stephen, he'd never know after all.

Sarah tilted her head in query. 'Stevie?'

'Stephen Melville Evans. You don't know him?'

'Yes,' she said irritably. 'Everyone knows him, but I've never heard him referred to as *Stevie*.'

'We met in Spain. It's more casual there.' I smiled. 'He's such a sweetheart and will be so embarrassed to have got it wrong, but don't worry I'll set him right.'

'I don't know why he'd have thought such a thing.' Sarah's expression relaxed again now I'd accepted my error. 'Ruth would be mortified if she heard.'

Since it was obvious that she had done a very good job of keeping her relationship with Alan Brandon a secret, I doubted if anyone knew. Apart from Teagan. She had to have known since Ruth had spent time in the house with him. The photograph I'd seen was proof of that. But if Teagan had designs on the man herself it wasn't the kind of gossip she'd have wanted to spread. Perhaps instead she'd put aside her hatred of Claire and informed her of the developing relationship between the couple in the hope she'd have the power to end it.

Intrigue. It fascinated me.

As if to steer the conversation down a less contentious avenue, Sarah waved an arm around the garden. 'It's a perfect place for an artist, isn't it? What's your preferred medium?'

Hoping I knew enough about art to keep a step ahead of her, I said, 'Oils.'

'Like Monet, my favourite artist. You must show me your work someday.'

'I'm a long way from Monet.' My laugh was genuine, she'd never know how far. 'Anyway, I gather you're the real artist. Making a living from it too. Enviable.'

I'd said exactly the right thing and her face flushed with

pleasure. The right thing to get her off the topic of art, but the wrong thing to get her started on. It was incredible how much a woman could bore on about knitting… on and bloody on she went until, if I'd had a needle, I'd have put it to good use and perforated the windbag.

Between her droning and the heat of the sun, exhausted as I was, I could feel my eyelids begin to droop. 'More tea?' I asked so abruptly it startled her into silence. 'Sorry, I've been remiss as a host, you must be desperate for another drink.' I was, for a glass of wine or a very large G&T. 'There's no ginger left, but there's mint.'

'No, but thank you, I really should be going.' Sarah glanced at her watch, her eyes widening at the time. 'Goodness, we've been nattering for hours.'

She had anyway. 'It's been lovely to have had company. And I do really appreciate you enlightening me about the situation between Claire and Hannah.'

'Just keep it to yourself, won't you? I wouldn't like either of them to think I was gossiping about them.'

'My lips are sealed.' I smiled and got to my feet, afraid she would change her mind and stay longer.

She reached for her hat, pulled it down tightly, and stood. 'Thanks so much, I've had an interesting afternoon.'

I walked her to the door. Because we seemed to have developed a certain rapport, I took the chance and asked, 'You didn't simply wander along here, did you?'

A wave of colour washed across her cheeks. Not the pretty pink of pleasure that had brightened her pale face earlier, this was the dark red of embarrassment. I could see why she stayed in the shade. The colour didn't become her.

She pulled her hat down tighter, bending the brim to shield her eyes. 'No, I didn't.' She pointed through the open door to the bay trees. 'Someone mentioned you'd replaced the pretty cottage garden with artificial grass and fake bay trees. I didn't believe anyone would be...'

Her voice faded, the missing words *so stupid* floating in the air. She fluttered her hands, obviously mortified, having enough sense, at least, to stop making the hole she'd dug any bigger by pretending she was going to say something else. 'I'm sorry. I didn't mean to offend you.'

Were they all laughing at me? These women who extended a hand of friendship only to slap me across the face with it. 'No offence taken,' I said, with a laugh that sounded as fake as the damn Astroturf. 'It's all about respecting choice, isn't it?' I was pleased to see the colour on her face deepen further as this pointed remark sank in. 'Claire asked me about it yesterday. I don't think she approves either. I assume she's the "someone" you're talking about.' It was a guess. Claire hadn't mentioned it, too ladylike to criticise it to my face, happy enough to talk about it behind my back.

'Yes, but just in passing, you understand... it wasn't that we were talking about you or anything...' Sarah's colour stayed high as she tried desperately to redeem herself. 'I bumped into her in the newsagent's earlier.'

And they'd talked about me. Me and my appalling garden. And they'd laughed at me.

Claire would be sorry. They'd all be sorry.

They didn't know who they were dealing with.

CHAPTER TWENTY

I resisted the temptation to slam the door as Sarah walked the short garden path between swathes of my lush green fake lawn. Perhaps I should have asked the company for a dried-up shrivelled brown alternative to use in this heatwave.

Back inside, I headed straight to the fridge, spent seconds weighing up the options and decided on wine for convenience and speed. I filled a large glass almost to the top which took half the bottle. After hours listening to Sarah, I needed it, and bloody well deserved it.

It was peaceful in the garden now. I moved one of the seats to catch a little of the late afternoon sun and sat to enjoy my wine. The day was still hot, but not unbearably so. Or maybe what was keeping me cool were the gulps of icy white wine washing down my throat.

It wasn't a good idea to drink, not tired as I was, and especially not on an empty stomach. But I needed its temporary solace.

The afternoon had been a disappointment. I'd wanted to find some dark intrigue. Something spicy enough to take my mind off things, not two sad thwarted romances. Three if you counted Teagan's obsession.

I sipped my wine, slowing down as the alcohol filtered through to my bloodstream and rushed to my brain to muddle my thoughts. Why had Ruth and Hannah turned up at Claire's craft evening? What had they hoped to achieve?

It puzzled me that Sarah hadn't known about the relationship between Alan Brandon and Ruth. Teagan had her reasons for keeping it quiet. Jealousy is a great motivator. But Broadway was a very small town. Did nobody suspect? Sarah lived outside the town, it was feasible she'd not heard the gossip.

My thoughts came back to Stephen Melville Evans and his reaction to Ruth's name. He would be a similar age to Alan Brandon. Perhaps he'd heard gossip and didn't approve. Any thought of going to try to wheedle information from him was quickly discounted. Men of his calibre weren't the type to gossip.

The wine glass was empty, my thoughts completely tangled. Sarah didn't appear to be friendly with Ruth anymore. So why was it Ruth and Hannah had stayed friendly enough to have arrived at Claire's house together?

I tapped the empty glass against my lips. I only had Ruth's word for it that she'd had a relationship with Alan Brandon. The photograph may have been totally innocent. Maybe she had been burying the truth in a convenient lie and her relationship wasn't with Alan but with Hannah.

Or maybe I was simply trying to fill my head with thoughts about anything else so Kasper wouldn't sneak in and fill me with regrets.

Regrets are for fools who live their lives looking in the rear-view mirror. Whack. I wasn't a fool. I'd done what I'd done. No going back.

I did go back to the kitchen though, more wine seemed in

order. There wasn't that much left in the bottle, so I took it with me and returned to my seat in the garden. My mobile was on the table. I should ring a takeaway and get some food but couldn't find any enthusiasm, my appetite suppressed by the grape. Instead, I reached for the mobile and dialled Kasper's number and waited for my cue to leave yet another pathetic message before hanging up with the usual declaration of love.

Another week and I'd go home. Back to London and sort things out. Put this *cosy* cottage on the market. Get back to my life. It would be a relief to stop trying to make the dull days in Broadway exciting by inventing intrigue.

I played with the stem of the wine glass, sloshing the last of the wine around in the bowl, careful not to spill any. The loose strings of Hannah, Ruth and Claire's stories bothered me. I had a week, perhaps I'd keep myself occupied by tying them up.

Or cutting them off.

I liked to have options.

CHAPTER TWENTY-ONE

I sat in the garden till the light faded and my head was spinning from a combination of alcohol and tiredness. It was time to crawl into bed.

I left the empty bottle and glass where they were, grabbed my phone and got to my feet, my free hand braced on the table to steady me. The cottage seemed a long way away. I hadn't switched on a light and the path to the back door was hidden in shadows. The cottages to either side were shrouded in darkness, both, like mine, holiday retreats for out-of-towners who seemed to rarely visit. Certainly, in the time I'd been there nobody had stayed in either.

The night was still, punctured only by the distant mournful sound of an owl. My London friends wondered that I wasn't nervous here alone but the quiet suited my current mood. Time enough to return to the manic cacophony of city life. Time enough. I took a deep breath, the perfume of some night-scented flower tickling my nose.

Such a pretty scent but I knew the truth: they didn't fill the air for human delight. I'd put solar lights out when I first arrived and was both mesmerised and horrified by the size of the moths that fluttered around them once night fell. I removed the lights, leaving the insects to descend upon those odoriferous flowers instead.

The thought of those large hairy ugly insects landing on me sent me lurching towards the door. I caught my foot on a loose patio slab and stumbled forward, my hand reaching for something solid in the darkness. Finding nothing, I staggered, tried to get my balance and grunted as my shoulder and arm connected painfully with the rough Cotswold stone of the cottage, the mobile I was carrying sent flying.

Stunned, I stayed where I was until a sharp pain made me push away. I touched my arm and felt the stickiness of blood, the roughness of broken skin. 'Damn!'

In the kitchen, with the door shut, I switched on the light and surveyed my injury. Long bloody scratches, some scrapes. I pulled a clean tea towel from a drawer and wrapped it around the worst of them.

The back door was locked before I remembered my phone lying outside somewhere. I banged my head on the wood in frustration and tried to open the door again but after two attempts gave up. The phone would be fine. It was in a case. Slugs might investigate but I doubt if a bit of slime was going to bother it.

My shoulder ached from where I'd slammed against the wall. It took me a few minutes of frantically searching drawer after drawer to find some painkillers. I popped two out of the foil and swallowed them dry, then thought better of it and grabbed a glass. If I didn't drink some water, I was heading for a colossal hangover. One glass was all I could manage. I refilled it to take with me but when I looked up the stairway, I put it down on the floor. Ascending the steep staircase in my current condition needed both hands.

Never had a bed looked so inviting. I pulled my dress off and tossed it into a corner. It was quickly followed by my underwear. The tea towel had fallen from my arm, I wrapped it around again, switched out the lights and lay down with a grateful sigh. It was too hot for even the sheet I'd been using the last few nights.

Exhaustion weighed me down. Surely sleep would come.

It should have done but my restless brain had other ideas. Those strings were dangling, tantalising me. Why had Claire ended her relationship with Hannah? Sarah said she'd left suddenly and never returned in all those years – that didn't strike me as an amicable separation.

If Ruth was telling the truth about her relationship with Alan, and despite Sarah's denial I was convinced she was, had Claire deliberately come between them... because she didn't approve of her father's plans to marry a woman her age... because Claire wanted the role as lady of the manor for herself... or was there something more to it?

Perhaps I was simply making intrigue where there was none. To fill my head with white noise instead of the dangerous thoughts that were still trying to force their way in.

That stupid meaningless affair I'd embarked on had been a bit of fun. Nothing more.

Kasper and his damn pride.

I thought he loved me enough to forgive me.

How wrong I'd been.

92

CHAPTER TWENTY-TWO

I must have fallen asleep at some stage because when I opened my eyes it was daylight. I wasn't sure how long I'd slept, but it hadn't been enough and my brain felt woolly when I sat up. Or perhaps it was the effects of alcohol on an empty stomach. That day, I promised my poor body, I'd eat and not drink.

With a head full of good intentions, I swung my feet to the floor and stood. Too fast. I winced with the pain in the shoulder and arm that had hit the wall the previous night. I looked down at the scratches and scrapes and the lovely purple shade that had exploded from shoulder to elbow. It hadn't felt so bad after the painkillers and the anaesthetic effect of the alcohol but now it ached like hell. None of the scratches were deep. They looked raw and nasty but at least the bleeding had stopped.

When I looked at my bed, I groaned. The few hours' sleep I'd had were obviously spent twisting and turning and although the bleeding had stopped it had continued for long enough to streak my expensive linen sheet with lines of red. Grunting with annoyance, I pulled it off, took it to the bathroom and threw it into the bath. Hopefully a soak in cold water would rescue it. I filled the bath, sloshed the sheet around a few times and stood.

That was as much as I was going to do.

The exertion made me hot and sticky. I could have done with a shower but was afraid to start the scratches bleeding again. Instead, I did my best with a damp flannel. It would have to suffice. I slipped on another of my loose linen shift dresses, this one with elbow-length sleeves to hide the previous day's stupidity and headed downstairs.

The stairway led directly into the living room, ending only feet from the porch door which I'd left open. To my surprise, there was a letter sticking through the letter box. None of my London friends had the address and I knew it wouldn't be from Kasper.

I pulled it out and looked at it. No address. Just my first name scrawled across the poor-quality envelope. Curious. I took it with me to the kitchen and left it on the table. Not until I'd rescued and cleaned my slug-slimed phone and made coffee and toast did I reach for it. I tore it open and pulled out a single sheet of paper. There wasn't much written on it. A few blunt words lacking any subtlety.

You're not wanted here, troublemaker, go back to London.

It hadn't been signed. No surprise there. I balled the sheet and tossed it towards the rubbish bin. It missed by a mile – much as the words had done. Seriously, did the writer really think mere words would force me away? I chewed on the last piece of toast and drained the coffee pot. More caffeine was needed to get my thoughts in order.

It looked as if my questions had upset someone. *Trouble-maker?* Perhaps Sarah and Ruth had been talking... but to whom?

I smiled as I looked to where the scrunched-up ball of paper sat. Some actions have the opposite effect to what we hope. The note certainly did. If someone felt the need to warn me off, then there was something to find out... something more intriguing than failed love affairs.

Sarah's arrival the day before had changed my plans, I'd follow through with them that morning. Drive to Willersey and try to find Hannah. I had an idea she might be the key to everything.

I left the house at ten. The thick walls of the cottage kept it cool and made me forget how hot it was outside. I had a quick reminder when I opened the front door and the heat hit me like a blast from a furnace. Hot and humid, perspiration was pinging before I made it to my car. It was parked in the sun, the door handle blisteringly hot. I pulled the door open as far as possible, reached in to insert the car key, then opened all the windows hoping for a draught to cool the interior. It wasn't happening. I felt the leather seat and groaned. Way too hot to sit on. I headed back into the cottage for something to cover it.

I waited till the worst of the heat had left the interior before climbing in. The air-conditioning had the car cool within a few minutes and I could relax on the short drive to Willersey. It was only a couple of miles to the town, but I'd only driven for a few minutes before I was stuck behind a laden farm vehicle doing about five miles an hour. On the twisting narrow roads there was nowhere I could overtake. Rather than railing at my bad luck, I used the opportunity to admire the countryside. There had been little rain for weeks and the land was looking parched. I've no doubt lush green would have looked fabulous but for me the scorched vegetation blended in better with the Cotswold stone houses.

When the farm vehicle turned into a field, I should have been able to speed up but suddenly I was there, in Willersey, awed by yet more beautiful Cotswold stone buildings, driving as slowly as I could.

There was no better way to find out information than over a drink so when I saw the Bell Inn with outdoor seating overlooking the village green, I indicated and pulled into a parking space. Unfortunately, I was driving. Despite my preference for breaking rules rather than keeping them I held myself in too high esteem to risk my life for a glass of wine, but they'd have coffee.

I pushed the door open into a small, charming pub and crossed the flagstone floor to the bar. Mid-morning it was quiet. The bartender's attention was on whatever programme was running on a computer sitting on the counter. His brown eyes flicked up, then lingered before a smile crooked his lips. 'Hi, what can I do for you?'

There was a hint of suggestion in his words. I wondered how often it was successful. He was maybe twenty, goodlooking in an obvious kind of way, with an arrogant sense of his own importance telling me as clearly as if written across his forehead he'd be selfish and useless in bed.

'A coffee, please.'

'A cappuccino?'

Yes, I guessed he'd like women with plenty of fluff. 'A double espresso, please.'

He obviously realised his charm was wasted on me because when he asked me where I'd be sitting his words were sharper.

'Outside.'

'Okay, I'll bring it to you.'

'Thanks.' I'd probably lost any opportunity to get information from him, but anyway I doubted if women like Hannah appeared anywhere on his radar. No matter, I'd have my coffee, admire the view and consider my options.

The espresso was good, and it was pleasant to sit looking across the green to the pond where a family of ducks added to the scene. Picture-postcard perfect. I guessed it was what most people would think sitting there, the sun beating down, the scene almost idyllic. Not me though. I was wondering what secrets the two women standing on the far side of the green were sharing. Whose lives they were ripping to shreds with careful words. And the man who passed... feet dragging in the dust, eyes fixed on the ground, an almost visible cloud of weariness hanging over him... was he contemplating his demise, wondering if the duck pond was deep enough, or if the distant woodland would be a better place to end his misery?

People and their wretched lives fascinated me.

When they'd gone... those women, that pathetic man... the stage was empty, and I could relax. Tiredness weighed me down, apathy wiping away any desire to proceed with my half-baked plan. I ordered another coffee and would probably have been quite happy to sit there for the rest of the day, sipping one after the other, if I didn't get the distinct skin-crawling feeling someone was staring at me. Trying to be casual about it I looked around but whoever was assessing me was out of my line of vision.

After the early morning missive advising me to get out of Dodge, I was perhaps right to be wary. I hadn't considered looking in my rear-view mirror as I'd driven there so perhaps someone had followed me, curious as to where I was going. Someone... one of the art group or Teagan. They would know why I had come to Willersey. I'd spoken to Claire, Ruth and Sarah, only Aileen and Hannah remained.

The feeling I was under observation served to shift my

apathy. Plus, there was only so much coffee I could drink. I settled my bill with the sullen-faced boy behind the bar who appeared to take rejection badly. Poor thing, hopefully he'd learn.

Forgetting him before I'd left the bar, I stood outside and scanned the road in each direction. If someone was observing me, they were being careful. It helped to know the area, and I wondered if it was Hannah. She might have been forewarned by Sarah, Ruth or even Claire that I was asking questions.

Leaving my car where it was, I walked the short distance to the petrol station. Like many small towns, there was a handy convenience store selling a wide range of products. I put my face mask on, headed inside and pottered around it until the two customers who were queuing to pay had left.

I took the items I'd randomly selected to the counter. 'Hi, I'll take these please.'

'That'll be four ninety-five,' the assistant said. 'D'you want a bag?'

'Please, thanks. I never remember to bring one.'

'People never do but they don't seem to mind paying the extra for one.' She put the packets of biscuits and loaf of bread inside a carrier bag and handed it across.

'The biscuits are for a friend if I can find where she lives. You know how it is when someone says they live at such-and-such address and you think it'll stick in your head so you don't bother writing it down.' I shook my head at my stupidity.

'You don't have her phone number?'

'Ha, I wish I'd been that sensible!' I moved a couple of steps towards the door before turning. 'I don't suppose you know her. Hannah Woods?'

It might have worked. I could have been that lucky, but the woman shook her head. 'No, sorry, not a name I know. I haven't lived around here that long.'

Just my luck. I gave a wave, left the shop and headed back to my car, the bag drooping from one hand. When I opened the boot, a gust of hot air hit me. Chocolate biscuits weren't the most sensible thing to have purchased. It was hotter than hell, the chocolate would melt in seconds. Yet another stupid decision. I slammed the boot shut, pushed damp tendrils of hair from my face and looked around. Not a sinner to be seen but I still had that sensation of being stared at. I leaned against the car, jerking away in a hurry when I felt the hot metal.

The idea of driving around in the hope of finding where Hannah lived didn't appeal in this heat. I checked my watch. Midday. I wasn't particularly hungry, but lunch would pass some time.

I headed back into the pub where the sullen boy had been replaced by an older man who smiled warmly as I approached the bar.

'Hi,' I said and tried the same story of a forgotten address. 'I don't suppose you know her... Hannah Woods?'

'No, don't know the name, I'm afraid.'

'No worries. I'll get some lunch and maybe I'll remember it.' I scanned a menu. Typical pub fare with a variety of sandwiches and pies. I wanted something lighter. 'You don't have salads of any sort, do you?'

'Just what's there.'

I pointed at one of the sandwiches. 'Okay, I'll have the avocado, prawn and tomato sandwich. Is it possible to hold the cucumber?'

'Yeah, no problem,' he said, scribbling my order down on a notepad.

'Could I have some lettuce instead?'

'Sure.' Another scribble.

'And if you could hold the bread too, that would be perfect.' I met his raised eyebrow with a smile before adding, 'And a cappuccino, please.' I waved towards the door. 'I'll be sitting outside.'

The seat I'd had earlier was now in full sun. I moved to one under a parasol which wasn't ideal since it was fixed in place and not at the correct angle to prevent rays beating down on the table. The heavy wooden chair was in the shade but even that didn't offer much respite from the midday heat, and I could feel prickles of sweat between my breasts and under my arms. After lunch, I'd give up, go home and have a cool shower. And a glass of chilled wine.

It was the sullen boy who brought my lunch out. I swear he smirked when he put the cappuccino in front of me. I ignored him and waited till he'd gone before pulling the plate of food towards me. It was exactly what I'd wanted, light and tasty.

I'd finished and was sipping the coffee when movement on the other side of the village green caught my eye. Perhaps she'd not expected me to look up when I did because she didn't duck out of the way. A sneer curled my lip as I raised a hand in greeting.

I wondered if she'd pretend not to see me or if she'd slink away afraid of confronting me. Neither happened and after the briefest of hesitations, she lifted her chin and crossed the green.

CHAPTER TWENTY-THREE

I kept the cappuccino held against my lip to hide the grin as Ruth approached looking guilty and defensive. Obviously hot too: her hair was plastered to her skull, dark sweat marks spread outward from the armpits of her T-shirt, a trickle of moisture tracked through the too-heavy make-up she used, leaving a curious slug-like trail from her hairline down her cheek to her chin. Too-tight navy trousers, bunching unattractively near her groin, wouldn't have helped. And I bet they were polyester.

'Hello, fancy meeting you here.' I put the coffee down and waved to a seat on the other side of the table. 'Why don't you join me?'

Ruth took one look at the seat in the full sun and raised an eyebrow before moving to an empty table and dragging the unused free-standing parasol over. 'I'll get a drink; you want anything else?'

'A mineral water. Sparkling, please.'

She nodded and vanished inside, returning a short time later with a glass and small bottle in one hand. 'Here you go.'

A fat slice of lemon and a few cubes of ice half-filled the glass. I poured the sparkling water over, conscious of the woman sitting opposite watching my every movement. Looking up suddenly I met her eyes and smiled. 'I can almost imagine it's a gin and tonic, can't I?'

She didn't reply or echo my smile.

It wasn't until the older bartender arrived with a pot of tea that she seemed to relax. Maybe it was the mundane actions of pouring tea and milk into the cup that restored a sense of normality to the proceedings. She certainly appeared less hot and flustered but her eyes still bounced away from mine. It was too hot to pussy-foot around. I put my glass down and folded my arms across my chest. 'Why are you following me?'

Perhaps heat made people less willing to dissemble. She took another sip of the tea, then placed the cup carefully on the saucer. 'You've been asking a lot of questions.'

'I told you, I'm interested in people and what makes them tick.'

'A nosy parker.' Her voice was scathing as she let her eyes drift over me, her mouth twisted in a sneer.

Her dislike was water off a duck's back to me. I've put up with a lot worse to get what I wanted. Done a lot worse too. 'Sarah told you we spoke. I didn't think you were close anymore.'

'We're not but we go back a long way. Plus, we're Broadway, we'll always close ranks against an outsider.'

I was tempted to hum the 'Duelling Banjos' theme music from *Deliverance* but was afraid it would go over her head. 'I simply asked if she could explain the sense of animosity I felt between you and Claire.'

'So Sarah said.' Ruth picked up the pot and poured herself more tea. 'She's always been incredibly gullible. She told me the sob story you gave her to encourage her to tell secrets that weren't hers to tell.'

'As I told yours.' I held her gaze, unblinking.

Her face twisted, and for a second I thought she was going to throw the tea in my face. 'You had no right to tell her about my relationship with Alan.'

I raised an eyebrow. 'It would have come out, surely, when you married. Anyway, she didn't believe me. Thought I'd been listening to gossip. I resisted the temptation to tell her that I'd heard it from you.' I gulped a mouthful of the fizzy water, too fast, the following belch loud enough to draw attention from nearby diners. 'Always a bad idea to swallow sparkling water in a hurry.' I put the glass down. 'I was surprised Sarah didn't already know about your relationship, that you hadn't told her.'

'My private life is just that... private.'

'Teagan must have known. She obviously doesn't gossip.' I waited for a comment and when none came, added, 'Sarah thinks Teagan might be in love with Alan Brandon herself.'

To my surprise, Ruth appeared genuinely amused.

'Sarah got it wrong?'

'Definitely. The only thing Teagan loves is her role as house-keeper. It's why she stays, despite her hatred for Claire.'

I must have looked puzzled by this because she laughed again. 'Don't tell me that you with your exceptional skill in reading people didn't see the animosity between those two.'

'Actually, I thought it was aimed at me, but Sarah did tell me yesterday about Teagan blaming Claire for the mother's death.' I rolled the glass around the wet circle it had made on the wood of the table. 'Teagan could get a job elsewhere, couldn't she?'

'She has a certain standing in the community in Broadway, she'd find it hard to replicate that elsewhere.'

My interest in Teagan, not strong to start with, had waned by this stage. I was much more interested in finding out about the relationship between Hannah and Claire. 'Had Teagan anything to do with the reason Hannah and Claire split up?'

The cup rattled on the saucer as Ruth put it down. She

picked it up again, stared at the saucer then put the cup down more gently. 'I thought I'd cracked it.' Her voice was barely a whisper, her sigh loud and long. 'Some things are best left in the past. Sarah had no right to bring it up. It's history. Stirring things up again will only result in further pain, and there's been enough already.'

So abruptly she got to her feet, I was startled. 'Go back to London, Jocelyn. You're out of your depth here. Go home before you cause additional heartache.'

Her flat shoes stirred up wisps of dust as she walked away. Then she was gone, and I was left with my thoughts.

Out of my depth, was I?

But didn't that suggest there were depths to explore?

One of my favourite occupations.

CHAPTER TWENTY-FOUR

When I went into the bar to pay my bill, I was amused to see Ruth had left me to pay hers too.

My curiosity about the relationship between Hannah and Claire hadn't ebbed. In fact, Ruth's intervention had increased my interest. But I wasn't doing any further digging that day, the heat had drained what energy I had. I'd enjoyed my time sitting there though, and my lunch, small though it was, was good. Perhaps I'd return the next day and maybe I'd have better luck in locating Hannah.

Before I left, I went back to the convenience store for milk and other supplies. I didn't bother with any chit-chat this time, taking my purchases and heading back to the car. It was early afternoon, even hotter than it had been, my car almost breathing flames. I opened all the doors and stood nearby in the shade to wait for the inside to be bearable enough for me to climb in.

There was no delay on the return trip to Broadway and a short while later I was pulling up outside my cottage. I didn't notice the front door was open until I was right in front of it, my keys already in my hand. Automatically, I stepped back and looked around, wide-eyed and alert. There was nobody around, nobody to call to for help. My mobile was in my bag. I didn't bother reaching for it. Who was I going to call? Not the police. I didn't want them poking and prying into my life.

I moved to the door, put my hand to it and pushed gently. It swung in as much as it could with the clutter behind it. 'Hello?'

No answer. That didn't reassure me. If there was a burglar, he was unlikely to reply. I stepped inside, stood there waiting with my head tilted, listening.

The cottage was solid, thick-walled. And quiet. If there was someone there, either they were standing as quietly as I was, or they'd gone. Slowly, I moved into the living room and once again, cocked my head to listen. There was nobody in the kitchen, the back door still locked tight.

Returning to the living room, I looked up the stairs. 'If there's anyone up there, you'd better get out while you have the chance. I've phoned the police. They'll be on their way.' Silence. One step at a time I headed up. There was little place to hide in the small rooms. I opened and shut the wardrobe doors, even bent down to peer under the beds.

My footsteps down were even slower, my face creasing in puzzlement. Had I left the front door open or had that faulty catch simply not shut properly? I tried to recall the moment I'd left, but like many things you do automatically I couldn't precisely remember the details.

I inspected the door. The lock was intact, no sign it was forced or tampered with. A quick check of all the rooms showed me that nothing had been disturbed, nothing missing. It appeared as if I'd gone out without making sure the door was shut behind me. I did have a lot on my mind. It was possible.

Or maybe someone had a key to the cottage. It was an outrageous idea, but was it possible? Everything appeared as usual, however careful scrutiny on a second sweep showed me what I'd missed the first time. As an interior designer, I liked things just so, and now I could see the cushions were slightly out of line, the pile of books slightly askew. Everything a little *wrong*.

Someone had done a good job of looking around. Exploring my life. One of my arty friends getting payback for my nosiness perhaps... a game of tit for tat.

A game.

And perhaps whoever it was, had left the door open deliberately to let me know they knew how to play.

They thought they were being clever. They hadn't a clue who they were up against.

CHAPTER TWENTY-FIVE

The truth amused rather than irritated. I wondered what they'd made of my silk underwear, the sex toys in the drawer of my bedside locker, the selection of erotic novels on the bookshelf in my bedroom.

Which of the women had it been? Not Ruth. She wouldn't have had time. It didn't matter. There was nothing in the cottage of any concern, nothing to tell anyone more about me than I wanted them to know. I was far better at keeping secrets than they.

I fished inside my bag for my mobile, checked for messages, answered a couple from friends who wanted to know when I was coming back to the land of the living. *Soon*, I replied to each without giving specifics. There was no message from Kasper. I sent him a version of the same one I'd been sending for days then dropped my phone on the sofa beside me.

I'd liked to have packed up, got into my car and left Broadway for good but it was too soon. I needed to stay away for another few days. To be absolutely certain. To give Kasper time.

I shook my head and got to my feet. Thinking about Kasper always made me restless. It didn't used to. When we'd first met, everything seemed so straightforward, so *easy*. He was desperate to replicate the happiness he'd had with his first wife, Laurie, and initially I was content to fall in with his idea of what a happy marriage should be. But I'd expected excitement, expensive dinners in Michelin-starred restaurants, weekends in five-star hotels, holidays to luxurious destinations, not the dull monotonous plodding lifestyle of a housewife married to a workaholic.

He really shouldn't have been surprised when I found excitement elsewhere.

Another few days and it would all be fine. I simply needed to be patient.

Fill my head with other things.

That took me back to Hannah, Claire and Ruth.

If Ruth was to be believed, Claire was virtually keeping her father a prisoner to prevent the relationship between him and Ruth from developing further. Perhaps Alan Brandon was sicker than was realised. He'd recovered from Covid but I'd read about the long-term effects, what they were referring to as Long Covid. Perhaps the man was too unwell to fight for his rights.

A sudden thought made me smile. Perhaps he was dead, and Claire and Teagan were conspiring to keep it covered up. I imagined him in his room, tucked up in his bed, slowly mummifying.

How terribly Gothic that would be.

The thought amused me as venturing into the macabre often did. My friends accused me of having a warped sense of humour, they weren't aware, luckily, just how twisted it could be.

Had I not been confined to Broadway, I suppose I wouldn't have given these women and their pathetic secrets and lies another thought. But I was stuck there and needed entertainment. Anyway, Ruth's behaviour in following me and her attempt to warn me off had done what nothing else had... it intrigued me. As did the search of my home.

There was more to these women's stories than met the eye and finding out what it was would keep me amused until it was safe to leave.

Another idea took root, making me frown. I had no feelings for any of the women I'd met. I neither liked nor disliked them although, if I were pushed, I'd have had to admit to finding Claire's belief in her superiority a little grating. Of any of them, I supposed Ruth was the one I disliked the least. In fact, I quite admired her sneaky surveillance of me in Willersey even if I did catch her out. Perhaps that was why the idea had popped into my head. Not altruism, nobody could ever accuse me of that, maybe it was simply pleasure at the thought of getting one over the lady of the manor.

I wasn't sure how I was going to do it, but that had never stopped me before. I smiled at the thought of how success would impact the women. Claire and Teagan in particular, and that made me more determined to go ahead with the idea that had come to me... to resurrect Ruth and Alan's romance.

It was only five thirty. Plenty of time to give the rolling ball a shove. I found it was better to fly by the seat of my pants rather than plan so without further ado, picked up my bag and headed out. A couple of minutes later, I was knocking on the door of the manor house.

CHAPTER TWENTY-SIX

I expected the door to be opened by the grim-faced Teagan so was pleasantly surprised when I saw Claire, whose expression, although not precisely welcoming, was an improvement on the housekeeper's.

I'd arrived with no plan, but in the few seconds before the door opened, I came up with something so radical, even for me, that I struggled to hide my smile. 'I'm so sorry to arrive unexpectedly,' I said, holding a hand over my mouth and squeezing my eyes shut, wishing I'd had the foresight to rub a little chilli pepper in my eyes before I'd left the cottage. It was the downside of winging it. I couldn't manage tears, but made my lower lip quiver pathetically when I took my hand away. 'It's just that I didn't know who else to turn to.'

I was about to say my cottage had been broken into and luckily stopped myself making such a catastrophic mistake. Because I hadn't called the police, had I? And she'd wonder why, and I couldn't tell her the last thing I wanted in my life was the police sticking their beaks in my business. Any of my business. I had to think on my feet but that was one of my fortes. 'I think someone has been in my cottage and I'm so scared.'

It went against everything I believed in to play the part of a helpless vulnerable pathetic female, a role that would have had anyone who knew me in convulsions, but I was never shy of doing something contrary to my nature in order to achieve the end I wanted.

Claire reacted as I expected her to, her expression changing instantly to one of sympathetic support. 'Oh, my goodness, you poor dear, come in.' She reached for me, wrapping an arm around my shoulder, bracing herself when I let my knees buckle a little... for added effect.

My head was down, and I was squeezing my eyes as tightly as I could, hoping to wring a little moisture out before we left the dimly lit hallway or at least have them looking a little reddened.

I must have done a good enough job because Claire sat on the sofa beside me and fussed over me, making supportive meaningless sounds that set my teeth on edge. 'Have you rung the police?'

With a snuffling snorting noise, I searched my pockets for a handkerchief. Claire had leaned away at the noisy contribution to my role as tear-wracked female and she shuffled further away as I blew my nose loudly. Only a fear I would start a nosebleed, which I was prone to, stopped me from continuing my nasal orchestral manoeuvres.

Perhaps I was enjoying myself a tad too much. Reining in my amateur dramatics, I gave my nose a final wipe and answered the question. 'No, I didn't. I feel so silly. You see, there wasn't a break-in, I–' Another snuffle, and lower lip tremble showed her how distraught I was. '–I accidentally left the front door open when I went out, or I must have done, it was open when I returned, and the lock wasn't broken or anything. I was annoyed with myself for being so careless, then I saw someone had been inside.' I dabbed my dry eyes with the balled-up tissue.

'I didn't ring the police, nothing was taken, but someone had been pawing at my things, it made my skin crawl to think some pervert had been looking through my underwear.'

I managed to keep a close eye on Claire's face despite my dramatics, and I'd have sworn she knew nothing about my intruder.

Her expression was one of sympathy and horror. 'How can you be so sure someone was inside?'

I sniffed and sat back, a hand resting across my forehead. 'Little things. Cushions out of place, books out of alignment, drawers not shut all the way. I *knew* someone had been there.'

'But nothing was taken?'

'Nothing. So there didn't seem any point in phoning the police. I was fine until I saw the person had been rifling in my underwear drawer. That's when I knew I had to get out of there and I couldn't think of anywhere to go apart from here.' I managed to inject my words with just enough pathos to make Claire sound like my saviour.

'I'm glad you did, that must have been scary.' She waited a beat. 'If you don't mind me saying, it was rather foolish to have left your front door open when you went out. I know it's not London, but that doesn't mean we don't get the odd crime, and an open door would be a siren call to the wrong person.'

If there was one phrase that galled me, one that should be banned from the English language, it was *if you don't mind me saying*. Was there ever anyone who didn't mind? 'I know,' I said, hiding my irritation in yet another snuffle. 'I must have been distracted by the heat, or something. I'm not usually so foolish.'

Claire nodded, patted my knee lightly, then got to her feet. 'I'll get you a nice cup of tea. Nothing better to calm the nerves.' She left me sitting on the sofa and vanished through the door to the hallway.

Had I been truly upset about the ordeal of having an

intruder, a cup of tea wouldn't have calmed me in the slightest. A gin and tonic or a very large glass of wine would have been my preference. But Claire knew best.

I half expected her back within seconds having given the tea order to her minions. When she hadn't returned a couple of minutes later, I guessed she was making it herself. It was tempting to have a snoop while I had the chance but if my plan worked, I'd have lots of opportunity later. No point in risking it all now.

It was several minutes before the door opened. Perhaps she was allowing me private time to calm down further. But that wasn't my plan. I rubbed my eyes and did the lower lip tremble as she set the tray down on the coffee table between us and looked at me.

'Such an upset for you.'

Perhaps my amateur dramatics were more restrained than I'd thought. Upset? Or was Claire the mistress of understatement?

'Yes, I'm feeling quite shaken.'

Claire sat opposite me this time... not beside me, as if to distance herself from having to offer further reassurance. She poured the tea, added milk and handed the cup and saucer across.

I reached for it, allowing my hand to tremble so the cup rattled ominously on the saucer. 'Sorry,' I said, putting it down carefully and shaking my head. 'I'll be okay in a sec.'

'Have a biscuit. The sugar will be good for the shock.' She pushed the plate towards me. 'They're lemon, gluten-free. Teagan always makes too many and they're so good I can't resist them.' She picked up one and demolished it in a few bites. 'Not good for my waistline.'

'I couldn't eat. I feel quite weak, actually.' I reached for the cup and saucer with two hands. The china rattled gently, enough to make a point of my decrepitude.

'Drink your tea then, it'll help.'

I almost smiled at the hint of desperation that had crept into Claire's voice. Perhaps it was dawning on her that she could hardly throw me out in my sad pathetic state. As I brought the cup to my lips, I wondered about dropping it with a cry of despair. My mother's voice drifted to me over aeons of time as it often did. Too often. I'd not seen her for years, and her words still echoed loudly in my head. *You never know when enough is enough, Jocelyn. Whack.*

I listened to her, as I often did, drank my tea and put the cup back down with only the merest tinkle as it touched the saucer. 'It's hard being on my own when this kind of thing happens, you know?'

Claire reached for another biscuit and nibbled the edges before speaking. 'I didn't like to ask–' She tilted her head towards my left hand. '–you wear a ring, but you've not mentioned a husband.'

I twirled my wedding and engagement ring around my fingers, the two-carat diamond catching the light from the lamp Claire had switched on before she'd left to get the tea as if afraid to leave me alone in the twilight. 'We're going through a rough time. I thought the move here would bring us closer, but we had a big row and he decided to stay in London until we decide where our future lies.' I crooked my index fingers in the air around those final four words, as if to distance myself from the sadness of them. 'I thought we'd be together forever, you know, but now, I'm terrified he'll suggest we separate.'

'Oh dear, I am so sorry.'

'I'm not used to being alone. We've been together forever. So this...' I held my hand over my mouth and half-shut my eyes. 'I'm not sure I can go back to the cottage.'

I couldn't see her expression. After a suitable amount of time, I lifted my chin and shook my head. 'You have been so kind, I don't know what I'd have done without you tonight but now, I'd better go.' I reached into my pocket for my mobile. 'I'll see if the hotel has a room. For tonight. Hopefully tomorrow, in the bright light of day, my fears will seem groundless.'

I searched for the hotel in question. 'Here it is. I'll give them a buzz.'

'They'll probably be full.'

'No harm in asking. If they are, there's a B&B on the way out of town, perhaps you'd know the name.'

'One night,' Claire said as if coming reluctantly to a decision. 'Stay here, we've plenty of room.'

I widened my eyes, as if that idea had never crossed my mind. 'Goodness, I couldn't impose. You've already done so much.'

'It's no imposition. Honestly.' The last with such emphasis I wondered who she was trying to convince, me or herself. 'It will take me a second to make up a bed for you. And I can loan you a pair of PJs.'

I let my shoulders droop and did my lip trembling thing again. 'That would be so unbelievably kind. I think a night feeling safe and secure would recalibrate my brain and allow me to focus anew in the morning.'

'That's settled then.' She didn't sound too happy about it, and her smile was forced. It became almost painful to watch as a further thought hit her, her expression contorted by conflicting emotions. 'You've not had dinner either, I suppose.'

'No, I was going to have something later.' I shook my head. 'I'm really not very hungry though.'

'Nonsense, you need to eat something. Teagan is out for the evening. She left a lasagne and I have no doubt she's left too much, she always does. We can share it.'

My plan had worked better than I'd expected. Now I had to make the most of the opportunity.

CHAPTER TWENTY-SEVEN

To my surprise, we ate in the kitchen. 'We rarely use the cavernous dining room,' Claire explained as she led me through a doorway to the back of the hall and down a narrow dark corridor. 'Here we go.'

The kitchen was a large bright room furnished in a pleasing combination of old and new. A huge American fridge-freezer hummed quietly in the corner, but the room was dominated by a pine table, scarred from time and use. It was surrounded by eight matching chairs, two of which held long-haired felines. They lifted their heads to stare at me with vague curiosity without stirring further.

Claire ran a hand along the length of one. 'I hope you don't mind cats.'

'No, I love them,' I said truthfully, reaching a hand down to caress the nearer one, rewarded by the rumble as it purred in return.

'Usually, if Teagan's here, I'll have my meal on a tray in front of the TV.' Claire smiled as if to say she was as common as the rest of us. I found it more interesting to hear she didn't eat with the help. Remembering Teagan's sour face, and what Ruth and Sarah had said about the relationship between the house-keeper and lady of the manor, I suppose it wasn't too strange.

Claire put the lasagne in the oven then turned to me. 'I'll just go and get that room ready for you while that's heating up.'

If she was hoping I'd insist on making the bed up myself, she'd be waiting a long time. The role as pathetic victim was a new one for me. I was enjoying the novelty of it almost as much as having the lady of the manor waiting on me. 'I'm putting you to so much trouble.'

'Not at all. I'm delighted to be able to help.' There was little enthusiasm in her words, less in the forced smile.

As soon as her footsteps had faded, I gave the kitchen a quick once-over but bar some ancient food-stained cookery books there was nothing of interest to be found. No, the excitement of discovery was going to come later.

The lasagne was good although it would have washed down better with a glass of wine rather than the water I'd been offered.

'I have some work to do,' Claire said when we'd both finished. 'I'll show you to your room. There's a TV so you can snuggle up and watch something to help you relax. It's en suite too, so you can lock your door to feel safe and you won't need to open it till morning.'

I possibly wasn't the most perceptive woman in the world but even I could hear the message hidden in the polite words. *Everything is in your room, don't come out.*

'You've been unbelievably kind; I can't thank you enough.' I pushed my plate away and got to my feet.

'Glad I was able to help.'

It would have fit better with my impression of her... the lady of the manor with the slightly superior air... if she'd left the plates where they were for the help to deal with on their return, but my character assessment was dented when she stood, took the plates and cutlery and placed them all into the dishwasher.

She was back in her grand lady role as she led me into the hall and up the staircase. We didn't, as I'd expected, stop on the landing but continued up a slightly narrower, less impressive stairway to the second floor. I wondered if this was the servant's domain and was half expecting to be shown into a tiny room with a narrow bed and functional furniture, so was pleasantly surprised when she opened the door and stood aside to let me in.

The room was possibly as big as the ground floor of my entire cottage and was breathtakingly elegant. A wooden floor was partially covered by a rug, its muted colours screaming antique, and partially by an enormous bed with beautifully carved pencil posts. Two large bay windows opposite were hung with heavy curtains. An ornate wardrobe took up most of the space along the far wall. Comfortable chairs and occasional tables filled the rest of the space.

'This is charming.'

'Thank you.' Claire inclined her head slightly in acknowledgement of the compliment then crossed the room to a door in the opposite corner. 'The en suite.'

It had obviously been added at a much later date and was a perfect contemporary addition, marble and glossy wood, a huge shower, free-standing bath, a shelf holding white fluffy towels.

One night. I'd have happily stayed there forever.

Claire pulled one of the wardrobe doors open sending a slight musty smell wafting over us. Inside, all but one of the shelves were empty. She pointed to it. 'It's a long way to the kitchen so there's a kettle, tea, coffee etc here, and I've added a jug of fresh milk for you.'

Everything I required. No need whatsoever to leave the room.

'I've left pyjamas for you too.' Claire pointed to the folded bundle on a corner of the bed. 'Now, if you've everything you need, I'll leave you to relax.'

'Everything I could possibly need and more, thank you so much.' I was gushing but I was sincerely impressed with the room. Once Claire had left, I explored every crevice and item. The curtains, I discovered, were silk. A little moth-eaten in parts, but still stunning. I kicked my shoes off and walked bare-footed across the rug to the wardrobe. Clothes hangers swung gently when I opened the other doors but apart from them it was empty.

I pulled a chair over and stood on it to check the higher shelves, sliding my hands over the smooth wood, finding only a faint trace of dust for my trouble. I sat and examined the tray Claire had indicated. Every type of tea and coffee I could possibly require. Maybe it was always kept there for visitors, it was, after all, a long walk to the kitchen. As well as the milk, Claire had also left a plate of biscuits, carefully covered in cling film. I peeled it back, pulled one out and sat nibbling it as I thought.

I discounted the possibility Claire was simply being kind by making sure I didn't need to go rambling in search of anything. She'd been forced to offer me succour for the night, her reluctance had been evident. Short of locking me in, there wasn't much else she could do.

A large flat-screen TV was positioned like a piece of art over the fireplace, the remote on the mantelpiece underneath. I wasn't interested in watching anything, but I turned it on. If Claire passed by, it was better if she thought I was happily occupied.

I crossed to the window and gazed over the garden

spreading out from the rear of the property. Broad steps, lit by solar lights, led down from a wide patio to a path that meandered through flower beds bordering a velvety green lawn. *Real grass.* Further away, trees blurred the boundary. It was all idyllic and once again I felt a stirring of envy. I also understood, perhaps, why Claire was determined to keep Ruth from marrying Alan. To keep this... I too would have done whatever was needed.

Snooping and sneaking and all underhand things are best done in the shadows and that night I was in luck. The long period of hot dry weather appeared to have come to an abrupt halt. As I stared out the window, clouds rolled overhead. A wind had picked up too and blew through the garden with the glee of a naughty child, pushing plants over, blowing leaves from the trees. Rain came, gently at first, then it gathered speed and strength as darker clouds filled the sky, switching out the light, making me shiver.

It would have been nice to have sat and had a glass of wine to watch the drama, a cup of coffee didn't really fit the bill. I snorted a laugh at the thought of heading downstairs in search of alcohol, imagining Claire's snooty reaction. A rumble in the distance made me swallow my laughter and gulp. I wasn't keen on thunder and was more than a little nervous of lightning. I undid the curtain ties and searched for a pulley. Not finding one, I reached for the silk and pulled the curtains across, closing out the storm.

Despite the rain, there was no let-up in the humidity. I pulled the front of my linen dress and flapped it, trying to cool down. With the curtains pulled, the room was even warmer. Feeling increasingly sticky, I headed into the en suite and pulled off my dress and underwear. The bruising on my shoulder remained colourful but I was relieved to see the scratches on my arm had scabbed over.

I switched on the shower, adjusted the temperature of the water and stepped under the powerful spray. It was the perfect antidote to a sticky day. I stayed until I felt cool and refreshed, then naked and wrapped in a fluffy towel, I padded back to the bedroom and picked up the pyjamas Claire had left. Expensive, fine cotton. They were fresh and comfortable against my skin.

Although dark enough, it was still too early to start my exploration. Plus, there was the worry that the storm had disturbed the household. I needed to wait till it had moved away, till Claire, her father, and Teagan were certain to be asleep.

There was a crime thriller on the TV. Full of loud voices and screwed-up faces. I left it playing to hide the sound of the thunder that had rolled closer, louder, a crack of lightning on its tail to send a shiver of anxiety slithering down my back.

Trying to take my mind off it, I sat on the bed and propped the big feather pillows behind me. My phone was on the bedside table. I picked it up and checked for messages before sending a version of the same message I'd sent to Kasper every day since I'd arrived in Broadway.

Of course, he didn't answer.

I tossed the phone on the bed and snuggled into the pillows. The bed was comfortable. The last few sleepless nights were catching up with me and I yawned, snuggled down a little more. Yawned again.

My eyelids drooped and I knew there was a danger I'd fall asleep. Did it matter? I'd never sleep the night through, and the later I headed out on my exploration the better. As if given permission, I felt sleep suck me into its clutches.

CHAPTER TWENTY-EIGHT

Sleep only lasted till the next crack of thunder made me jerk upright. Frustrated, I pushed the duvet back and climbed from the bed. Maybe the storm had made everyone else snuggle down in their beds and it was safe to go snooping.

My leather-soled shoes were bound to make noise if I walked on wooden floors and since Claire hadn't loaned me slippers, I decided to go barefooted. It might work in my favour anyway. If I were caught wandering, I'd plead sleepwalking and my bare feet and pyjamas would better support my story.

I listened at the door, my ear pressed to the wood. But there wasn't a sound to be heard. My fingers gripped the smooth doorknob and turned, one way, then the other. It didn't matter. The door wasn't opening. Claire had locked me in.

It took quite a bit to surprise me, still more to shock. And here I was both surprised and shocked that she would do such a thing. I'd underestimated her determination. It wouldn't happen again.

There was nothing to do but to return to bed, and to my surprise, after several minutes spent planning my revenge, I fell asleep.

It was the distinct sound of a door creaking that woke me, eyes flying open, clarity coming with a blow. Someone had come into the room. I shut my eyes again, snuffled a little and burrowed into the pillow.

Whoever was there did what I'd have done, they waited to ensure I'd gone back into a deep sleep before moving carefully around the bed.

There was a shuffle of feet on the rug, the almost imperceptible sound of someone breathing, then, as they moved closer to me, their face only inches away, I caught a whiff of something unclean and struggled not to gag.

It was seconds before they moved away. I listened for the sound of the door opening and when it didn't come, listened more intently and risked opening my eyes. The heavy curtains had shut out any light from the outside and only the stand-by light from the TV gave any illumination, the red light making everything seem unworldly.

Moving a little, I could make out a hunched figure near the window. I bit my lip to stop a nervous giggle. I'd wandered into a Gothic novel. An old manor house, a storm, a creepy madwoman sneaking around my room.

It had to be the housekeeper, Teagan. With her grim dour face, she'd be the perfect villain.

A rumble of thunder came again. The storm wasn't over yet. It was followed by a bolt of lightning that caused a faint line to appear above the curtains. It startled the figure into loosening their grip on what they were holding and there was a series of thuds and jangles.

My handbag!

Was my visitor simply a thief? If so, they'd be sorely disappointed, I'd only a few quid in my purse.

Convinced by this stage it was Teagan, it was tempting to leap to my feet and tackle her. I could drag her to the ground and get a few punches and kicks in before releasing her. I could. But I could also get hammered by someone high on adrenaline. Weighing up the options, I took the coward's way out and stayed snuggled into the pillow while she scrabbled around on the ground to find the items she'd dropped from my bag.

I stayed where I was for several minutes after she'd tiptoed from the room. I wasn't sure how late it was. The TV had shut down, so I'd slept for at least an hour making it perhaps eleven. When I was sure the intruder was gone, I swung my feet to the ground and switched on the light. Blinking, I looked at my watch. Later than I'd assumed. Almost one.

My bag was on the table where I'd left it. Had I been as heavy a sleeper as my intruder had expected, I'd never have known it had been interfered with. In the same way as I'd never have been aware my cottage had been searched, if they hadn't left the front door open. I'd thought that was deliberate... maybe it wasn't, maybe my intruder had simply made a mistake; unaware the catch on the door was faulty they'd scarpered without checking.

But why?

What could I possibly have that someone would be searching for?

And not just anyone... it had to be either Teagan or Claire.

I was used to being in control, to being the manipulator not the manipulated. Now someone was pushing my buttons and I didn't like it one bit. It made me uneasy. On edge. A dangerous place to be for a woman with my secrets.

It struck me that I hadn't heard a key turning in the lock. Perhaps, having seen I was sound asleep, they'd decided it was safe to leave it. Slipping from the bed, I hurried across to test my theory and grinned in satisfaction when the doorknob turned easily.

It was too soon after my unwanted visitor to go exploring and, afraid to lie down since the comfort of the bed appeared to induce sleep, I decided to make a drink. The milk looked a little dodgy after hours in the warm musty wardrobe, so I drank black coffee, sipping it slowly as I tried to unravel the conundrum... what was my unknown visitor looking for?

Thirty minutes seemed a reasonable amount of time to allow whoever it was to settle down for the night. The caffeine didn't bring clarity. Neither did the second mug but drinking it and eating the remainder of the biscuits helped the minutes tick by.

The doorknob turned easily under my hand. Outside, I shut the door carefully, then stood trying to orientate myself. Light was coming from the stairwell Claire had brought me up the evening before. In the other direction, a short corridor faded into darkness. I had my phone if I needed light but there was safety in the night, hiding places in the shadows. I moved slowly along, my hand on the wall as I felt my way. Reaching the next door, I stopped and held my ear to it. I wasn't sure what I expected to hear... snoring perhaps? But there was nothing. My hand was damp... humidity, not fear... I wiped it on my pyjama leg before trying the doorknob. It turned easily.

But it was fear, not humidity, that sent my heart thumping as the door creaked loudly. I held my breath, prepared to turn and run like hell back to the safety of my room if there was any indication I'd disturbed anyone. But there was only silence and I slipped inside. The room was to the front of the house, open curtains allowing light to filter through from the street lights outside. Enough to show me the room wasn't occupied. Shutting the door behind me, I crossed to a dresser and opened the top drawer. It was empty. There didn't seem to be any point in searching further and I retraced my steps.

It was the same story in the next two rooms. Each was furnished in a similar style to the one I was in, each was clean, both were empty. Understanding hit me; they were all reserved for visitors. This was why Claire had brought me to this floor. When the corridor ended in a solid wall, forcing me into an about-face, I returned along the corridor and hesitated outside my room. Despite the caffeine and the hour or so's sleep, tiredness was beginning to weigh me down. It would make my reactions slower. Make this daft idea riskier.

Only the knowledge that this was my only opportunity encouraged me to continue. At the top of the dimly lit stairway, I stopped again, listened for any sound, then step by step descended to the first floor.

It would have been safer if I knew how many people lived in the manor house. Claire and her father. Teagan too, but who else? Shame I hadn't asked Claire earlier, but regrets weren't going to help me now.

The first floor stretched both ways and without a clue, I took off in one direction. Sufficient light came from behind me to show two doors on one side, three on the other. Having seen the attractive view over the rear garden from my bedroom, I guessed the bedrooms facing that direction would be both Claire and her father's preference. But assumptions were dangerous, so I took care opening the first door on the road side, pleased to be proved right when it was empty.

I moved on to the next, this one on the garden side. It was beginning to feel like a game of Russian roulette, my breath catching as I slowly turned the doorknob, and holding as I opened the door. At last, I caught the distinct scent of human life.

I opened the door wide enough to slip inside, closing it quicky behind me then waiting as my eyes readjusted to the darkness of the room. The layout of the room looked to be much like mine and all the others I'd seen. I smiled slightly as I guessed what had happened. They'd employed a designer to decorate one room, then did every other room in its likeness. Boring but cost-effective. I didn't complain, it made searching the room so much easier.

I approached the bed first. Although the face was almost buried in a pillow, I recognised Claire immediately. Her hair was sticking out at angles and she was snuffling softly. The coverlet was obviously too warm and she'd kicked it off, the sheet underneath rucked up to show a long bare leg and the curve of her buttock. It surprised me that the conservative-looking woman slept naked. I'd already decided I'd fallen into the dangerous sin of underestimating her and this confirmed it.

If I learned nothing else from my risky adventure, I'd learned this.

The drawers of her bedside table were tantalisingly close, and my fingers itched to open at least one, but the contents could rattle, the drawer might creak, it wasn't worth the risk. I crossed to the open door of the en suite. Pushing it shut behind me, I used the torch on my mobile and checked out the bathroom cabinet. The usual suspects: half-used tubes of cortisone cream, an unopened box of paracetamol and a half-empty one of ibuprofen, some over-the-counter sleep remedies she'd probably discovered, as I had, didn't work. That was the sum total of the medication.

What had I expected? A shelf of Class A drugs?

I shut the door, turned off my phone and went back to the bedroom. One final glance at Claire and I crept from the room.

There were more empty rooms before I found what I'd subconsciously been looking for. *Alan Brandon.*

CHAPTER TWENTY-NINE

I knew as soon as I opened the door someone unhealthy was occupying the room. The overpowering sickly smell of reed infusers couldn't hide the underlying stink: a combination of body odour, urine, and the gut-churning stench of shit.

My hand stayed on the doorknob as I battled the desire to flee. I wasn't sure I wanted to know the details of whoever was hiding in this room. Curiosity won in the end and with great reluctance I shut the door behind me. The odour immediately intensified, caught in my throat and forced me to swallow convulsively.

A night light cast a strange orange glow over the room. I could see immediately the layout was different. No antique bed here, no rug on the wooden floor.

Less furniture. More space.

More equipment.

A hospital bed sat almost in the middle of the room. In the latter days of my grandmother's life, when a stroke had stolen her mobility, she was lifted from bed to chair by means of a mechanical hoist similar to the one that stood to one side of the bed.

Other pieces of equipment meant nothing to me. They probably didn't mean anything to the man lying in the bed either.

The man watching me.

'Marcie.' Only one word, feeble and faint, but taking so much effort, he shut his eyes and panted.

Marcie? I ran the name through the Rolodex in my head. *His late wife.*

I moved closer into the circle of light but if I thought a clearer view of me would provide him with clarity, I quickly discovered my mistake.

'Marcie!' This time the name was tinged with longing. 'I thought I'd lost you.'

'No, I'm Jocelyn. A friend of your daughter's.'

His hand reached out with unexpected speed and grabbed hold of mine. Gnarled bony fingers damp with sweat and goodness knows what else, the nails tipped with dark rims the cause of which made my skin crawl to contemplate. I tried to pull away from the fingers locked around my wrist and failed. 'You must be Alan.'

It had to be, but this cadaverous creature, with a lax jaw and watery unfocussed eyes, bore little resemblance to the elderly handsome man in the photographs I'd seen in Ruth's house. Ones taken only the year before.

He unlocked his grip on my hand and moved those terrible fingers up and down my arm in a hideous caress. 'Marcie, I've missed you so.'

'Mr Brandon... Alan... I'm not Marcie, I'm Jocelyn.'

'You were always such a tease. Come and give your husband a kiss.' He puckered up his dry lips, his fingers closing around my arm, pulling me closer. A foul rancid smell was expelled from his mouth, a nauseous stink coming from under the bedclothes. My stomach was churning. If I didn't move away, I was going to throw up.

Luckily, the exertion appeared to have exhausted him. The grip on my arm eased, his fingers fell away, and I stepped back taking shallow shuddering breaths as his hand reached out again, seeking contact, fingers creeping over the sheet like hideous B-movie arachnids. I took a step further away.

'Feed the baby, Marcie—' The words were barely audible. '— then come to bed. I'm very tired.'

Marcie, his late wife. The baby... Claire?

It was clear why Ruth hadn't been allowed to see him, why he was being so protected. There were those who lived well with dementia for a long time, but, as with any disease, there were those who didn't.

I looked around the room, at all the various pieces of equipment and supplies required to look after someone as dependent as it appeared Alan Brandon was, then back to the man lying in the bed. A wraith of his former self.

Was this why Claire had prevented Ruth from visiting?

What would Ruth think now of the man she professed to love?

In sickness and in health. But Ruth and Alan weren't married. She'd no obligation to him, even if she'd been allowed to lend a hand with his care.

Maybe Claire was simply trying to protect the memory of her father.

And maybe none of this had anything to do with the intruder who'd searched my cottage and bedroom... looking for something.

I took another look at the extremely ill man and shook my head. I was missing a piece of the puzzle and had no idea what it could be.

A few minutes later, I was back in my room. There was no temptation to search the rooms on the other side of the first-floor corridor. I'd discovered what they were hiding. *The secret of the manor.* It almost made me smile.

But only almost. What had started as a way of occupying myself while I waited till it was safe to go back to London had become something else. I needed to know why someone found it necessary to search my belongings, and more importantly, what they'd hoped to find.

I'd discovered one of Claire and Teagan's secrets. Now I needed to find out the rest.

CHAPTER THIRTY

Although my head was spinning from my exploits, I was tired enough to fall into a deep sleep and woke only when fingers of light pushed around the edges of the curtains. I stretched and curled up, forgetting for a moment where I was, what I'd seen.

It would have been nice to have stayed within the comfortable arms of that lapse, my eyes shut, pleasantly dozy, but then the memory of Alan's hideously wasted body came to me in full inglorious colour, and I was suddenly wide awake. It was probably my imagination, but I fancied the smell of his room lingered on me, infused into the cotton of the pyjamas I wore. It hastened my departure from the bed and into the bathroom for a long hot shower.

Lacking options, I dressed in the previous day's underwear and dress. My handbag was still where the intruder had left it. The interior of it as much of a mess as usual. If I hadn't been disturbed, I'd have been none the wiser. I scrabbled through the contents for the comb I knew was somewhere inside, resorting to emptying everything on the bed to locate it. I pulled it through my wet hair, then slicked it behind my ears. That was as much styling as it was getting that morning.

I checked my watch. Only eight o'clock. I'd no idea what time Claire and her housekeeper rose but I guessed they'd be up early to tend to Alan. A final check of the room to ensure I had the few belongings I'd brought with me, and I opened the bedroom door.

The house was quiet. I walked to the stairway and listened again before heading downward, slowing as I reached the first floor before continuing to the hall below. It was eerily quiet. I looked the way I'd come and wondered if I should go back, make myself a cup of coffee in my room and maybe watch TV till later.

Perhaps that's what I'd have done if I hadn't heard a crash followed by the distinct sound of someone swearing loudly.

I followed it to the kitchen door, took a deep breath and pushed it open.

Teagan was squatted down picking up the broken shards of a dish. She looked up as I entered, no surprise on her face at my arrival. She merely frowned and muttered a warning. 'Be careful, it's gone everywhere.'

It seemed to be a safer option to stay where I was, watching as she picked up the larger pieces with her fingers before brushing the smaller bits onto a dustpan. 'I think that's it,' she said, getting to her feet and peering around the floor.

There was a shard under the table. 'Missed a bit.' I pointed. 'Under the table.'

She didn't seem particularly grateful, frowning and reaching with the brush to catch the errant piece.

'What have you broken this time?' Claire's long-suffering voice came from behind me without warning, startling me.

Teagan glared at her without replying, then turned to empty the contents of the pan into a bin in the corner of the room.

Claire squeezed past me and crossed the room to switch on the kettle. 'And you've been overdoing it with the garlic again.' She looked back to me. 'Every time Teagan goes to her friend's house for dinner, she comes back stinking of garlic.'

I remembered the noxious breath of the woman who'd bent over me earlier that morning and was pleased to have my guess confirmed. 'You must be surprised to see me here this morning.'

She looked at me, giving a sniff of contemptuous loathing. I might have been offended if I didn't think being hated by the likes of Teagan should be taken as a badge of honour. 'Claire told me last night,' the housekeeper said, turning away. If she'd been told about my ordeal, there was little sympathy in her voice. Perhaps Claire had done a less than convincing job in detailing how upset I'd been.

'It was quite distressing. I don't know what I'd have done if Claire hadn't been so kind and invited me to stay.' I looked across to where my saviour was spooning coffee into a cafetière. She said nothing nor did she look in my direction, her whole focus on the difficult task of pouring boiled water into the pot. Perhaps she was worrying I'd want to stay a further night.

It was tempting to see how she'd wriggle out of it had I asked, but I resisted. 'A good night's sleep has restored my equilibrium. That bed is so comfortable, I don't remember the last time I slept so well.'

It was obviously what Claire was hoping to hear. I wondered if she'd known about her housekeeper's early morning visit to my room, if in fact she'd been the instigator. 'Oh, that's good,' she said, turning with the coffee pot in her hand. 'Please, sit down, have some breakfast before you go.'

Before you go. It was almost amusing.

I was relieved but disappointed to see Teagan leave the room. I might have learned something from listening to their tiresome sniping. I wouldn't from Claire's careful conversation.

She fussed around, making toast, offering me cereal. 'Or I could fry some eggs?'

'Toast and coffee is fine.' I waited till she sat with her own breakfast of the same before bringing the conversation around to her father. Directly, no time for shilly-shallying if I wanted answers before I was shown the door. 'I heard your dad caught Covid but made a good recovery. He was lucky.' I smothered a piece of toast with marmalade and waited for her comment. But she was good, she merely nodded and said nothing. 'Doesn't he come down for breakfast?'

'No, he has it in his room.' Obviously feeling this needed some elaboration, she added, 'Covid took a lot out of him, he's not been very well since.'

Not very well? Claire was the mistress of understatement, the man I'd seen only a few hours before looked as if he was in death's waiting room. 'Perhaps I could pop in and introduce myself, thank him for allowing me to stay?'

Claire lifted her cup and made a show of draining it before getting to her feet. 'That's not necessary, thank you, he's not aware you stayed and not up to receiving guests for the moment.' When it was obvious to her that I wasn't getting her not-so-subtle message, she pointedly checked her watch. 'I'm sorry to rush you but I have a lot on today so must get going.'

'No problem.' I popped the final piece of toast in my mouth and washed it down with the remains of the coffee. 'That's me done.'

'I'll show you to the door.'

If there'd been an eject button, she couldn't have got me out of the house faster. There was no further conversation, even when I offered my gratitude for her help. Perhaps she could hear the insincerity behind the words because she said nothing, merely smiling as she opened the front door and shutting it before I'd barely made it through.

CHAPTER THIRTY-ONE

After a night spent in the spacious rooms of the manor house, it was difficult to walk into my tiny, tiny cottage. I stood in the living room and felt the walls closing in, the furniture crowding me. I wasn't usually given to panic but fingers of it prodded and squeezed until I couldn't breathe. I needed to get outside.

Hurrying to the back door, I screamed every swear word I knew when the key wouldn't turn in the lock, my hands trembling, fingers damp and slippery. 'You shit!' I banged the door, jiggled the key again. Violence worked, the door swung open, and I fell into the garden, taking noisy gulps of air as I stumbled forward.

The memory of Alan Brandon with his scary, skin-crawling dirt-topped digits and the gut-twisting stink of death was to blame. That was all. *Nothing else.*

Another few days and I'd be heading home. Our apartment in London wasn't perhaps as spacious as the manor house but by city standards it was enormous. Once home, I could settle the situation with Kasper and start planning a better life for myself.

This creepy small town wasn't for me.

And once I was gone from it, whoever was curious about me, whoever was trying to find my secrets, I'd be leaving them behind. Wouldn't I?

I slumped onto the nearest garden chair. The storm hadn't lasted or done much good. The grass was still burnt umber, the air still humid. Another hot sticky day stretched ahead of me.

A vague idea that I should go to bed and try to catch up with some of the sleep I'd missed over the last few days was quickly dismissed. There were too many jarring ideas rattling inside my skull to allow me to switch off. With a sigh, I headed inside. If I wasn't going to sleep, I needed coffee.

I took a mug into the garden, sat with my elbows on the table as I sipped, my eyes growing heavy in the sunshine. Maybe I could sleep there. Like a cat in a sunbeam.

Pushing the mug to one side, I crossed my arms on the table and laid my head down. The warmth of the sun and the quiet of the garden worked in my favour. I drifted off on a dream of better days ahead, and of Kasper... always of him.

Slipping into the past, to when we were new together, hours of lovemaking, so much laughter. We often showered together, soapy hands exploring, sex against the wall as the water beat down on us. I could feel him, feel the water...

The water. My eyes flew open, and I jumped to my feet as the rain bounced off me and hammered on the table. My dress was already soaked through, my hair rat's tail tendrils. A boom of thunder chased me to the house, a crack of lightning lighting up the doorway as I raced through.

British weather! I grabbed a tea towel and wiped it over my face. Another flash of lightning sent me scurrying away from the window and through to the living room where I pulled the curtains against the storm and switched on the lights.

The cold wet material of my dress clung to my back, making me shiver despite the warmth of the day. I peeled it off as I headed up the stairs, dropping it and my underwear into the laundry basket in the bathroom before switching the shower on and turning up the temperature.

It was a good shower. Strong and powerful. And the dream I'd been dragged from so abruptly returned full colour, making my skin quiver with desire. It drove me to my knees, made me curl up with longing as the water continued to pound my skin.

Regrets were for fools, but it was time I faced it... that's exactly what I'd been, when I'd risked my marriage for the sake of brief if exciting liaisons. I pushed wet hair from my face, got to my feet and switched off the shower. Wrapped in a bath towel, I went through to the bedroom and dragged a T-shirt and leggings on over damp skin without bothering with underwear. I wasn't going to be going anywhere or entertaining anyone.

Thunder rumbled as I went barefooted down the stairs. It was a day to be staying inside. In London, I'd have spent a couple of hours in our home gym, then chosen a movie from our vast collection. Later, I'd have ordered a takeaway from one of several in the neighbourhood and when it arrived, I'd have opened a bottle of wine to go with it.

And I'd have curled up with Kasper and we'd have relaxed together.

Here, I stood in the middle of the living room and cursed my stupidity. For insisting on buying this blasted cottage. For wrong decisions. I was never happy with what I had, that was my problem, always looking for something with more glitter, more sparkle.

I flopped onto the sofa and switched on the TV in a search for entertainment. Finding nothing that appealed, I reached for the small box of DVDs I'd brought from the apartment the weekend Kasper and I had spent in the cottage. Romantic comedies he'd enjoyed as much as I had. His laughter infectious, making me smile.

The smile faded and in a sudden burst of emotion, where regret seemed to have the upper hand despite everything my mother had tried to drum into me, I threw the box across the room, the DVDs flying in every direction.

I left them where they fell, switched off the TV and picked up the book I was reading but when I opened it the words blurred on the page. Tears of frustration. I dashed them away, dropped the book on the sofa beside me and rested my head back.

The storm was still rumbling, the rain dancing on the window a soothing sound. I might have drifted off to sleep if someone hadn't hammered on the front door.

It was followed by a louder ear-splitting boom of thunder, and as I stood and stared at the door with wide eyes, I had the craziest idea that thunder had come to earth and was begging to be let inside. Lightning followed, backlighting the curtain, making me take a step away. The rain was suddenly heavier, the noise as it threw itself at the window unbelievably loud. I'd have looked out if the lightning didn't scare me.

With bizarre thoughts floating in my head, I moved towards the open porch door and peered at the front door to make sure it wasn't being broken down, giving a headshake at my stupidity and relaxing a little so that when the hammering came again, hard enough that I swore the door shuddered, I yelped in fright and scarpered to the far side of the room.

Kasper?

Had he come to forgive me or get revenge for what I'd done?

CHAPTER THIRTY-TWO

A modicum of sense forced itself into my befuddled brain. It wasn't likely to be Kasper at the door, nor was it likely that Thor himself was demanding access, although I had to admit had Chris Hemsworth been hammering on my door in his Thor costume, I'd have rushed to let him inside. When the banging came again, I crossed to the porch, tripped over shoes I'd abandoned in the middle of it and swore loudly.

Loud enough to be heard by whomever was on the other side of the door despite the storm that was howling outside. 'Hello, hello. Jocelyn, let me in.'

A woman's voice. Impossible in the shrieking storm to identify whose, but I didn't care, weary and befuddled as I was, I didn't want to speak to any of the women I'd met. It was tempting to run up the stairs and lock myself in the bedroom rather than having to answer and deal with whoever it was and whatever they wanted.

It wasn't a desire to be of help that pushed me towards the door but the sound of desperation in the voice, audible even over the noise of the storm. It roused my curiosity.

I hesitated with my hand on the catch as I remembered

knocking on the manor house door the night before. My desperation would have sounded equally genuine but it had been a lie. Perhaps this was too. I needed to be careful; it could be the person who had searched my cottage and my room at the manor. I didn't know why, or what they'd been looking for, but neither had been done to extend a hand of friendship.

Forewarned is to be made careful. I opened the door, gasping as the wind tried to grab it from my grasp. 'Quick, come inside.' I waited till the dripping wet body squeezed past before pushing the door shut.

'I'm ruining your carpet.'

I turned to see the wet, pathetic woman dripping water in a puddle at her feet and swore loudly. 'In the kitchen.' I waved to the door and ran upstairs to grab an armful of towels from the airing cupboard.

'Here.' I handed her a large bath sheet and wrapped another around her shoulders. She was wet through, but I couldn't bring myself to offer her a change of clothes. I wasn't Claire.

Instead, I left her drying herself as best as she could while I put the kettle on. 'Would you like tea or coffee?'

To my surprise, she shook her head. 'Do you have anything stronger?'

She was too busy mopping her dripping hair to notice my raised eyebrow. After all, why not? I opened a cupboard and took out a bottle of whisky.

'Sit,' I said, putting two glasses on the small kitchen table.

She put a fresh dry towel across the chair seat before sitting. Half-dried curls bounced around her face, she reached up to push them behind her ears, and straightened her rain-spattered spectacles.

I handed her the tea towel. 'Dry your blasted specs, you look ridiculous.'

She didn't take offence and did as I asked. 'Thanks.' She

scrunched up the towel and put it on the table beside her then picked up her drink, her nose crinkling as she held it to her mouth.

'Relax,' I said when she hesitated. 'I'm not trying to poison you. It's simply a hot whisky.' When I saw her blank face, I frowned. 'Whisky, hot water and sugar. There should be a slice of lemon beaded with cloves but you're out of luck. There's lemon but no cloves.'

She took a sip and nodded. 'It's good, hits the spot.'

I swirled mine around the glass and took the chair opposite. 'Not being rude or anything, Hannah, but what the hell are you doing here?'

Instead of answering, she tipped the glass into her mouth, draining it. Or maybe that was her answer.

I followed her example and got up to get the bottle. This time I didn't bother with the water or sugar. 'Before you get completely wasted, you'd better tell me what you want.'

The night we'd met in the manor, I'd noticed that Hannah's face tended to colour easily. Alcohol, embarrassment or perhaps anger added to it, and her cheeks flamed red. I sipped my whisky and waited for her to either explode or explain.

Alcohol loosened tongues and gave fools courage to speak. I watched her mouth move as she framed the words she wanted to use, trying them on for size. When she finally released them, they were mundane. 'You've been asking questions.'

I could have gone with the trite, *I'm naturally curious,* or the rude, *so what*, instead I shrugged and took another sip of my drink.

'Worse, people have been telling you secrets they'd no right to share.'

'Sarah told you?'

'Sarah and Ruth. We look after each other here in Broadway.' Hannah knocked back the second whisky. 'I didn't need to be reminded of something that happened so long ago... you've no right to be stirring up trouble.'

'I wasn't aware I was,' I said calmly. I reached for the bottle and topped up her drink wondering vaguely how she was going to get home to Willersey. 'I saw how you looked at Claire and wanted to know what was going on so I wouldn't put my foot in it.'

Anger squeezed Hannah's face into ugly lines. 'That's rubbish. I don't look at Claire any differently to anyone else.'

'Perhaps being an outsider, it was easier for me to see. Sarah was being kind in enlightening me, that was all.'

'Sarah...!' Hannah shook her head in obvious frustration. 'She'd have been better off keeping her mouth shut.'

'She said you were devastated when Claire finished the relationship with you.'

Hannah took another mouthful of the whisky and this time reached for the bottle herself and poured a larger helping. She didn't replace the lid, tossing it across the small room towards the sink where it landed with a noisy rattle.

'On a bender, are you?'

My question appeared to go over her head. She swirled the whisky around the glass before taking a sip. 'Sarah was wrong about Claire finishing things between us. She didn't, I did.'

'Ah, so that was why Claire left Broadway.'

'Yes.' Hannah sat back. 'My parents were horrified by our relationship. They were traditional folk, and I was their only child. No son to take over the farm, just me, and there were expectations.'

'And Claire didn't want to be a farmer's wife?'

Hannah snorted. 'You've met her, could you see her in that role?'

The lady of the manor... mucking out pigs, feeding hens and

whatever else farmers' wives did. The thought made me smile. 'Not really.'

'I told her that I'd been for counselling, that I'd been mistaken about my feelings for her...' Her voice faded.

When the silence stretched too long, I gave her a nudge. 'She believed you?'

Hannah sighed. 'Not at first but then I told her...' A tear ran from the corner of an eye and trickled down her cheek, followed shortly by its twin on the other side.

'You told her?'

'I'd been to see a counsellor...'

It was like pulling teeth. 'Yes, so you said, so what?'

'The counsellor was an early proponent of conversion therapy. By the end of six sessions with her, I was convinced my feelings for Claire had been an aberration.'

Once again, I was both surprised and shocked by the turn of events. I'd heard of conversion therapy, the heinous practice of trying to change an individual's sexual orientation by psychological intervention. Although banned in many countries, to date it was still legal in the UK. 'You told Claire?'

'Yes.'

The pieces all fell together like dominos. 'The counsellor... it was Ruth, wasn't it?'

Hannah reached for the bottle. 'Yes. Yes, it was.'

CHAPTER THIRTY-THREE

I shook my head. 'No wonder Claire was horrified when she heard about the relationship between her father and Ruth.'

Unlike Sarah, Hannah wasn't ignorant of the relationship between Ruth and Alan Brandon. 'I'm sure she was stunned. Then mad at Teagan for not having told her what was going on sooner.'

'Why hadn't she?'

'I'd guess because between Claire and Ruth, it's a toss-up as to who Teagan hates the most.'

Maybe it was the whisky, or weariness, but my brain was finding it hard to keep all the strands from tangling in a knot. I squeezed my eyes shut as I tried to work it out. 'I don't understand, surely if Teagan had told Claire what was going on, she would have come home and put an end to it.'

Hannah shook her head emphatically, making her drying curls bounce. 'I forget you haven't met Alan Brandon. He is a man who knows what he wants. Stubborn, if you like. If Claire had come home and interfered, he'd have dug his heels in even more.' She shook her head again and sipped her drink. 'No, I think Teagan hoped the relationship would simply fizzle out and things would return to normal.'

'Then Covid came along with chaos on its tail.'

'Exactly. Alan was very sick for a while. He recovered but he's in the vulnerable category so they're being very careful. I don't think he's been out of the house since. Hopefully he's happily pottering around the garden getting his strength back.'

Remembering the cachexic face of the man and the smell of death that hung over him like a pall, I doubted if *happily* was an appropriate word. 'He could see Ruth now though, couldn't he, if he wanted to?'

'Teagan insists he's not well enough for visitors. Short of breaking in, there's not a lot Ruth can do but wait. Hopefully things will change soon.'

'Hopefully.' Perhaps my voice carried more than an element of doubt because Hannah looked at me with narrowed eyes.

Or maybe it was the whisky because her voice was slurred when she said, 'They'd hoped to be married by now. They've already done some of the legal stuff, wills etc.'

'Wills?'

'Yes, marriage changes a will, don't you know that?'

I looked at my glass. How much had I drunk? Too much, or not enough. I drained what was left. 'I know that, but they weren't married.'

'They wanted to get the legal stuff out of the way so they could relax and enjoy the wedding. So they made wills–' Hannah crooked her index fingers in the air, swaying alarmingly as she did so. '–in contemplation of marriage. Perfectly legal.'

Perfectly legal. But neither had anticipated Covid. 'Does Claire know?'

Hannah choked on the mouthful of whisky she'd taken, thumping herself on the chest, starting to laugh then becoming almost hysterical. I thought about slapping her across the face, the way they do in movies, anticipating the crack of my hand against her cheek with a modicum of pleasure but as I prepared to strike, she took a deep breath and regained control. *Pity.*

'God, no!' Hannah said, flapping a hand in front of her face as if the slight breeze might sober her up. 'No, but she'll know he'd make a new one when he wed since a wedding invalidates previous wills.'

'So did he leave everything to Ruth?' I tried to sound suitably sombre as I contemplated the impending death of Alan Brandon and the consequences which none of the players in this increasingly far-fetched family drama had foretold. 'Or perhaps he wanted to keep the manor house in the family and leave it to Claire?'

Hannah shook her head. 'No, he'd never do that. Claire, despite her lady-of-the-manor persona, doesn't give a toss about the house, never has. She's been trying to get him to sell it for years. A couple of the hotel chains have made approaches, you see. It's in the ideal position right in the centre of town and that garden in the rear stretches back a long way. Alan knows if she inherited the house, it would be gone as fast as you could say *prime location.* Ruth, on the other hand, has a deep love for the town and its history. She'll be a perfect lady of the manor. They'll be very happy there together.'

'And you don't resent her for what she did to you?'

'What she did to me?' Hannah shook her head. 'She didn't *do* anything to me, she merely helped when I asked her to. Twenty years ago, there was support for the idea of conversion therapy, she was only doing what she thought was right. Anyway,' Hannah raised her glass again, 'Claire and I were doomed from the beginning. Tradition is an anathema to her. To people like Ruth, and me, it means everything. I've been happy with Doug. He's a good man. And I love my children.'

'Are you saying the conversion therapy worked?'

She reached for the bottle again, slopping more into the glass. 'Whether it worked or not, wasn't the point. The therapy gave me time to decide what I wanted my future to be. I would never have been happy in London; Claire would never have been happy living on a farm. I gave her a reason to leave that worked, but...' She gulped more of her drink.

I finished the sentence for her. It was easy. 'You've never stopped loving her.' It seemed to be clear the conversion therapy hadn't worked on Hannah. I wasn't surprised. Trying to change someone's innate sexuality was as impossible as it was wrong.

Hannah smiled drunkenly. 'Some people only fall in love once; it seems I'm one of them.' She waved her glass, the whisky lapping over the side and dripping down her hand to the table. 'I have no regrets for the choices I made though.'

I remembered seeing the way Hannah had looked at Claire, but I'd also seen the way Claire had looked at Hannah. I didn't understand it then, maybe I did now. Longing and loss.

Emotions I knew well.

I looked across the table at my uninvited guest. 'You had no regrets, Hannah, but what about Claire?'

CHAPTER THIRTY-FOUR

Maybe that was a question for a sober moment because Hannah didn't seem capable of answering. Neither, it turned out, was she capable of standing, because when she tried, when she muttered almost unintelligibly that she'd better head home and struggled to her feet, she dropped to the floor in an untidy heap of limbs and damp towels.

There are melancholy drunks and there are giggling ones. It seemed Hannah was the latter, her shoulders heaving as she tittered uncontrollably. I hadn't drunk as much but it was forty per cent proof on a near-empty stomach, and I was feeling the effects. Not totally inebriated perhaps, also not sober enough to deal with the heaving body on the floor. I left her there and swayed into the living room to collapse on the sofa.

It would have been nice to have given the implications of what Hannah had told me some consideration but that was beyond my brain's capability. I pulled my legs up, rested my head against a cushion and, to the sound of the rain pelting the window behind me, fell asleep.

When I woke, my head was thumping. With the curtains shut, it was difficult to figure out how much time had passed but there was no rim of light around the curtains, so I guessed it was late. It was quiet too. Either there was a lull in the storm, or it had finally blown itself out.

Despite my sore head I remembered the earlier conversation and frowned. *Conversion therapy*. Hannah appeared to have forgiven Ruth for her part in the attempt to change her sexuality, but I doubted if Claire had, and I bet she viewed ending the relationship between Ruth and Alan as suitable revenge.

But Ruth held the winning hand, she'd inherit when Alan died and there wasn't anything Claire could do about it.

I wondered if she knew that Hannah had lied about having been converted... that she'd used it as an excuse to end a relationship she'd decided was impossible. The expression on Claire's face when I saw her looking at Hannah... I'd seen longing and loss but wasn't it edged with something darker? Perhaps she knew Hannah's lie and hated her for it.

There was no sound drifting from the kitchen. Hannah was probably still on the floor, hopefully sleeping off the effects of the alcohol. She wouldn't be sober enough to drive, but there were taxis in Broadway, I'd happily call one for her.

I reached for the lamp and switched it on, wishing it was as easy to throw light on the goings-on in Broadway, because there was something missing... some final piece of information. Impossible to think with a sore head, I swung my feet to the ground, waited until the world stopped spinning and struggled to my feet.

If the continuing quiet was an indication, the storm appeared to have died. Stumbling to the curtains, I parted them and peered through. Ominous heavy clouds hanging low in the sky told me I was being optimistic... merely a lull, not the end. I held my watch up to check the time, surprised to see it was almost 8pm. I'd slept for hours, thanks to whisky's anaesthetic.

In the kitchen, Hannah was still on the floor. She'd spread herself out, her head resting on her bent arm and looked surprisingly comfortable. It was tempting to nudge her with the toe of my shoe, but I needed to get my head to stop thumping first. I opened a kitchen drawer and rummaged among the clutter for the paracetamol I knew was there somewhere. It was shoved to the back. I pulled it out and popped two pills, swallowing them down with a gulp of water from the tap.

It seemed sensible to leave the packet on the table for Hannah when she woke, she'd be in need of relief. Back in the living room, I sat cradling a glass of water in my hands and rested my head back willing the ache to subside. Although Hannah's revelation had explained the dynamics between the main players, it didn't explain why Teagan had searched my room, or why she or Claire had searched the cottage. I didn't like mysteries when I was the focus, it was unsettling.

The answer would be to leave Broadway and never return. Except I couldn't leave just yet. It was too soon.

Damn Kasper!

I threw the glass across the room, an arc of water following in its wake. I half expected the noise as it hit the wall to wake Sleeping Beauty in the next room but there was no sound of her stirring.

Did it matter that someone had been snooping into my affairs? Nothing had been taken after all. But it was unsettling to think that someone was looking at me with suspicious eyes. It was what I did, I wasn't used to the situation being reversed.

If I didn't have secrets... hadn't done things... if my life was simpler... then it wouldn't matter.

But I did have secrets, I had done so many things, and my

life was anything but simple. So, yes it did matter. I had to find out who and why, and deal with it. It was what I did after all.

Make everything work in my favour.

CHAPTER THIRTY-FIVE

It was another hour before I heard Hannah groan. I'd been wrestling unsuccessfully with my thoughts and welcomed the distraction.

She was lying flat on her back when I went through, a hand over her eyes, one leg under one of the chairs, the other under the table. Her face was unnaturally pale. I hoped she wasn't going to be sick. The look and stink of vomit made my stomach churn.

I lifted the chair out of the way, the rattle making her open bleary eyes to peer at me. 'How much did I drink?'

I spotted the whisky bottle on the counter. It had been full when I'd opened it. There was about two inches left. 'A lot,' I said reaching a hand down to help her stand.

'Thanks.' She tottered when she stood, and I hurriedly pushed a chair behind her.

I slid a glass of water and the paracetamol towards her. She eyed the packet suspiciously, picked it up and read what it said, turning it on its end to check the use-by date. I'd not checked myself and had no idea how old they were.

'Out of date the end of the month,' she said, taking out the foil and pushing two tablets into her hand. She tossed them into her mouth and drained the glass of water. 'I don't normally drink.'

'Probably just as well because you don't seem to know when to stop.'

She shrugged off my criticism. 'Sometimes things get to me.'

I was curious about something. 'Why did you go to Claire's art night? It was asking for trouble, wasn't it?'

Hannah's smile was sweet. It lit her face and transformed her from plain to startlingly attractive.

I tilted my head to look at her, unusually curious about this woman. 'And another thing, why do you wear those hideous, ridiculously large specs that take over half your face?'

'Shit, don't spare my feelings, will you?' But she looked amused rather than offended. 'I'll trade you the answers to your questions for a cup of tea.'

'Ha, deal!' With the kettle on, I searched for something to eat. There was bread in the freezer I could defrost, and tinned salmon in the cupboard. A few minutes later, I put a plate of salmon sandwiches and a pot of tea on the table. 'I'll expect to be told everything in return for this,' I said, adding mugs and a jug of milk.

We ate in silence for a while, then Hannah held the mug of tea between her cupped hands and smiled at me. 'You interest me, Jocelyn. I never really know what you're thinking.' She sipped her tea. 'Me, on the other hand, everything is written on my face, I can never hide anything.' She took off her spectacles, held them by one arm and swung them gently. 'These are my shelter.'

I blinked in surprise. 'They're not prescription glasses?'

'Nope.' Her expression slipped into lines of sadness. 'It was after Claire left. I felt everyone's eyes on me, watching me as I struggled to get through the days of sadness and excruciating loss. I got the first pair from a charity shop. They had prescription lenses but weren't very strong. Then I found where I could get plain glass ones from a mail-order company.'

'That's the craziest thing I've ever heard.'

'Even crazier, nobody else knows. It's quite liberating to be able to tell someone the truth.'

I looked at her in disbelief. 'Nobody knows? Not even your husband?'

'No. Doug is the sweetest man, he wouldn't understand.' She laughed. 'He'd think I'd lost the plot.' She looked at me with a suddenly serious expression. 'Not many people would understand, but I think you do, don't you?'

The need to hide behind a mask? Oh yes, I understood. 'Yes.' I didn't qualify my answer. I understood why Hannah hid behind a mask... to prevent a harsh world seeing her vulnerability... but she'd never understand why I did, never understand it was to hide the reality of who I was. I was Dorian Grey's portrait in the attic. She'd never understand that.

'I knew it,' Hannah said with a satisfied nod. 'I felt a certain connection.'

I busied myself taking my empty plate to the dishwasher, pouring more tea and adding milk. All to keep hidden the sudden flush of tears her words had caused. We could never be friends, me and this *nice* woman. And for probably the first time ever, I wasn't using the word as an insult the way I'd been so painfully taught to do. *Nice.* Genuine and kind. Hannah looked at me, but she didn't see me, she didn't even realise we spoke a different language.

'What about my other question?' I asked, trying to get the conversation on a safer topic. 'What made you join Claire's art group?'

'Ruth asked me to.' Hannah reached for another sandwich,

demolishing it in a couple of bites before brushing crumbs from her fingers. 'I refused at first–'

'But then she told you about her relationship with Alan?'

'That's it. She called to the farm one day and asked to speak to me. We weren't friends any longer, not really, and I hadn't seen her for months. We sat over a pot of tea, and she told me all about it.' Hannah smiled and shook her head. 'Ruth in love was a revelation. I was a little stunned. She was desperate to see Alan and thought the craft night was a way in.'

'But she didn't get to see him, did she?' I was curious as to whether Ruth was aware of Alan's condition.

'No, she didn't. The first night we went she asked to go to the loo. She knew where it was, since she'd spent time in the house, but Claire insisted on showing her and waiting for her in case she got lost on her return. It was almost funny.'

I imagined Ruth's frustration at being so well blocked. 'I suppose short of pushing Claire over and making a run for the stairway, she couldn't have done much.'

'Exactly,' Hannah agreed.

I looked at her. She was right, she had one of those faces where every emotion was clear, colouring her eyes in tones of sorrow and refiguring her lips in a twist of pain. 'It wasn't the only reason you went though, was it?'

'I should put my glasses on, shouldn't I?' She hung her head for a second, her hair swinging forward to provide a mask of a different kind. Finally, she swept the mass of curls behind her ears and looked at me. 'Claire left Broadway the day after I told her I'd changed. Left and never came back. Not even for her mother's funeral. When she did return, Covid had impacted our lives and restricted our freedom. Shops were shut so I'd less reason to come into town too. When Ruth asked me to go along...' Hannah sighed, a long low sound. 'I wanted to and didn't want to. I wasn't lying, Claire is the only person I've ever truly loved. I was also afraid to see her in case my feelings hadn't changed.'

'And they hadn't?' I didn't really need to ask; I could see the answer clearly written in her eyes. It fascinated me, this ability to love so deeply. It's not something I was able to do, it required too much selflessness.

'No,' Hannah said. 'My feelings hadn't altered at all, but hers had. I saw such hatred in her eyes it made me weak. Hatred for me, hatred for Ruth. I knew then Claire was never going to allow a relationship between her father and Ruth to continue.'

'Claire still believes Ruth's conversion therapy worked?'

Hannah shrugged. 'I never told her otherwise. She'd have heard about my marriage to Doug too. The perfect heterosexual couple providing the children my parents desperately wanted to secure the future of the farm.'

'You could tell Claire the truth now, leave Doug and your children to look after the farm, make a new life for yourself with her. Don't you deserve it at last?' It seemed clear to me. If you wanted something you went after it with everything you had, let nothing stand in your way.

A strange expression crossed Hannah's face. It took me a second to interpret it, pity wasn't an emotion usually directed my way.

CHAPTER THIRTY-SIX

'Why not?' I genuinely couldn't understand why Hannah would pass up the opportunity to find happiness after years of putting everyone else's needs first.

'Why not?' She laughed as if puzzled, the sound fading as she realised I was serious. 'Claire may very well be the love of my life, but Doug is my husband, my partner, the father of my children. We've been through tough times over the years, and every time, we got through them together. He's a genuinely good guy who has always loved me, and if I left him, it would break him to pieces. I'd never do anything to hurt him.'

'You sound like you're in love with him.'

Hannah's chair fell backwards as she stood abruptly. She caught it before it hit the floor and stood with a hand resting on it. 'Life is never that simple.' It was a minute before she dropped back onto the chair. 'We were happy till Claire came back to Broadway and unsettled everything.'

'Reminding you how much you loved her?'

'Doug doesn't know about Claire. There was a bit of talk at the time. It died quickly when she left and by the time he came on the scene, it was yesterday's news.' Hannah smiled. 'If he heard rumours he's never said, but I don't think he'd have believed them anyway. We had a very physical relationship right from the beginning.'

'So, what's worrying you now?' I smiled at her look of surprise. 'As you said, your emotions are written clearly on your face.'

'Claire was never one for half measures. She loved completely; I think she hates with equal dedication. She's determined to end the relationship between her father and Ruth, keeping them apart in hopes that it will fizzle out. We... Ruth and I... think Alan might be suffering from Long Covid because otherwise he'd never have left her hanging like this. They were very much in love; I've never seen Ruth's face light up the way it did when she spoke about him.'

The truth about Alan's condition was itching to be let out but then I'd have to confess to sneaking around the manor house in the middle of the night. Plus I'd have to explain why I'd been staying there in the first place. It was all too exhausting. 'So that's what you're worried about? Ruth and her romance?' I was getting bored with it all.

Hannah didn't have my skill for reading expressions or for interpreting tone of voice and obviously saw my question as indicating interest. But her answer surprised me. 'Not just that.' She pushed to her feet again, and obviously feeling right at home, filled the kettle and switched it on. It wasn't until her hands were curled around a fresh mug of tea that she answered. 'As I said, Claire was never one for half measures. She won't be happy destroying Ruth alone; she'll also want to destroy me.'

I couldn't help it, I laughed. 'Aren't you being a bit melodramatic? What could she possibly do to destroy you?'

Hannah's smile was bittersweet. 'All she'd need to do is stay around here.'

'Ah.' I couldn't think of anything else to say. I'd have known how to get rid of someone who got in my way, I'd done it before, but I guessed this gentle woman was never going to do what I'd done.

Unable to offer her advice she'd take, I changed the subject to something concerning me. 'Do you know who owned this cottage before we bought it?'

Surprised by the abrupt change in conversation, she looked blankly at me for a moment before shaking her head slowly. 'No, I don't. Why?'

'Someone let themselves in yesterday and searched the place, I was wondering who'd have had a key.'

'I'm surprised you didn't have the locks changed when you moved in. Whoever the previous owner was, they'd probably have given neighbours spare keys in case of emergencies.'

Kasper had suggested having the locks changed and I'd poo-pooed the idea, unwilling to face yet another workman when all I'd wanted to do was spend a relaxing few days. 'Kasper didn't think it was necessary.'

Hannah reached for the teapot and topped up our mugs. 'I'd have thought, in your line of work, you'd be more cautious.'

I was lifting the tea to my mouth and stopped with the rim of the mug resting on my lips to look across the table in surprise. 'My line of work?'

'Private investigator.'

I put the mug down carefully. 'What are you talking about?'

She seemed taken aback by my sharp question. 'You said... at the craft night... remember?'

'I didn't say any such thing!'

'You did!'

She said it with such emphasis that I shook my head. 'You must have misunderstood, I'm not a bloody private investigator.'

'But...'

I watched her squeeze her eyes shut, as if that was going to get her stupid brain working more efficiently. A private investigator? What had made her think such a ridiculous thing?

'It was when–' She opened her eyes and nodded. '–you'd been asking questions and someone, Sarah I think, or maybe it was Ruth, commented that you were very curious about everyone. You laughed and said something about it being the downside of being a private investigator.'

My jaw dropped, cartoon-like. I remembered. 'I was being funny. Please don't tell me everyone thinks the same.'

I could tell from Hannah's suddenly wide eyes that they did. All those stupid women were convinced I was a private investigator.

Was that why Teagan searched my room, why she or Claire had searched my cottage? They thought I was a private investigator and were concerned I was looking into something involving them.

But what could I possibly be investigating?

CHAPTER THIRTY-SEVEN

'I'm an interior designer,' I said. 'I'm not now nor ever have been a private investigator.'

Mortification painted bright-red stripes across Hannah's cheeks. 'I'm sorry. Perhaps we didn't understand your brand of humour.'

Perhaps? I'd had enough. I was weary and wanted Hannah gone so didn't bother with being subtle when I asked, 'How are you getting home?'

'My car is parked down the road.' She screwed up her nose. 'I'm not sure I'm safe to drive after all that whisky.'

I reached for my mobile. 'I'll get you a taxi.'

'Couldn't I stay? I won't be any trouble.'

'No, that's not possible. Anyway, what would darling Doug say if you didn't arrive home?' When there was no answer, I raised my eyes to the ceiling. 'You told him you were staying over, didn't you?'

She smiled her sweet smile again and I realised she used it as a very effective tool to manipulate. Maybe she was nice, but she wasn't a bit stupid. And strangely, because I'd been dead set against it, I found myself smiling in return and shaking my head almost in disbelief. 'Right, you can have the spare room, I suppose, but you'll have to make the bed up yourself.' I wasn't doing the lady-of-the-manor bit and making it up for her. My kindness had limits.

My capacity for tea also had limits and I shook my head when Hannah asked if I wanted more.

'You don't mind if I help myself, do you?'

She hadn't asked the previous time she'd made tea but perhaps she was sobering up and regaining her social skills. 'Knock yourself out,' I said, waving her towards the tiny kitchen. 'There's bread in the freezer if you want to make another sandwich.'

I left her to it and went upstairs to take a sheet and pillow-cases from the airing cupboard. As I crossed the landing to the small spare bedroom, humming drifted up from the kitchen. It was a tune I recognised but couldn't name. A sad mournful tune that brought me to a halt, unaccustomed envy sweeping over me for the ability to love so deeply.

The spare bedroom was small, more suited for a single bed than the double I'd insisted on. I dropped the pile of folded linen on the mattress but at the door, looking back, it looked so mean-spirited I huffed in exasperation and quickly dressed the bed, leaving a towel folded on top. I might have congratulated myself that I was being as good a hostess as Claire, but I couldn't bring myself to offer one of my silk pyjamas.

'Wouldn't fit her anyway,' I muttered as I shut the door and headed downstairs.

Hannah was sitting with a sandwich in one hand and a mug of tea in the other. 'You're almost out of butter.'

Ignoring her comment, I opened the fridge and took out a bottle of wine. 'You want a glass?'

'Lord no, I've drunk more tonight than I've drunk in the last year.'

I could feel her eyes on me as I poured, her critical attention making me fill the wine glass almost to the brim. 'Cheers,' I said and lifted it carefully to my lips, taking a large slurp before putting it down.

'I was thinking,' Hannah said, nibbling at the corner of her sandwich. 'I didn't think it mattered to any of us that you were a private investigator... that we thought you were,' she amended hurriedly. 'But obviously it did if someone broke in here and searched through your stuff. I'm trying to think who it could be.'

'I know who it is, or I think I do anyway.'

'Really?' Her eyes widened.

What did it matter, I wasn't going to be in Broadway much longer. 'I had my suspicions, so decided to do a bit of *private investigating*.' It sounded so much better than snooping and I could see from Hannah's expression that she was interested. 'I pretended to be very upset about the intruder and called on Claire–'

Hannah's eyes widened further. 'You went to the manor house?'

'It's not Buckingham Palace!'

'I know, but here in Broadway, it might as well be.'

'Do you want to hear my story or not?' I waited till she'd nodded emphatically before continuing with my tale, leaving out the bit about snooping around the rooms and finding Alan Brandon. 'I was asleep. Not very deeply obviously because I heard the door open and someone come into the room. I kept my eyes shut and pretended to be out for the count. They stood over me for a few seconds to check.' I shivered slightly, remembering the feel of that odorous breath on my face. 'Then they moved away and searched my handbag.'

'Wow!'

'It was Teagan.'

'Or Claire?'

I reached for my wine and took a sip. 'No. Next morning, Claire complained about Teagan eating too much garlic again. That's when I knew who'd been in my room.'

'But what was she looking for?'

'I've no idea, but maybe it's something to do with them thinking I'm a private investigator. Perhaps they think I'm investigating them.'

Hannah pursed her lips. 'Teagan is full of her own self-importance. She likes to know what's going on and what everyone is up to. She was probably simply taking the opportunity for a nosy.'

It was possible, hadn't I done exactly that? 'Would she have keys for this place?'

'Wouldn't surprise me. The cottage isn't far from the manor. Teagan would have known who lived here before you, maybe well enough to have been a keyholder. I wouldn't put it past her to sneak around.'

I smiled at the dislike in Hannah's voice. 'You don't like Teagan much, do you?'

'She thinks her long association with the manor house and the Brandon family entitles her to respect, and to a position in the community I, and quite a few others, don't think is warranted.'

'Are you saying she has ideas above her station?' I raised an eyebrow.

'An old-fashioned notion but yes, in this case, I think it's appropriate.'

'But if she'd married Alan Brandon, wouldn't that have changed things?'

'Married Alan! Are you crazy, that was never on the cards.'

I shook my head. 'From what I heard, Teagan had her eyes on him, and the prize of being lady of the manor, and she blames Ruth for scuppering her dreams.'

Hannah's eyes looked ready to pop from her head. 'That's why she hates Ruth? I always wondered. Teagan and Alan? No, I don't believe it. Where did you hear that?'

I frowned, trying to remember who I'd heard this juicy piece of gossip from, then my brow cleared. 'It was Sarah. She also told me Teagan blamed Claire for Marcie Brandon's early death but maybe she was wrong, maybe Teagan hated Claire for coming home and upsetting her plans.'

'No, the timing is way off. When Claire came back, Ruth and Alan were already engaged.'

'Yes, but we were all aware a lockdown was coming. Teagan probably envisaged days when she and Alan were alone. She'd have thought she'd plenty of time to work on him. I bet she was swanning around the house, practising for the role she'd always lusted after.'

'Then Claire came home and relegated her back to the position of housekeeper.'

'And Teagan would have hated her even more.'

CHAPTER THIRTY-EIGHT

We mulled over it for a while longer until Hannah's eyes began to droop and our ideas were becoming increasingly bizarre.

When she headed off to bed I sat with my glass of wine and tried to make sense of it all. But alcohol and logical rational thinking never went hand in hand. I soon gave up and went to bed.

I didn't have to peer in at Hannah to know she was sleeping the sleep of the innocent, the sound of her snore hit me as soon as I stepped onto the landing.

The cottage was too small to accommodate such noise. It was tempting to shake her awake, tell her I'd changed my mind, but I imagined the look of reproach in her eyes and couldn't bring myself to do it. It was unusually kind of me.

Without bothering to undress, I lay on top of the bedcover and shut my eyes. Usually after a surfeit of alcohol, I'd fall asleep quickly, and wake after a few hours. That night, between the noise from my unwanted visitor and the scrambled thoughts in my brain, sleep was impossible.

Then I remembered I'd not checked my phone for messages,

nor had I sent Kasper the daily update. It was a waste of time but it seemed an essential step. I swung my feet from the bed and reached for the mobile I'd left on my bedside table.

There were a couple of messages, one inviting Kasper and me to a cocktail party the following night. Such short notice was a clear sign we weren't originally on the invitation list and were being asked at the last minute to make up numbers. I deleted without bothering to answer and blocked the sender.

There was nothing from my husband.

I understand you're hurt and don't want to speak to me, but we must at some point. I'll be home in a few days. I hope by then you'll have decided to forgive me, x

I read the message over, added another *x* and pressed send.

Sleep wasn't likely to come. Instead, I went downstairs, filled another glass with wine and took it into the garden. It was still warm enough, although the storm had taken the edge off the heatwave. I did a quick sweep of the table and chairs for the dreaded slugs and snails but found none. I guessed the hedge-hogs I'd seen on numerous occasions had feasted on any to be found.

There wasn't much light pollution in Broadway, the night sky startlingly beautiful. I stared up at the million pinpricks of light wondering if it was possible to pick the one star that made dreams come true.

And if I could by some miracle locate it, what would I wish for? To turn the clock back to the time before I made my first mistake, or the second, or any of the subsequent ones? I thought of Kasper's handsome face, his warm hands, his kindness. Maybe that last mistake was the one I'd choose to change.

I laughed at my fantasy, took a sip of the chilled wine and relaxed. I couldn't change the past. I'd made my choices... my mistakes... along the way and learned to live with them. I'd live with the last one too.

Putting Kasper to one side of my jam-packed brain, I thought about Teagan, Claire and the rest of the women here in Broadway. Outwardly they'd seemed such a boring, dull lot with small-town mores and even smaller aspirations. I thought they'd bore me to death. But now, the undercurrents of hate and intrigue fascinated me.

In a few days, I'd be heading back to London to face intrigues of my own.

When my eyelids began to droop, I decided it was time to try to get some sleep despite the rumbling from the spare bedroom. I'd barely touched the wine. Back in the kitchen, never one to waste good alcohol, I pressed clingfilm over the top of the glass and stuck it into the fridge.

I had switched out the light and had my foot on the first step when I was startled by shouting from outside. I moved closer to the front door and pressed my ear against it. Unable to hear anything, I stepped back and slowly, quietly, opened it, and peered around the edge.

The street was empty. I was about to shut the door when a harsh shout came again.

Frowning, I opened the door wide and stepped outside, walking on the balls of my bare feet as if that would make it more unlikely that I'd step on a snail... or worse, a slug. I stopped at the gate. In the circle of light provided by a street light I made out a bulky figure standing in front of the manor house, a hand raised in a fist.

For a few awful stomach-dropping seconds, I thought it was Kasper. The same build and height. The same anger in his voice the last time we were together. I knew if I went nearer, if I got close enough to see his face, it would be creased in anger, his eyes laser beams of disgust. Perhaps it was why I couldn't resist opening the gate and walking barefoot up the wet dirty street. When the figure turned towards me, and I could see his face, I came to an abrupt halt. He was a stranger. Not Kasper. For a moment, I felt bereft.

It possibly wasn't the cleverest thing to approach an angry man in the middle of the night but there was something rather pathetic about him, and although I wasn't in the least soft-hearted, I wasn't immune to a man in need. It often worked in my favour. It had with Kasper when we'd met. 'Are you okay?'

It was perhaps unsurprising he looked nervous. A bare-footed woman walking down the middle of a street in Broadway in the wee hours of the night wasn't a usual sight. Perhaps he thought he was seeing ghosts. 'I'm Jocelyn.' I waved back to the cottage. 'I live there, I heard you shouting.'

He turned back to face the manor house. 'I'm looking for my wife.'

This completely threw me. Had I missed something. 'Claire?'

'Not that bitch! My wife, Hannah. I know she's in there. With *her*.' There was such hatred in that final word I took a step backward.

This was Hannah's gentle husband, Doug? I held up a hand, appeasing, unsure if I could get through his anger. 'You're wrong, she's not there.'

His eyes were fixed on the upstairs windows. If he'd heard my words, if they'd managed to pierce the blanket of rage he wore, they didn't seem to be having any effect. I looked back to the cottage. Perhaps it would be best to wake Hannah and get her to come out to calm him down, but before I could decide, I saw something that made me squeeze my eyes shut in disbelief. A squad car. In sleepy Broadway. In the middle of the damn night.

Doug's shouting had obviously disturbed others, people who

had no fear of becoming involved with the police. I didn't fear them, not precisely, but I was understandably wary of dealing with them... in any capacity.

I hurried to Doug's side and put my hand on his arm. 'Hannah's not in there, she's in the cottage with me.' His anger didn't disperse, worryingly it seemed to increase. I hurriedly added, 'She's asleep in the spare bedroom.'

The police car was almost alongside. I tugged Doug's arm. 'No point in getting arrested. Come on, you'll see Hannah in a sec.'

Her name seemed to work as a draw and he came with me. The police car pulled up alongside, the driver's window sliding down, a grim face peering at us. 'We've had reports of a disturbance.'

I linked my arm in Doug's. 'Oops,' I said, grinning widely. 'Sorry, we've been singing. Didn't think it was that loud. We'll be quiet. Promise. Anyway–' I pointed to my front door. '–we're just home.'

An untrustworthy lot, the police. They waited until we went inside before moving away.

I flicked on the light.

'Who are you?' Doug leaned back against the front door as I stood in the porch brushing dirt from my feet.

'Jocelyn. A friend of your wife's. I met her at the craft night.'

He eyed me suspiciously. 'Just a friend?'

I rubbed my foot on the doormat to dislodge some unknown sticky substance, wishing I could wipe away the tiredness sweeping over me as easily. 'If you're asking if your wife and I are lovers, then the answer is no. We're barely acquaintances, and if I'd known she snored like a hippo I'd never have invited her to stay.'

This succeeded in smoothing the lines of anger from his face. 'That's my Hannah.'

With my feet as clean as I could get them, I went into the living room, leaving Doug to follow.

A big man, tall and wide, he took up more space than there was to spare. I waved him to the sofa. 'Sit, for goodness' sake, you're making my small room seem even smaller.' I took the seat opposite and assessed this new addition to my household. He was handsome, a little weather-worn, but he'd kind eyes, and creases around his mouth said he smiled easily. 'Why did you think Hannah was at the manor house?'

He wiped a hand over his face. 'I had a call. A woman. She asked if I knew what my wife was up to. She hung up before I could ask what she was talking about.' He adopted a man pose, spreading his legs, resting his elbows on his knees and linking his hands together to hang between them. 'I knew.' He looked across at me then and frowned. 'Or I thought I did.'

'You knew about Hannah and Claire?'

'Of course I knew! You think there weren't several people who rushed to tell me when we first got together, then several more who made it their business to whisper a warning in my ear when we said we were getting wed.'

'Hannah thinks you don't know.'

'She has a good line in believing what she wants to.' He bounced his joined hands. 'I thought if I loved her enough everything would be okay, and it was, at least till that cow arrived back in Broadway.' His smile was wistful. 'I'm not deluded. I know Hannah loves me, but Claire is the love of her life, I can't compete with that.'

I stared at him with eyes gritty from exhaustion. Why had I got myself involved with these people? How did I, without a benevolent bone in my body, land myself with Hannah and her love-smitten husband?

I was too tired to come up with an answer.

175

CHAPTER THIRTY-NINE

I stood and went to the kitchen, returning seconds later with the whisky bottle and two glasses. 'Hannah polished off most of this earlier which is why she's sleeping soundly. You may as well have a glass, you can either crawl in beside her, or have the sofa. No point in heading home now.' When he didn't demur, I poured two generous glasses, then when there wasn't enough left to warrant keeping it, emptied the rest of the content on top.

'Thanks.' He picked it up, looked at it suspiciously for a second, then emptied half in one mouthful.

I sipped mine as I considered what he'd said. I'd never had a man who loved so unconditionally, so absolutely. I don't know if Hannah realised how lucky she was.

'I wonder who rang me.' He swirled the whisky around his glass, staring into it as if the answer was inside. He wouldn't be the first person to look for a solution in alcohol, nor would he be the first to realise any answer it gave was a lie.

My guess would be Claire. She may have seen Hannah pass and wondered where she was going. The curve of the road gave a clear view of my cottage, I pictured Claire peering through the

176

rain to see Hannah hammering on my door. Love, hate and jealousy would have fought for domination, hatred winning when I opened the door and welcomed her inside.

Loathing would have curdled Claire's brain, and jealousy driven her thoughts, to make her pick up the phone to tell Doug the lie she believed. Unfortunately, she didn't tell him where Hannah was, and Doug had reached the wrong conclusion.

'Claire,' I said, unsurprised to see Doug nod in agreement. 'What are you going to do about it?'

He swilled the remainder of his whisky around in the glass. 'Not much I can do, is there? I love Hannah but I'm not such a fool to think I can compete with a woman she's loved most of her adult life. The children are grown, there's nothing to hold her here any longer.'

It never ceased to fascinate me how easily people gave up rather than fight for what they wanted. I stared at the man opposite, his beefy shoulders, colossal hands, firm chin. The picture-perfect epitome of the hero of every action movie, and now here he was like one of those stupid villagers in *The Magnificent Seven*, willing to give up rather than fight.

It was left to me to take the Yul Brynner lead part, or perhaps Steve McQueen? With my experience, I could easily handle the two.

'If Claire left Broadway, Hannah would soon forget about her.' I sat forward, forcing Doug to meet my eyes. 'She told me she loves you and the life the two of you have built together. I don't think she's any desire to leave you, but she's drawn like a magnet towards the memory of her first love. If Claire were no longer around, Hannah would go back to treating the memory as just that, a memory.'

'Yes, but it doesn't look as if that's going to happen.' He looked slightly embarrassed when he admitted, 'I've been asking around, seems like Claire's home this time for good.'

'She might be encouraged to leave again.'

He looked at me in confusion, then laughed uncertainly. 'What, like be run out of town? Like witches of old?'

'I think they used to kill witches, actually,' I said, unperturbed by his sharp tone. It didn't seem sensible to say there were other ways to get rid of Claire if she couldn't be encouraged to go by gentle means. This big man before me might indeed be the ideal hero, but in my experience, heroes rarely wanted to take that final step to ensure success, too bound by morals.

Morals never got in my way.

CHAPTER FORTY

I left Doug finishing the last of his whisky and headed to bed, hoping my clearer thoughts would allow me to get some sleep. Whether it was that or the extra drop of whisky, I don't know, but suddenly it was morning.

It was voices that woke me, a deep one that had my eyes flick open on a startled breath. Kasper? I lay, unable to move as my brain tried to catch up. It was the second voice, raised in agitation, that made the pieces click into place. Not Kasper, Doug. And Hannah. I wondered if she had a hangover.

I didn't have one despite all I'd managed to drink, but that didn't mean I wanted to listen to loud voices. Not this early. Not ever, they brought me back to places I didn't want to visit.

Curling my pillow around my ears didn't make much difference and once again I cursed my stupidity for buying such a teeny tiny cottage in the Cotswolds when, for the same money, I could have bought something spectacular in Italy.

Plus, I wouldn't have become embroiled in the twisted lives of these people. I conveniently forgot I'd wanted some distraction, always ready to forget what didn't suit me. I threw back the sheet. Since I was stuck in Broadway for a while yet, I might as well see what I could do to sort out the pair of lovebirds below.

There was no doubt in my mind that there was something to be done, but then I wasn't stifled by the rules and regulations nice people like Doug and Hannah would feel obliged to adhere to.

I pulled a robe on and went down. The couple had made themselves at home and were sitting at the small table with a pot of coffee, a plate of toast and the minuscule amount of butter that remained.

'If I'd known I'd be catering for a crowd, I'd have gone shopping.' Sarcasm was wasted on most people, it didn't draw as much as a raised eyebrow.

'It's okay, we found some marmalade to make up for the lack of butter,' Hannah said.

'I was being sarcastic, actually, but don't let that worry you.' I reached for a mug and poured coffee for myself before Hannah made the mistake of offering me some. In my cottage. At my table. My damn coffee.

'We've been a terrible imposition.'

If she was waiting for me to say not at all, she'd be waiting a long time.

'And it was extra kind of you to go to Doug's rescue.'

I reached for a piece of toast and sat. 'He was shouting loud enough to wake the town; you'd have heard if you hadn't knocked back the whisky like you had. I could have left it to the police, but...' I shrugged. Let them believe I was too nice to get the law involved.

'We're glad you didn't, it would have been embarrassing and had people talk.'

Doug snorted. 'You don't think they'll talk anyway.'

Hannah glared at him. 'If you hadn't been so stupid and got

your boxer shorts in a twist, they'd have nothing to talk about, would they?'

I lifted a hand, palm out. 'Please, if you're going to have a domestic, could you take it elsewhere?'

They had the grace to look embarrassed, an unattractive flush marring Hannah's cheeks.

'No, we're good,' Doug said, lacing hands around his mug of coffee. He gave Hannah a sheepish glance. 'I *am* sorry, you know, I shouldn't have listened to that spiteful cow on the phone.'

I popped the last piece of toast into my mouth and brushed crumbs from my fingers. 'He's told you, has he?'

'That he knew all about me and Claire, you mean?'

I resisted a sarcastic, *what else,* took a mouthful of coffee and waited.

Hannah looked from me to her husband, her gaze softening as she stared at him. She winked, bringing a smile to his face before looking back to me. 'Yes, he told me. I suppose I should have known. Maybe I simply wanted to believe that people weren't gossiping about me back then.'

When Doug snorted again, she reached over and thumped his arm. 'Right, okay, I was blind to the sideways glances and deaf to the whispers because it was easier for me.'

He caught her hand, kept it in his big paw and smiled at her.

I wanted to put two fingers in my mouth and do a pretend heave. Hannah must have read my expression and guessed my reaction. Her colour rose again and she pulled her hand away. 'We should be going.'

'Yes.' I wasn't in the mood for the social niceties. But I was curious. 'What now? It looks to me as if your marriage is strong enough to survive Claire living in Broadway, am I right?'

Hannah's face tightened. She couldn't have missed Doug's

suddenly intent expression but she didn't look at him. Didn't give him the reassurance he was desperately seeking. Finally, into a silence that was bristling with tension, she muttered, 'Of course.'

Two words left open to interpretation. Of course it was, or of course it wasn't. I read doubt in both faces. A hint of desperation in his, sadness in hers. Maybe I was wrong, maybe their marriage wasn't strong enough, or maybe Hannah was simply lost in the fantasy of the road not taken.

For as long as Claire was in Broadway, that wasn't going to change.

The answer seemed simple. Claire had to leave.

I looked from Doug to Hannah and decided I'd nothing to lose by helping them out.

CHAPTER FORTY-ONE

D oug and Hannah left a short time later. I watched them walk away, as much distance between them as the footpath would allow.

I lounged around for the rest of the morning, trying to come up with a plan but my thoughts were tangled with the continuing puzzle of what Teagan was looking for when she searched my room. If it was her who had searched the cottage.

I had a couple of days to sort everything out. Then I'd be leaving Broadway for good. I'd get a removal company to pack up anything I wanted. I looked around the living room and shook my head. On second thoughts, I'd sell it furnished. The few personal items that were there would easily fit in the car. Anything else could be dumped.

It was a relief to have made the decision. It would be a further relief to get back to London and to get the next difficult part done with. I sighed and pushed a hand restlessly through my hair. Doug had reminded me a little of Kasper. Not in physique, Kasper was a trimmer, fitter man, but in the simple belief that love could conquer all.

Kasper had been stunned to discover I'd cheated on him.

The concept of fidelity had never been one I understood nor felt obliged to adhere to. After all, joining a library didn't mean you couldn't buy the occasional book. My regret was for having to admit it to him, but I'd been left with no choice.

He'd only ever been gentle and calm so the shouting, red-faced angry man who'd accosted me on his return that particular day was a revelation. Admitting to an affair was preferable to telling him the truth, and anyway, although I'd not been with a man that day, I had on many previous occasions.

My argument that my liaison had meant nothing didn't pierce Kasper's carapace of self-righteousness. Doug's shouts on the streets of Broadway had nothing to the bellows that ricocheted off the walls of the apartment and I was inordinately grateful for the soundproofed walls which meant the neighbours couldn't hear. Or complain. Or be a witness.

Retreating to the Cotswolds had been my solution. I smiled slightly as I thought of Kasper all alone in our spacious apartment. Distance and time, they were the perfect *dual* solution.

A few more days, I'd go back and everything would be okay.

Until then, I might as well have some fun. Sort out Hannah and Doug's life. Find out what Teagan was up to. My being a private investigator wouldn't have made any difference unless she or Claire had something to hide.

I rested my head back on the sofa and stared at the ceiling. Something was bouncing around the edges of my mind, tantalising me, something someone had said recently that perhaps might be more important than I'd originally thought.

It was frustratingly close but wasn't getting any closer. I knew the best thing to do was to stop trying, to let my thoughts drift to something else. Unfortunately, that happened to be Kasper, and I wasn't sure that was the best place to go.

The solution seemed to be to get out of the cottage, go for a walk and see if my head cleared enough to give the lurking thought room.

Ten minutes later, I headed out, taking extra care to ensure the door clicked shut after me, although if someone had a key it seemed a silly precaution.

Midday in a heatwave probably wasn't the best time to go for a ramble. I'd brought a wide-brimmed hat with me to provide a circle of shade and I chose the shadier side of the street to walk along.

I'd no destination in mind, but when I found myself at the other end of the town within shouting distance of Ruth's house, I wondered if that enticingly close thought had directed me there. I'd walked further than I'd planned, and I was hot and sweaty. The recent heavy rain hadn't washed away the dust and it caked my shoes.

I stamped my feet as I stood on Ruth's doorstep waiting for her to answer. She would, I was sure. She'd have heard about Doug's scandalous display from someone and that he and Hannah had spent the night in my cottage. I admired her garden as I waited, the mix of colours was pleasing. I wasn't a gardener, and couldn't have named most, just the one in the corner with the pretty pink blossom. I recognised it from an article I'd read not too long before. Prettier in reality, I thought as the sound of the door opening drew my attention.

The phenomenon whereby what you were trying to remember pops into your head when you are thinking of something different always fascinated me, as it did now. That ghostly thought I'd been trying to grasp solidified as I stared at Ruth's unwelcoming face. It made me give an abrupt laugh, startling her.

'Sorry, sorry,' I said, raising my hand. 'I had a strange thought. Actually, I think it might interest you.'

It would take a far tougher woman than Ruth to resist the

temptation to find out what I was talking about, never mind getting the lowdown on what had gone on the night before. She looked over my shoulder as if to check there was nobody to see her weakness before standing aside to let me in.

This time, and I wasn't sure if it was classified as an elevation or demotion, she brought me into the kitchen, a generously-sized room obviously added to the original house and looking out over a lushly-planted garden.

I stepped closer to the window and stared out. 'You've obviously got green fingers.' A trite comment but appropriate and it softened her set expression a little.

'It's my passion.'

Passion. I looked at the neat woman with her overplucked eyebrows and severe haircut and wondered if she'd really been in love with Alan Brandon. Would she be devastated to know how poorly he was or was it the position of lady of the manor she'd lusted after. 'What about Alan?'

Ruth jerked as if I'd slapped her, then pulled her shoulders back and lifted her chin. The very picture of indignation. 'Excuse me?'

'Was there passion there or was it more a platonic relationship? He is far older than you so I wouldn't be surprised if it was the latter.'

Her mouth opened and shut without a word being said. I doubt if she'd often found herself speechless and was unaccustomed to the sensation. It seemed a good idea to make the most of it before she recovered the use of her tongue. 'I know about the wills you each made, and how much you love Broadway and the manor house. Under your care, it would never, I'm guessing, be turned into a hotel.'

'Absolutely not.' Here at least, Ruth was able to make a comment. 'That was Claire's crazy idea. The manor is a home, it will stay a home.'

'Because you'll be in line to inherit it when you marry Alan.'

Ruth looked at me through narrowed eyes, her mouth working to find the correct answer. 'I don't know what concern it is of yours, but yes, that's right.'

'And if Alan dies, it'll be yours too.'

A wave of emotion passed across Ruth's face rendering her features suddenly softer, warmer, loving. Perhaps there was no great passion between her and Alan, but it seemed the love was real.

'I know he's a lot older than I, but he's a fit, active man.' She turned and sat at a pine table positioned to make the most of the view over the garden, waving me to the seat opposite. 'At least he was when last I saw him. He had Covid but didn't need to be hospitalised and as far as I know he's doing well.' Anger hardened her face. 'There's no reason why I couldn't visit him. I've had both my vaccines but Claire spouts about his vulnerable state and refuses to allow it.'

'I think I might know why.'

There was longing in her face that made me shiver. I'd never felt that way, if I wanted something, I took it. I was never beholden to anyone.

I don't know why I wanted to assist these people... Ruth and Alan... Hannah and Doug. Weak fools, they didn't deserve my help. How my friends in London would laugh when I regaled them with my Broadway stories... they would laugh but would they also secretly envy... as I did?

'I have a confession to make,' I said slowly. 'I met Alan recently. A couple of days ago. It struck me he didn't have long.'

Euphemisms are never a good idea when emotions are tumultuous. Ruth's expression remained blank.

'He's dying, Ruth.'

CHAPTER FORTY-TWO

'D ying?' Ruth's voice cracked on the word. 'That can't be, he recovered from Covid. I know he did.'

'Yes, I'm sure he did. He's not dying from the virus though, at least I don't think so. It looked to me as if he has dementia and I've never seen anyone so thin so there may be other underlying issues. I just know what I saw... a man who isn't long for this world.'

'I don't understand.'

How could she with only half the story. It was time to tell her about my escapade in the manor. This time, I wouldn't leave my snooping out. 'Let me explain, but first, did you think I was a private investigator?'

She stared at me as if to challenge the change of direction but when I met her gaze without backing down, she nodded. 'Yes, I did because that's what you told us. Remember? On Wednesday at the craft night. You said–'

'For goodness' sake, I was joking!' I'd raised my voice, her face tightening in response. 'Sorry, sorry, it's simply so ridiculous you all believed it.'

She shrugged. 'Why wouldn't we?'

That made me laugh. 'Yes, I suppose you're right. Anyway, I'm not now, nor ever have been a PI, okay?'

'What's this got to do with Alan?'

I folded my arms on the table in front of me and leaned forward onto them. 'Someone broke into my cottage and searched it. I pretended I was scared as a result, descended upon the manor looking for help and persuaded Claire to let me stay overnight. She did so reluctantly and went to a great deal of trouble to ensure I didn't need to leave the room during the night. Later, when they thought I was asleep, someone came into the room and searched my handbag. I don't know what they were looking for. It wasn't until yesterday that I learned everyone believed me to be a private investigator. It completely puzzled me and that's why I came out for a walk, in the hopes that my thoughts would settle.'

'And did they?'

I smiled. It must have been slightly demonic because I saw a glimmer of fear cross her face. I had that effect on people sometimes. 'Not until my wandering led me here, and not until I stood on your doorstep.'

I was, perhaps, making it all needlessly dramatic for my entertainment but I was enjoying myself, and her reaction. Eyes rounded, lips slightly parted. Hanging on my every word. She was exactly where I liked people to be. 'I think Claire found out about Alan's new will leaving everything to you.'

'Alan is an incredibly honest man, he's not capable of deception. He'd have been upfront with her, would have wanted her to know his plans.' Ruth sighed. 'He was aware how she felt about the manor, knew she'd sell it given half a chance.'

'And would he have been as equally candid with Teagan?'

'No, of course not. Despite Teagan's genuine regard for Alan, she was never more than a servant to him. For him, class was everything.'

'He didn't know she was in love with him?'

Ruth laughed, a genuine sound that relaxed her expression and put a twinkle in her eyes. 'Teagan loves herself, and what she thinks is her position in Broadway. A figment of her imagination, you know, most people laugh at her and her pretensions. But they do it behind her back. She's a nasty piece and people know to be wary.'

I tapped my fingers on the table. I was on to something, I knew it, I simply needed to knit the strands together. For my theory to be credible, Teagan had to be involved. 'If Alan told Claire, perhaps she told Teagan.'

'Why would she, they can't stand one another.'

There was something... a hair's breadth out of reach. 'Tell me,' I said slowly, an idea formulating out of the many strands of information. 'If you and Alan married, and even if you don't, if you inherit the manor, what would happen to Teagan?'

Darkness crept over Ruth's face, tightening her mouth, chilling her eyes. 'When I live there, with or without Alan, there'll no longer be a need for a housekeeper. Teagan would be offered statutory redundancy. Everything as it should be. She'd be out, and I assure you nobody within a hundred-mile radius of Broadway would offer her a position.' There was no hiding the venom in Ruth's voice.

'Why do you hate her so?'

She shut her eyes and I didn't think she was going to tell me. It was pure curiosity on my part, I didn't really care and was growing weary of it all. I was about to get to my feet, when she opened her eyes again and spoke.

'Teagan hated the relationship between Claire and Hannah. She considered it a crime against nature and whispered her hateful ideas into the ears of anyone who would listen.' Ruth dragged a hand down her face, looking suddenly older, sadder. 'I didn't know until much later, until it was too late to stop.'

'The conversion therapy was Teagan's idea?'

'Yes. I'd written an article for a science journal. I didn't know it was one Alan subscribed to, nor that Teagan found them fascinating. When she read my article, she first tried to persuade Claire who laughed and told her it was nonsense.'

'But Hannah was more gullible.'

'Gullible?' Ruth shook her head. 'No, not so much gullible as desperate. Neither Alan nor Marcie cared a hoot about Claire's sexuality, but Hannah's parents did. They were obsessed with securing an heir for the farm.' Ruth held a hand up. 'And before you even think of mentioning surrogacy, forget it, it wasn't mentioned back then, and adoption was out of the question. The Woods wanted blood heirs. They'd found it hard to accept not having a male heir, you know, and had pinned all their hopes on Hannah meeting the right man. She told me they'd never acknowledged her relationship with Claire although they would have known about it. Claire and Hannah didn't hide it, which was rather brave of them really.'

'From what I've heard about Teagan, I can't believe she encouraged Hannah to go to you for this conversion therapy out of the goodness of her heart or out of sympathy for Hannah's parents, am I right?'

'Teagan is a nasty old bat, I'm not sure she has a heart, and I'm positive she's never wasted a shred of sympathy on anyone. No, she wanted to destroy their relationship because she simply didn't approve. That Claire was devastated didn't bother her, but I don't think she expected the outcome.'

'That Claire would leave and not return?'

'Exactly.'

I looked at Ruth. Did she feel guilty for her part? I'd nothing to lose by asking. 'But some of the blame for her leaving was on your shoulders, wasn't it? For trying to convert Hannah?'

Ruth's laugh pealed out, startling me. 'Gosh, I'm sorry, how rude you must think me.'

Like most people, and possibly more than some, I didn't enjoy being laughed at and felt anger uncurl. 'I seem to have said something amusing.'

Ruth leaned forward and patted my arm. 'I am sorry. Let me explain. That article on conversion therapy had been written a year before. By the time of publication, I no longer believed in its validity and wrote a disclaimer in the following month's edition, but by then it was all too late.'

I'd always prided myself on my poker face but it obviously let me down. 'I'm not surprised you look puzzled,' Ruth said. 'Hannah did come to me for conversion therapy, and she even believed it was what she got–' Her voice faded, a smile playing on her lips.

I was fascinated. An expert at dissembling, at manipulating, at getting the end I desired by any means possible, it surprised me there were others out there who were like me, or worse. I leaned closer, my eyes fixed on Ruth's face. 'But she didn't?'

CHAPTER FORTY-THREE

For a moment, I thought Ruth wasn't going to answer, then she shrugged and smiled. 'I need a drink,' she said, taking me completely by surprise. She stood and crossed to the fridge. 'Glass of wine?'

I was never one to turn down the offer of a drink, especially if it was going to oil the wheels of conversation. 'Sounds good.'

She returned with a bottle of chilled wine and two glasses. Condensation ran down the outside of the bottle and pooled on the table. I wanted to warn her it would stain the wood but for the first time since I'd come to Broadway, I realised these women were as bright if not brighter than I was. Just not as mean.

Ruth poured wine into both glasses, lifted hers and gulped down half before putting it down and looking at me. 'Hannah didn't get conversion therapy for two reasons. One, as I've already said, I no longer believed in its validity and two, because she didn't need it in any case.'

My indrawn breath of disbelief dragged a portion of the mouthful of wine I'd swallowed along with it. The resulting coughing fit was as inelegant as it was noisy. I put my glass down and banged my chest with the flat of my hand, coughing and hacking as I tried to catch my breath. 'Sorry,' I said finally, wiping tears from my eyes. 'I'm sorry, you caught me by surprise.'

'Obviously.'

'Please, go on.'

'People like Teagan think sexuality is black and white. Men love women, women love men. Full stop. There are others, more enlightened, who acknowledge that men can love other men, women other women, but even that is too simple. Sexuality isn't that black and white, and nowadays most people recognise that it's more fluid. Twenty years ago, Hannah fell in love with a woman who incorporated everything she herself wanted to be. Claire was different back then; free-spirited, enlightened, clever, worldly-wise, exciting. Hannah climbed into a box marked lesbian because she thought loving Claire meant she had to. All I did in counselling her was to show her she was wrong, that she could find a man to love just as well.'

'That's common sense, not conversion therapy.'

'Exactly. But I gave Hannah what she wanted. A reason to end a relationship she knew wasn't right for either of them.'

'And then she met Doug.'

'Yes, only a year later. Doug was the perfect choice. He even took the name, Woods, so the children would carry the family surname. He saved the farm too. Woods Farm has been in that family for centuries, but Hannah's parents ran it the way it was always run and, as a result, they didn't have tuppence. It was Doug who turned the place around, invested in technology, new breeds. Went organic when it was considered a ridiculous idea and they've reaped the rewards since.

'I've met him, he seems like a decent bloke.'

'He is and he adores Hannah, always has.'

'And she loves him, I could see that, so why is she so worried about Claire being back in town?'

Ruth drained her glass and reached for the bottle. 'More?'

I slid my barely touched glass towards her and she topped it up generously. I looked at her in suspicion. Maybe it wasn't only me who used alcohol to oil the wheels of conversation. These women were sneaky, I needed to have my wits about me. I had secrets that needed keeping.

'Hannah said she'd been converted because it made it easier for her to end their relationship, but I know she was still desperately in love with Claire. There's a part of her that continues to be, and that worries her. I've tried to reassure her, explaining that first love often occupies a little piece of our hearts and minds forever.'

What a load of psychobabble! I hid my sneer. Now Ruth had started talking, I wanted to hear everything. 'Claire knew you were responsible for the conversion therapy; she must have hated you for it.'

'Hated me, hated Hannah for wanting it. Claire was devastated and left Broadway almost immediately.'

I tried and failed to imagine the lady of the manor looking distraught. She didn't strike me as the type. 'Do you think she still loves Hannah?'

Ruth lifted her hand and see-sawed it. 'Loves her, hates her.'

It was what Hannah had said and it was something I could understand. 'Yes, when love sours, it curdles you inside and taints every action, every thought, and there's not a thing you can do except to go along with all those creepy, treacherous, poisonous things it makes you do and–' I stopped abruptly when I saw Ruth's eyes widen.

CHAPTER FORTY-FOUR

'Ignore me,' I said with a laugh. 'I read far too many Gothic stories and drift into melodrama so easily.'

Ruth didn't look convinced, but then, she wasn't a stupid woman, she was right to be wary of me.

I picked up my almost-full glass and gulped a few mouthfuls. 'Getting back to Alan's will...'

Ruth sighed. 'What about it?'

'Would he have changed it to leave everything to Claire after she returned?'

'No, of course not. Claire's return hasn't changed anything.'

'Except to prevent you seeing him.' I couldn't believe she didn't see the truth that was staring her in the face. 'What if...' The ideas in my head were still a little tangled but I knew I was right. 'When I saw Alan, he was so confused, he thought I was Marcie. I'd guess you could probably persuade him to do anything, even to change his will. What if that's what Claire has done?'

Ruth's face was a picture of disbelief shaded with confusion. 'If he's as confused as you maintain, his solicitor would never have allowed him to make a new will, it wouldn't be legal.'

'Don't be stupid.' My words were harsh enough to make Ruth blink. 'It doesn't need a solicitor. You can download will forms on the internet.'

She still wasn't convinced. 'But they'd need the will witnessed. Claire or Teagan couldn't be witnesses if they're going to be beneficiaries.'

'Don't you read the newspapers? Covid has impacted everything including the writing of wills. They brought in new legislation to allow them to be witnessed by video link. All they'd have needed to do was to make Alan look presentable.' I flapped my hands out. 'Easy!'

Enlightenment dawned slowly. Perhaps it was harder for people like Ruth to believe that others were so downright conniving in their effort to get what they wanted. I understood completely. Credit to them, it was pretty ingenious.

'All they need to do is to make sure nobody realises Alan is confused until he passes away.' I saw the quick flicker of pain cross Ruth's face. 'I'm sorry, this must be hard to take but believe me, the man I saw isn't the man you remember.'

Ruth was struggling to believe, or perhaps accept, the reality of it. My sympathy for her was drowned by contempt that she'd not fought harder for what she wanted and allowed Claire and Teagan to win by default.

I was still puzzling things out in my head. 'I think it was that whole misunderstanding about my being a private investigator. You said you'd gone to the craft night in the hope you'd be able to see Alan and they prevented that. I bet Claire thought I was working for you.'

Ruth's face twisted as she tried to make sense of what I was saying. 'It's all so unbelievable.' She gulped some wine and wiped a hand over her mouth. 'Surely Claire wouldn't go that far.'

I bit my lip at her naivety. We'd paid over three hundred

thousand for our tiny cottage. At the most conservative estimate, the manor house must be worth four or five million. That kind of money would be an incentive to do almost anything. I'd done a lot more for a lot less so I knew what I was talking about. Ruth was made of different fabric though and I could see her struggle to understand.

'Wait,' she said, holding up a hand. 'No, that can't be right. She'd hardly have allowed you to stay at the manor if she was trying to keep Alan's condition a secret.'

'She didn't have much choice really, did she?'

'Yes, but she thought you were a private investigator, she would have known you'd go snooping around.'

I shook my head. 'She locked the bedroom door.'

Ruth gasped, her hand going to her throat. 'She did what?'

'Locked the door. I didn't know until later when I did, as you so elegantly put it, try to have a snoop around.'

Ruth's hand slid upward to cover her eyes. Perhaps she was trying to hide away from it all. Unfortunately, it wasn't that easy.

'But you said...' She dragged the hand down her face, pulling at her skin. Someone should have told her it was very bad for the delicate tissue, especially at her age.

'I said I went looking around, and I did, but not until after Teagan came snooping around my room. Remember I told you she dropped my handbag?' I waited until Ruth nodded before continuing. 'Well, I shuffled in the bed to give her the impression I was stirring which must have startled her. She waited a few seconds before scarpering but in her haste to get away she didn't lock the door behind her.' I swirled wine around in my glass before lifting it to my lips for a sip. 'I'd guess Claire was annoyed with Teagan to find it open when she came to unlock it in the morning, and was possibly worried I'd left the room, but I made a great fuss about telling her how heavily and well I'd slept. I think I convinced her.'

'It's all so...' Ruth clamped her lips together as she struggled with a range of confusing emotions. 'I don't know what to think really.'

'Thinking is one thing, more importantly what are you going to do?'

'Do?' She lifted the wine glass to her mouth, but she didn't drink, merely holding it there pressed against the full of her lip.

Apathy was an abomination. I wanted to shake her till her bones rattled. There was always something you could do to change the course of events. But I saw the truth in Ruth's eyes. She wasn't made of the kind of stuff people like me were. She'd do nothing, let Claire and Teagan win, and spend the rest of her life grieving for the man she loved, and the life she could have had.

Unless someone... like me... did something for her.

CHAPTER FORTY-FIVE

There seemed to be no point in sitting there any longer. Ruth was falling apart, and I wasn't sure I wanted to watch.

Draining my glass, I put it on the table. 'I'd better get going.' I stood and looked down at her in frustration. She'd cry when I was gone, but that would be as much as she'd be willing to do. Honestly, people like her really did make my blood sizzle.

'Maybe–'

She looked up at me with a glint in her eyes, surprising me so much that I dropped back onto the seat. Perhaps I'd underestimated her. I leaned forward, agog to hear what she'd planned.

'Maybe you could go to the police and tell them what you saw.'

I fell back, my mouth working as I tried to stifle the shout of disbelief. When she reached a hand across the table, I jumped to my feet knocking the chair backwards. 'You're out of your tiny mind!'

'They'd believe you, you've no agenda after all, why wouldn't they?'

No agenda. This stupid woman had no clue. 'You want me

to tell the police that Claire kindly allowed me to stay in her home, and to thank this pillar of society for her generosity, I sneaked around her house while she was asleep. When I discovered her father in an emaciated state, instead of ringing an ambulance or calling for help, I went back to bed, slept till morning, then a couple of days later I sauntered along to you and told you what I'd seen. Is that really your master plan?'

Colour flushed Ruth's face. 'I didn't think...'

'Obviously,' I said, folding my arms across my chest. I resisted the temptation to raise my eyes to the ceiling when she cupped her hand over her face and started to cry. Like most women, she didn't do so gracefully. Her shoulders heaved, a snuffling snotty series of sounds forcing themselves through her fingers.

I considered leaving to allow her to wail and wallow in private but just as I was about to make my exit, she took her hands away and looked at me. I'd have needed a platinum-coated heart not to have felt some sliver of sympathy for the sorrow I saw in her eyes. Just a sliver though, and it was piercing the wider slice of disdain I felt for her that she'd sit there snivelling instead of getting off her backside and doing something.

'I'm sorry.' She reached for a roll of kitchen towel that sat on the counter, pulled off a few sheets to wipe her face and blow her nose. 'I'm not usually given to tears.'

'They don't tend to achieve much.'

She seemed to find this amusing although I was being serious. 'That's one way of looking at it, I suppose.'

It was the only way, as far as I could see but I wasn't going to get into an argument about it. I tilted my head towards the door. 'If you're okay, I really should get going.'

'Yes, of course.' She put her hands flat on the table and pushed to her feet as if the weight of the world had landed on her shoulders.

I wanted to tell her, to explain, to make her understand that there was only one effective means of removing that weight. Doing something. Fighting back. Grabbing the problem by the neck and squeezing it, watching it as the life faded from it, waiting to make sure it was well and truly done for before accepting it was dead and gone.

It was the only way to deal with problems.

So much better than standing with reddened eyes, mucous hanging from one nostril, the glistening trail of snot on the back of her hand, looking pathetic and defeated.

It tugged at heartstrings I wasn't aware I had. 'Why don't you leave it to me. I'll think of something. Okay?'

Pitiful gratitude shone in her eyes for a second before it faded and she shook her head. 'I can't let you get involved with my problems, but thank you, I am grateful for the offer.'

'It wasn't made lightly, I assure you.' Perhaps it would have been better if I'd left it at that. Got out, left her and Hannah to drown in their own stupidity. But I hated the taste of defeat that soured my mouth. 'I promise you, I'll think of something. Having no agenda—' I smiled as I used her word. '—makes it easier for me. Honestly.'

She looked unconvinced.

'Trust me. I won't let you down.'

'Okay, thank you, see what you can do. I do appreciate it.'

She walked me to the front door.

The sun was beating down on her pretty garden. I stepped outside and turned to say goodbye. Before I did, I pointed to some flowers. 'I don't have anything as nice in my garden. Would you mind if I snapped off a few blooms to take with me?'

If she was surprised at the request, she didn't say. 'I could get the secateurs and cut you a bunch if you'd like.'

I shook my head and waved a dismissive hand. 'That's okay, honestly, I'll simply snap off a handful.' I crossed into the garden as I spoke and picked some daisy-like flowers, then broke a few sprays off the pretty, pink flowering bush.

A minute later, I had a generous bouquet. 'That's it,' I said, waving the handful at Ruth who stood hanging onto the doorway.

She was still standing watching me as I walked away. I wondered what she was thinking.

Whatever it was had little chance of coming close to the truth.

CHAPTER FORTY-SIX

B ack at the cottage, I filled the kitchen sink with water and carelessly dumped the armful of flowers into it ignoring the water that lapped over the side. It trickled down the cupboard door underneath and dripped onto the floor. Having lost any interest in the cottage, I couldn't bring myself to care.

The flowers could stay in the sink till I'd finalised my plans.

The garden seemed the best place to sit and think. My favourite seat under the tree offering shade. A slight breeze had picked up. It shushed through the tall grasses planted in pots on the patio, the calming relaxing sound an antidote to my churning thoughts. Philanthropy wasn't something I usually indulged in, and I wasn't sure why I wanted to make everything right for both Hannah and Ruth. I sighed and thought of Kasper. Maybe that was it, a bizarre attempt to make things right.

Happy ever after took hard work and wasn't for the faint-hearted. Sometimes, indeed most times, it required thinking on your feet and the ability to switch plans mid-stride. As I had done.

I pushed damp tendrils back from my face, lifted my hair to

allow the breeze to slip around my neck and cool me down. Switching plans had been a necessity. I'd made a mistake with Kasper. Almost ruined my future. But I'd turned it around.

Turned it around... my sigh was lost in the shush of the grasses, my regrets forced to the deepest, furthest reaches of my brain. Regrets were for fools who lived their lives looking in the rear-view mirror, weren't they? But sometimes, it was hard not to look back and see what you'd lost.

Happy ever after wasn't for the faint-hearted... women like Ruth and Hannah. But if I sorted my mess of a life out... if I'd managed to turn disaster into triumph... couldn't I do the same for these two helpless pathetic women?

I just needed to plan carefully.

My head was full of useless pieces of information acquired over the years from a variety of sources. I was an avid reader of books about war, particularly eighteenth and nineteenth century wars, and when I first stood outside Ruth's home admiring her garden, one of those trivial facts sprung into my mind.

From the Peninsular War of 1807 to be exact. One of the fascinating stories was of the death of a group of French soldiers who'd used twigs of freshly cut oleander branches as skewers to cook meat. One of those weird and wonderful facts that lodges in your head waiting to be of use.

I looked back towards the open kitchen door and smiled.

A clear plan allowed me to sleep well for the first time in days. I woke a few times, I always did, but that night it wasn't dreams of Kasper that disturbed me but plans for the rescue of Ruth and Hannah. In one of those wakeful moments, I also came to a decision. I'd go back to London the following day; I'd waited long enough.

Not directly, I needed to be clever. I'd ring my friend Tracy and ask her to accompany me in case dealing with Kasper became more awkward than I'd hoped.

Rising early, I didn't delay. There was a lot to be done before I left.

When we'd bought the cottage, not only did I have plans for tea parties on the lawn, but I'd pictured me baking the necessary cakes... luscious sponges sandwiched together with whipped cream and strawberries. That nonsensical idea... Mary Berry I wasn't... went no further than buying all the accoutrements required which had sat in the kitchen cupboards untouched ever since. With everything I needed on hand, I drank a black coffee for breakfast and set to work.

I'd done some reading about oleander following that story of the French soldiers and knew it tasted quite bitter. I also knew it was unaffected by heat. I flicked through the two cookery books I'd bought, pressing the second open at the recipe for lemon muffins. With my likeness for G&T, there were always lemons in the fridge. I read the recipe through and smiled. Lemon muffins were the perfect vehicle for the bitter oleander.

My flour wasn't gluten-free but I didn't think it mattered. There'd be no time to suffer the consequences, oleander was a quick, effective killer.

The recipe was easy to follow and an hour later I took the tray of muffins from the oven. They'd risen perfectly and looked, even to my critical eye, bloody amazing.

I broke one apart and nibbled a small piece to check that the bitterness wasn't obvious. It tasted lemony, nothing more. I spat the chewed piece into the sink and rinsed my mouth out.

There was a tin box of biscuits in the cupboard. I'd bought it at some stage, picturing afternoon tea in the garden, cups and saucers, pinkie fingers raised in the air. I was laughing at my fantasy as I peeled the tape from the edges of the tin to open it. The biscuits looked tempting; I picked up one and popped it into my mouth before chucking the rest into the bin.

I knocked a few crumbs into the sink before lining the tin with a couple of floral paper serviettes I found in a drawer. Six of the muffins fit neatly inside. It left three spare. I'd have to dispose of them carefully.

The baking tray I'd used was scrubbed clean and put away. I'd be leaving it behind with almost everything else. All I was taking were my clothes, some jewellery, a small painting I'd bought locally. Everything else could stay. I'd tell the estate agent to sell it as it was. I never wanted to see the damn place again.

Once the car was packed up, I leaned against it and stared at the cottage. It had been one of my crazier ideas. Small-town living wasn't for me. And despite their surprising complexities, neither were small-town people.

I picked up the bag holding the spare muffins and threw it into the boot of the car. It made sense to get rid of them back in London. The tin holding the others rested on the bonnet. I took it and walked the short distance to the manor house.

Despite the early hour, it was already blisteringly hot, and I stood as close to the front door as possible, my precious tin of goodies held in the shade of my body.

It wasn't the faithful henchman who opened the door, but the lady of the manor herself. 'Hi,' I said, in my best cheerful tone. *See how harmless I am.* 'I'm going home to London and wanted to drop in to say goodbye.' I held my offering forward. 'I baked these for you by way of a thank you. Lemon muffins. Gluten-free, of course. Enough for you and Teagan to thank you both for looking after me while I was here.' I took a step backwards when she took the tin from my hands. 'I was hoping to make another craft meeting but unfortunately my plans have had to change and it's unlikely I'll return to Broadway. Please say goodbye to the others for me.'

Claire held the container of muffins between her hands. 'I will. They'll be sorry not to meet you again.' She almost sounded sincere.

I couldn't think of anything to say that wouldn't sound false so settled for a smile as I reached out and tapped the lid of the tin with a fingernail. 'These are my favourite; I do hope you enjoy them.'

She held the tin closer to her chest. 'I'm sure I will, lemon is my favourite.'

'Oh, that's good.' She'd never know how good it was. My plan was fairly foolproof. Either she'd share them with Teagan, and both would die. Or she'd greedily eat them all herself, and Teagan would be blamed for poisoning her. There were plenty who'd testify as to how much the housekeeper hated her.

Either way would work, and I walked to my car feeling smugly satisfied that my plan was going to go so smoothly and both Ruth and Hannah would get their happy ending.

Outside the cottage, I perched on the wall and sent Ruth a message.

Returning to London. Permanently. But don't worry, I've cooked up a solution to your problem.

CHAPTER FORTY-SEVEN

I rang Tracy before I left Broadway. 'You free for lunch?'

'Jocelyn!' Her screech was ear-splitting. 'Girlfriend, you got tired of country living and returned to civilisation?'

'I'm on my way. Should be there–' I peered at the time on the dashboard clock and did a quick calculation. '–say one, the traffic is likely to be dire.'

'One it is. The usual place?'

Sushi and a chilled glass of Prosecco would be the ideal welcome back to the capital. 'Yes, that sounds perfect. I'll see you there.'

'Can't wait and I want to hear all about everything.'

'We can swap war stories. See you at one.'

I hung up, dropped the phone on top of the pile of bags I'd squashed onto the passenger seat and started the engine. Time to go home and face whatever lay in store.

Despite my pessimism, I made good time and took the opportunity to park the car in the underground car park of our apartment block. It was monitored so I felt no worry about leaving the packed car unattended. There was no temptation to go up to the apartment either. After lunch, I planned to persuade Tracy to accompany me. She could help me bring some of my stuff up. And be there when I confronted Kasper.

It was always good to have a witness.

The restaurant, Matsushisa Sushi, was only a ten-minute walk away, but the heat in London was excruciating and I was sorry I hadn't pulled a hat from my bag. Instead, I dashed from one side of the street to the other in a desperate attempt to stay in the shade.

A sign on the restaurant door informed customers that face masks were appreciated rather than obligatory. My face was slicked with perspiration and I hesitated, wondering if it mattered a whit. Then with a sigh, I pulled a mask from my bag and slipped it on.

Tracy was waiting at our favourite table, one with a view over an internal courtyard filled with potted acers of all sizes and shapes. The restaurant air conditioning was set high which was a blessed relief. I lifted the hair from my neck to cool my skin as I crossed the space to where my friend sat, her eyes fixed on the screen of her mobile.

She was one of those women who looked impeccable whatever the circumstances, a mere heatwave wasn't going to change that. Me, on the other hand... a glance in the glass told me that even in the soft-focus shimmer of the restaurant's lights, I looked ghastly. I lifted a hand to fluff my hair, then gave up. There would be plenty of time over the next few days and weeks to organise a hairdressing appointment, salon visit, and manicure.

'Hey, Tracy.' I pulled off my face mask and leant down to plant a kiss on her cheek.

'Jocelyn!' She leapt to her feet and enveloped me in a hug so tight I smelt her perfume on my clothes for hours after. 'It's so good to see you. Now tell me everything.'

'First, I need a drink.' I looked around for the waiter who appeared as if by magic and with little time wasted, we were soon in possession of glasses of Prosecco, the bottle resting comfortably in an ice bucket. I lifted my glass. 'Cheers!'

'Cheers, and welcome back, I missed you.' She took a minis-cule sip of her drink. My svelte friend was probably calculating how many calories were in it before she swallowed. I had no doubt that I'd be the one drinking the rest of the bottle.

'Still no word from Kasper?'

I'd told her about the row that had driven me to Broadway. 'Not a word. I'm hoping when he sees me, he'll remember how good we were together.' I waited a breath. 'I was hoping you'd come back with me. Kasper is fond of you. It might make it less awkward, you know, he'll feel obliged to be nice to you and it's bound to rub off on me.'

'Hmm, are you sure? It might be better to have it out with him in private.'

I reached a hand for hers. 'Please, Trace, believe me, it would make it so much easier. I know Kasper, he's got old-fash-ioned manners, he'd never dream of picking a fight with me in front of you. He'd consider it akin to washing dirty linen in public.'

She thought a moment before nodding slowly. 'Okay, if it's what you want, I'll come with you.'

I squeezed her hand and released it. 'Good, you can help me bring some of my stuff up from the car.'

That made her laugh, the slight tension disappearing from her expression. 'I should have guessed; you always have an ulte-rior motive for everything you do.'

I raised an eyebrow at the slightly catty remark but decided to ignore it. Tracy could take umbrage easily. She'd stormed out of restaurants and bars on more than one occasion having felt slighted at some remark or other. That these occasions often seemed to coincide with an expensive night out where I was left to pick up the bill had occurred to me, but I'd let it go. I could afford it, and like Claire, I quite liked playing Lady Bountiful.

Over dinner... the sushi was better than I remembered... I told her about Broadway. I thought she'd choke on her cucumber maki when I told her about the craft night I'd attended.

'You! What did you do? Crochet?' She snickered. 'No, better, knitting, I could see you curled up with a pair of knitting needles and a big ball of wool.'

'Art, actually,' I said. 'Sketching.'

'You!'

I wanted to tell her she didn't know me as well as she thought she did. Truth was, she didn't know me at all. 'No, it was an old sketch pad belonging to my ex. I simply drew over the lines he'd drawn. Nobody asked to see it so I was safe.' I shrugged. 'It was something to do one evening and I did meet a fascinating group of women. There are depths beneath the quiet exteriors of these townies.'

'I'm sure.' Tracy, who rarely left the city and then only if it was unavoidable, looked unimpressed. She glanced at her watch. 'Now if you want a hand dragging your paraphernalia to your apartment, we'd better hit the road. I promised to meet Salvatore later.'

I didn't ask who he was. Tracy went from one unsuitable, much younger man to the next, faster than any woman I'd ever met, and I'd long since learned not to bother trying to remember their names. She wasn't impressed when I told her she should call each of them Romeo. My argument that grand ladies of a previous time used to do the same with servants, calling them all Rose or some such name, didn't convince her.

Hannah's sweet smile popped unexpectedly into my head. I played with the stem of my glass before looking at my friend. 'Did you ever wish you could meet one man who'd love you forever?'

Tracy gave me a strange look. 'One man? Methinks you spent too long in the Cotswolds.'

I laughed. 'Perhaps... it's just...'

'What?' Tracy said with an impatient glance at her watch. 'Anyway, you've got the supremely gorgeous Kasper, haven't you?'

'Yes. Don't mind me – I'm being silly.' Silly to be suddenly swamped by regrets. Men like Doug would never love a woman like me.

My friend, of course, had a hat. A wide-brimmed affair so large it forced me to walk feet away so there was little chat on the short walk back to the underground car park.

'Here,' I said when I opened the boot. 'If you take this one, I'll take the suitcase. I can come back for the rest later.'

'Kasper will give you a hand, won't he?' Tracy took the black plastic bag I handed her, holding it gingerly at a distance from her body as if afraid the plastic would contaminate her pristine cream dress.

'Oh yes, I'm sure he will.' I heaved the suitcase out and slammed the boot shut.

The lift was nearby. Inside, I inserted the key that would bring it directly to the penthouse apartment I'd shared with Kasper since before our marriage. Tracy, like many of my other friends, was surprised I hadn't wanted to move from the home where he'd lived with his deceased wife. But why would I have wanted to do anything so crazy? The apartment was in a salubrious part of London, it was spacious and simply so fabulous I'd never consider moving. Anyway, it hadn't taken long to exorcise Laurie's ghost.

The lift opened onto a small hallway, one lavishly carved door opening from it into the apartment. Double locks ensured security. It took only seconds to realise the lower lock wasn't engaged.

'He's definitely home,' I said to Tracy as I slipped the Yale key into the top lock and pushed the door open. 'He'd never go out without locking up.'

The internal hallway was spacious, a stairway sweeping from it to the first floor where the reception rooms had floor-to-ceiling windows making the most of the views. The three bedrooms, each with its own en suite, and the bathroom were on this floor. 'Just drop that anywhere,' I said to Tracy and set the suitcase alongside. I glanced up the stairway. 'Kasper's probably in his office. He'll have his earphones on, so he won't have heard us come in.'

We climbed the stairs together, silently.

'Do you want me to wait in there?' Tracy nodded towards the living-room door.

I linked my arm in hers. 'You're not getting out of it that easily.'

There wasn't a sound to be heard from the room Kasper used as an office.

'You sure he's home?'

'He'd never go out without locking up, not even to go down to the concierge.' I hesitated between knocking on the door like a pathetic servant or barging in. Settling for a combination of both, I knocked and pushed the door open at the same time. I needn't have bothered; the room was empty. 'How odd.' I shut it and walked back to the living-room door.

I could never walk into this room without admiring the view

and even that day my eyes roamed over it with a possessive pleasure.

'He's not here,' Tracy said, jolting me from my reverie.

Stating the bloody obvious! 'No.' I turned away from the view. 'Perhaps he's gone for a lie down.' I smiled and nodded. 'That's it, I bet. He was probably up early making phone calls to one of his overseas contacts and decided to have a snooze. He'll be stretched out on the bed.'

I stepped towards the door, stopping when I felt Tracy's hand on my arm. I looked at her, puzzled. 'What?'

'You don't think...' She squeezed my arm. 'Perhaps you should leave it. He might not be alone.'

When I took off down the stairs, my feet barely touching the ground, Tracy was close behind. Maybe she thought I'd kill him if I found him curled up with some fancy piece. Perhaps I would have done, but when I threw open the bedroom door and saw my husband laid flat out on the ground, I knew infidelity wasn't the issue.

CHAPTER FORTY-EIGHT

I screamed and ran to his side, dropping to the floor and putting a hand on him, pulling it back with a cry of despair. 'He's cold, Tracy.' I looked back to where she stood inside the door, her eyes wide. 'He's dead. Kasper's dead.' It was only then that the smell of death hit me. The smell and more... I looked down with a grimace at the circle of fluids around his body and jumped to my feet, dark circles on my linen dress making me gag.

Gulping, I stood, twisting my hands, unable for perhaps the first time in my life to know what to do. 'What will I do without him?' I felt Tracy's arm slide around my shoulder, and she pulled me into a hug.

'We need to ring the police.' She held me close. 'He must have had a massive heart attack or a stroke. You always said he worked too hard.'

'Yes.' I snuffled into her neck. 'I tried to get him to take more time off. Why didn't he listen to me?'

'Come, let's go back to the living room, I can ring the emergency services from there.'

The awful stink of death, the mouth-twisting smell of decay

overpowered me. I heaved and ran from the room. Tracy caught up with me in the main bathroom, on my knees, my face over the toilet bowl. I reached for the handle, flushed, and took the towel Tracy pushed into my hand.

Holding it over my mouth, I got to my feet.

'Oh Jocelyn, I don't know what to say.'

I wiped my face and dropped the towel in the bath. 'There's nothing to say. My poor Kasper.'

I let Tracy take me by the hand and lead me back upstairs. She pushed me into a chair, then took out her mobile and made that call.

———

Dead bodies tend to get a fast response and it seemed to me that it was only minutes before the apartment was filled with the sound of voices. Tracy insisted on answering doors, filling the emergency services in, reporting back to me with every new arrival.

She made tea too but thankfully didn't go so far as to put sugar in it. But the heat of it was reassuring as I held it cupped between my hands listening to loud voices drifting up the stairs.

It was another hour before someone appeared in the open doorway. He knocked to attract our attention and I looked across the room to see a slim man with thin hair standing framed in the doorway. He wore a tan suit, white shirt and the most garish tie I'd ever seen. It was a bizarre addition to a dreadful day.

'I hate to intrude–' His voice was sympathetic but firm. '– but there's a few questions I need to ask.'

Tracy went to stand. 'I don't think–'

I put my hand on her arm to stop her. 'No, it's okay. Honestly. It's best to get this over with.'

The man approached holding out his identification. 'I'm Detective Inspector Cosgrave.'

I gave his card a cursory glance and waved to the seat opposite. 'Have a seat, I'll try to answer any questions you have.'

He gave the sofa a suspicious glance before sitting on the edge of the seat with a sigh that was decidedly weary.

I thought it was a bit rich that he seemed to be looking for sympathy, but it was always a good idea to keep on the right side of the law. 'Would some tea or coffee help?'

'Coffee would be good, thank you.'

Tracy got to her feet. I could tell she was relishing her role as supportive friend. 'I'll make some for all of us.'

The detective relaxed back in the chair. He flicked open the notebook he held in one hand before looking across to me. 'Can you tell me what happened, Mrs Dexter?'

It didn't take long to explain our movements from our arrival in the apartment to finding Kasper's body. '...then we found him, on the floor.' I held a hand over my mouth for a second, taking it away to shake my head sadly. 'It was the most awful sight to see him lying there.'

'And you didn't move him?'

'No.' I gulped and pressed my lips together before I was able to continue. 'When I felt how terribly cold he was I knew he'd been dead for a while.'

'Yes. Your friend told the uniformed officers that you'd been away for...' He glanced down at his notebook. 'Twelve nights.'

'That's right.' I struggled to keep my voice steady. 'We had a bit of a row. I decided to spend some time in our cottage in the Cotswolds to allow him to cool down.'

'Has a bit of a temper, does he?'

'No, not at all. Kasper is... was... the gentlest man you could meet.' I dropped my eyes to my clasped hands. 'It's not something I'm proud of. I had an affair.' I breathed deeply through

218

my nose to steady myself. 'It didn't mean anything, didn't last very long, but unfortunately Kasper found out. He was gutted.' I lifted my hands and dropped them to my lap. 'Angry, sad, disappointed. It was awful to see. I suppose I was running away from that when I went to Broadway.'

'Broadway? In the Cotswolds?'

'Yes, that's right. I was lucky, lockdown had been lifted so I was able to go.'

A clatter from the kitchen drew our attention briefly but neither of us acknowledged Tracy's apologetic wave. I waited for another question. The detective didn't appear that dynamic. I could almost guess what he was going to ask next.

'Did you ring him while you were away?'

So predictable, if the situation weren't so awful, I might have smiled. 'Yes, of course I did but he wasn't answering my calls. I left voicemails and sent him text messages every day.' I reached for my bag and rummaged inside for my mobile. 'I thought it would take him a few days to forgive me and when he didn't answer, it didn't really surprise me, but now...' I swallowed the lump in my throat.

'Just to be clear, you didn't actually speak to him from the time you left here?'

'That's right. I rang but he didn't pick up.' I handed the detective my mobile. He looked surprised but took it and flicked through the messages I'd sent to Kasper.

I wondered if I'd made a mistake when he handed it back to me, his eyes perceptibly sharper.

Tracy claimed our attention as she put a tray on the coffee table between us. 'Here we go.' For the next few seconds there was the palaver of adding milk and sugar as needed, Tracy handing the mugs around before sitting down beside me and patting my thigh reassuringly.

I sipped my drink and waited.

DI Cosgrave drank his as he flicked pages in his notebook. I wondered if there was really anything written there or if he was doing it for effect, to intimidate. If so, it was working. What could he have written that would fascinate him so much?

'The day you left, what time was that at?'

I squinted as if trying to think back through the passage of days to grab that piece of information, whereas in fact I knew exactly. 'I left here early morning, around seven, stopped for petrol along the way and got to Broadway a little before eleven.'

'And you didn't come back here at any point between leaving and returning today?'

I frowned. It wasn't a question I expected. 'No, I didn't. It's not that far, but too far to drop back for anything.'

'And when you and Ms Robinson discovered your husband, neither of you moved the body?'

'I already said we didn't. It was obvious he was dead.' I sighed and reached for my friend's hand, needing her support. 'Tracy helped me from the room, I was in shock I suppose.' I pulled at the material of my dress where the stains were evident. 'I didn't realise I was kneeling in...' I stopped, shook my head and gulped loudly.

'I'm sorry,' Cosgrave said. 'I don't mean to distress you. These questions are never easy but unfortunately we have a job to do.'

'I understand.' I rubbed my eyes with the tissue Tracy had put in my hand.

'It's a bit of a puzzle though.' Cosgrave reached into an inside pocket and drew out a plastic bag. He looked at it for a moment before pushing the tray out of the way and placing it flat on the table between us. 'We'll have to get a sample of your husband's handwriting, to prove he wrote this, but until that's done, we're going with the belief it's genuine.' He pushed it gently towards me.

'What is it?' Tracy's curiosity always got the best of her, one of the reasons she went from man to man hoping that Mr Right was hiding in the next.

Cosgrave looked at her before reaching for the paper so carefully preserved in the evidence bag. 'When the ambulance crew rolled Mr Dexter onto his back in preparation to move him, they found this under his body. A pen too. When they read the note, that's when the uniformed officers decided to call me in.'

Looking back to me, he tapped the note. 'He put the date and time on it. It's written on the back of a business letter he must have had in his pocket. The writing is a spidery scrawl, he's missed out words, abbreviated some, and others are hard to make out.' He tapped it again, his eyes never leaving my face. 'I've spent some time with it, Mrs Dexter, and I'm fairly confident I've got it right.'

Even if I could have found the words... any words... there didn't seem any point in speaking. It looked like Kasper was having the last laugh.

Cosgrave flicked the pages of his notebook, stopped, and folded it back on itself. 'An expert will examine the letter in more detail at a later point but I think I've managed to make sense of it. Let me read what I think Mr Dexter was trying to convey.' He peered at the page of his notebook. '*J hasn't called an ambulance.*' The detective looked up and met my eyes. 'I'm going with the idea that J is you, Mrs Dexter.' Without waiting for a comment, he continued to read. '*She's waiting for me to die, and I will, but she's not getting away with it, nor for killing L, she admitted to killing my precious wife, the only woman I've ever really loved. She–*' He stopped again. '–the next word was difficult to make out but I'm going with *gloated* because it seems to fit.'

I wondered if I was supposed to agree.

Cosgrave continued. '*She gloated about how cleverly she hid the car away in a lock-up. Don't let her get away with it.*' He shut the notebook and put it away. 'Mr Dexter's first wife was called Laurie, isn't that correct?'

I could feel Tracy's shocked eyes boring into the side of my head, the detective's suddenly excruciatingly sharp eyes piercing me in a search for my secrets.

He'd not find them.

CHAPTER FORTY-NINE

I met the detective's eyes and refused to look away, my expression fixed in neutral to hide the turmoil. It was easy when you'd done it as often as I had over the years. 'He must have used the last of his energy to write that.' I heaved a sigh packed as full of pathos as I could manage. 'Even dying, he couldn't forgive me, using his last moments to get revenge.' I shook my head, my lower lip trembling in sorrow. 'I didn't know him at all, did I?'

'That treacherous bastard!' Tracy shuffled over on the sofa and put an arm around me. 'How could he be so cruel?'

I buried my face on her shoulder and sobbed.

'He's accusing you of allowing him to die, and of murdering his first wife. That's a lot of hatred.' Cosgrave's voice was quiet but firm.

I straightened, pulled a tissue from my pocket and rubbed it over my eyes and nose. 'I knew I'd hurt him with that silly meaningless affair, but I had hoped we could get past it.' I sniffed and blew my nose. 'I suppose I'm lucky I can prove I'd left hours before he wrote that note, aren't I.'

'You could have driven back–'

'I didn't!' Perhaps interrupting the detective wasn't the wisest thing to do, nor to let my irritation show, but Kasper's note had thrown me. I'd never thought him capable of such treachery.

'You have a parking space here, I suppose?'

'Yes.'

'We'll check the CCTV cameras to confirm your departure time to keep everything above board.'

And no doubt he'd check to ensure I hadn't parked again later.

Of course I hadn't. That would have been incredibly careless.

I'd taken the train.

CHAPTER FIFTY

The day before *that* day had started well.

'I'll see you tonight,' Kasper said, bending to press a kiss on my lips. Barely awake, I'd raised a hand to run it over his smooth cheek.

'I'll organise something nice for dinner.' I didn't mean cook. It was the joy of living in London, so many restaurants did delivery.

Kasper smiled, knowing well what I meant. It was one of the things I loved about him, he was no fool. 'I have meetings in the city all day, so I'll look forward to that.'

I listened to his footsteps recede, the distinct sound of the front door opening and closing. Too early to get up, too alert to sleep, I lay listening to the sounds that drifted through the open window. Our bedroom looked out on the rear courtyard garden three floors below. Various trees, some several feet tall, provided enough shelter for sparrows, their twittering giving the impression we were anywhere but in the centre of London.

It would have been so easy to have put off what I'd planned for that day. But it had been months since I'd last visited and I needed to make sure everything was as it should be. With

Kasper out all day at meetings, it was too good an opportunity to miss.

There was no point in putting it off any longer. I'd get it done, come home and organise something extra special for dinner. Decision made, it was still several minutes before I threw the duvet back and scrambled from the bed. I didn't bother with a shower. When I returned I'd need to scrub myself clean. Instead, I pulled on the jeans and T-shirt I'd worn the previous day. No make-up, my hair pulled back into a low ponytail.

There was little risk involved but that didn't prevent anxiety making my stomach churn. I made coffee, took one sip and threw the remainder away. Afterwards, I'd treat myself to break-fast somewhere.

I slipped my feet into flat walking shoes and grabbed a rain jacket with a hood. No handbag. My purse tucked into one pocket, keys into the other. As inconspicuous as possible.

Our penthouse apartment was situated in Cleveland Row. A quiet street with little through traffic. We were lucky, it was one of the few blocks with underground parking. But I wasn't taking the car that day. It was a short, pretty walk along the edge of Green Park to the station of the same name. I kept my head down and walked briskly, but not fast enough to attract attention.

The station was busy with commuters and tourists. It was easy to get lost in the crowd, and I joined the stream that flowed down to the Piccadilly Line. The Tube was packed, sardine tight, and smelling as badly. Forced to stay on my feet, I hunched my shoulders and made myself smaller as we flew along.

There was no reason for anyone to be following me, no reason for anyone to be suspicious of my journey. My friends... and Kasper... might wonder what I was doing in this part of the city, might be slightly surprised by the excuse I had already formulated that I was exploring various London boroughs looking for inspiration. I'd practised saying it, adding suitably confusing references to industrial chic and post-industrial aesthetics, the kind of pretentious crap that convinced people you were talking sense instead of rubbish.

However, it was better and safer to avoid meeting anyone I knew. I'd chosen the day because of the weather forecast. Rain, or even the promise of it, meant I could have my hood pulled up without causing suspicion.

It was only seven stops to my destination. I kept my eyes fixed on the floor between my feet. When the Tube stopped, I moved to the exit, and slid out along with several other travellers, all intent on getting where they needed to be, nobody paying me any attention.

From Caledonian Road Station it was only a ten-minute walk to my destination. A light drizzle was falling. It was carried on a slight breeze and found its way under my hood, wetting my downturned face. I wiped a hand across my eyes, regretting the last-minute decision to leave my umbrella behind.

It wasn't heavy but the streets and buildings quickly turned a uniform grey, confusing me when I looked up blinking, disorientated.

Panic brought me to a halt and drew looks from a couple of teens who stood in a doorway sharing a cigarette with a distinctive sweet smell. I tugged the hood down further over my face, wiped my eyes with a damp tissue I'd found in the pocket of my jacket, and forced myself to move on, eyes darting from side to side looking for something familiar. It had been six months since my last visit to check and everything looked different in the rain.

Finally, as I was beginning to think I must have taken a wrong turn, I saw a building I recognised. It gave me new impetus and I hurried to cover the last few yards to my destination.

It was quiet. The absence of an on-site security man being one of the reasons I'd chosen this particular lock-up park. Apart from a CCTV camera near the entrance, there was no other surveillance.

The first time I'd come, shortly after I'd signed the contract for the lock-up, I'd parked the car out on the road. Far enough from the gate to go unnoticed, near enough to see if anyone was going in or out. One car arrived, and I waited anxiously for it to leave.

When it did, I wasted no more time. A bunch of black helium balloons tied together with string lay in the back seat footwell of the car. I grabbed hold of it, pulling it with me as I got out. The balloons waved and danced, hiding me from the CCTV camera. It was quick work to tie the string to the pole effectively blocking the camera's view. It wasn't a long-term solution but it didn't need to be. I opened the garage door, then hurried back for the car, drove it inside and locked up.

The balloons were dancing gaily as I left, there was no reason to remove them and I guessed they remained there till they eventually deflated.

That day there was no reason for such dramatics. The lock-up park was quiet. There had been no problems when I'd rented it, no complex paperwork, the rent paid a year in advance. Cash, no questions asked.

I reached the door, dug into my jeans' pocket for the key and slipped it into the lock. It took a bit of rattling and fiddling before it turned with a crunch, the sound loud enough to draw attention. I looked around before twisting the handle and pulling the door open. The old metal door groaned. I ignored it and stared at the car. Almost two years it had sat there waiting.

There was no long-term plan. I pulled the door shut behind me and reached for the light switch to illuminate the interior of the lock-up. There was nothing inside apart from the Citroën. It was an old car, bought cheaply from an advert in a local newspaper, paid for with cash.

Bought for a specific purpose.

I walked to the front bumper and ran a hand over the dent, peering at the dark splodges that were still clearly recognisable as dried blood.

CHAPTER FIFTY-ONE

I had considered trying to get rid of the car but there was still an element of risk that worried me. Blood was encrusted in the cracks and dents and I wasn't sure washing, even a powerful car wash, would remove all traces. Torching it was also risky. It wasn't something I could do myself, and who could I trust to do such a thing without becoming suspicious of my reason? The lock-up rental wasn't expensive. No questions were asked so it was simple to keep putting off making a decision about the future. All that was required of me was to pay the yearly bill and check the integrity of the premises every few months. Seemed better not to change what worked.

There was no need to hang about. I shut the door, locked it, and headed back the way I'd come. The forecast had promised rain all day but as often happened, it had lied, and on the walk back to the station the sun came out.

Perhaps I should have been more careful, kept the hood in place, but I was feeling pleased with myself that things were going as they were supposed, so not only did I push the hood back, I pulled my hair out, fluffed it with my hands and strode along as if I hadn't a care in the world.

I hadn't.
Not then.

They came a few hours later when Kasper walked into the living room, his face unusually grim. The dining table was set in front of the windows to one side of the huge living room, the fully integrated kitchen located to the rear where the takeaway from one of our favourite French restaurants was keeping warm. I was standing between the table and kitchen, a bottle of nicely chilled Moët in my hand when he came through the door. The candles were lit, their light reflected in the surrounding floor-to-ceiling windows. Leonard Cohen was growling softly from the discreet speakers. My long red silk dress was low-cut and clinging, and I knew I looked fantastic, so I expected to see a glimmer of appreciation on his face.

But instead, he stood glaring at me, his lips curved in a sneer. 'Doesn't this look the part. The adoring faithful wife ready with my pipe and slippers.'

I'd no idea why he was in a mood. It wasn't like him; he was normally the most placid of people. Even between the sheets, but I'd found a solution for that. I held the bottle of Moët forward with a smile. 'The twenty-first century equivalent of, anyway.'

He snatched it from me, and before I had a chance to remonstrate, flung it across the room. I'd already removed the foil and loosened the muselet, so when the bottle landed on the floor the cork fired out and hit the photo frame on the sideboard sending it flying.

Noise and chaos. Champagne spurting, then trickling. Kasper's face red with unaccustomed anger. Me, wondering what the hell was going on.

'I saw you,' he said as if that explained everything. 'Sauntering along with your hair mussed up, colour in your cheeks. Slut.' He stepped closer. The whites of his eyes were red, and spittle gathered at the corner of his mouth, white bubbles that made me wonder, oddly, if he'd been bitten by a rabid dog on the streets of London.

Then I remembered pulling my hood down as I walked away from the lock-up. I'd run my fingers through my hair and bounced along, full of satisfaction at a job well done. Probably with a big bloody smile on my face. *Stupid, stupid woman!*

I put a hand on his chest. 'Darling, you've put two and two together and got five. I was out exploring various London boroughs looking for inspiration. Industrial chic and post-industrial aesthetics are the way interior design is going now, I'm hoping to put a portfolio together, maybe start looking for a few clients.'

'A portfolio?'

'Yes.' I smiled at him.

'You must have taken lots of photographs then.' He looked towards the kitchen, then strode across the room and grabbed my phone from the counter. 'Show me the photos for this portfolio you're making!' He pushed the phone into my chest almost knocking me off my feet.

Photographs! Why hadn't I taken some damn photographs? I shook my head. 'I took some, but they weren't right, so I deleted them.' Anger flamed in his face again and for a worrying moment I thought he was going to hit me.

'You lying slut. I know you're having an affair.'

I wasn't... not that day at least, and anyway, I'd never have classified my liaisons as *affairs*. There were no dinners, lunches, rarely even a drink. What my encounters brought was the energetic raunchy sex I loved. I could have argued that they saved our marriage, but I didn't think Kasper would have understood I needed more than he was able to provide.

'Admit it,' he said, 'that's what you were doing in that part of the city, getting your bit of rough.'

His eyes sparked with more passion than I'd ever seen. If only he was like that between the sheets. Telling him the truth about why I was in that part of the city wasn't possible, and since he hadn't swallowed my lie about the industrial chic... why hadn't I taken some damn photos... I was forced to lie. 'Yes, but it didn't mean anything, Kasper.' I stepped closer to him, moulded my body along his, letting him feel what he'd miss if he pushed me away.

He grasped my upper arms, fingers bruising the soft flesh, lips curled in a snarl. I tossed my hair back and parted my lips, hoping the heat of his anger would turn to passion. It didn't. He flung me away. I stumbled to the floor and lay, legs akimbo, my dress falling open to expose my breasts. I saw his eyes widen and smiled seductively, reaching a hand towards him. 'I promise, it meant nothing, Kasper. And it won't happen again. It was a moment's weakness, that's all.'

There'd been several moments. Luckily, he didn't need to know that.

He turned away from me, then looked back with an expression of disdain colouring his face. 'I don't do seconds, Jocelyn. We're done. Pack your bags and get out.' He held a hand up. 'Before you ask where you should go, the answer is I neither know nor care.'

He walked away, leaving me stretched out on the floor, my mouth hanging open. This wasn't in the plan. I scrambled to my feet and ran a hand over the silk of my dress as I stared out the window. A view that never ceased to make my heart soar from sheer pleasure. I couldn't lose all of this.

A loud thud came from the room below. Our bedroom. Kasper was obviously taking his temper out on the furniture.

I crossed to pick up the champagne bottle, there was a little left in it. Ignoring the spillage soaking into the rug, I took the bottle to the table, emptied the remnant into a glass and stood staring out the window as I sipped. Planning was usually my forte but for the first time, I couldn't think what to do to make things right and even my favourite champagne wasn't inspiring me that evening.

I half expected Kasper to return, his anger abated... even a little. When thirty minutes passed and there was no sign of him, I put my empty glass down and sighed loudly. It obviously wasn't going to be that easy.

I sat on the sofa, curled my legs under me and rested my head back. It had been a long day and I was tired, so despite the domestic drama the comfort of the sofa got to me, my eyelids drooping.

The candles were still burning when I woke, the apartment quiet. I lifted my wrist, squinting in the half-light to see the time, my eyes widening to see it was 5am.

I stretched and got to my feet. Kasper hadn't come in to see where I was. Had he done, big on safety as he was, he'd have blown out the candles. Hopefully he'd be asleep and wake with some of his anger faded.

Perhaps I should slip into bed beside him, wake him the way he liked best. When he woke, I'd promise eternal faithfulness.

With the candles blown out, I headed downstairs to our bedroom. The door was shut but I was relieved to find it wasn't locked and opened it quietly.

To my surprise, the light was on, and the bed empty. My lips tightened but if he thought moving to the spare bedroom was going to deter me, he didn't know me very well. Nothing got in my way. More determined now, I'd turned away when a low moan startled me. I couldn't tell where it was coming from. When it came again, I tilted my head, listening. Kasper? Crying or moaning in sorrow. Poor man, he did love me so much.

Where was he? I looked towards the en suite but when the moan came again, louder, my head jerked to the other side of the bed and I hurried over to see Kasper on the floor, face down in the deep pile of the carpet. The thump I'd heard the night before! I rushed over and dropped to my knees. 'Kasper?'

When he didn't respond, I tried to move him. He was a big man; it was hard work, and my long dress hampered my efforts. Using my full body weight, I put one hand on his shoulder, another on his hip and pushed.

He flopped over, my impetus making me fall on top. I pulled back in a hurry and stayed on my knees looking at him. He was breathing... but it was a gurgle, a rattle. One eye watched me, the other was partially shut, his mouth askew.

'Kasper?'

He gurgled a reply through one side of his mouth, the other remaining drooped and useless.

A stroke.

Sometimes, I didn't need to make plans.

Sometimes they made themselves.

CHAPTER FIFTY-TWO

I reached into Kasper's inside jacket pocket, pushed aside pens and papers, and pulled out his mobile. Getting to my feet, I tapped the phone against my thigh. 'I should ring for an ambulance, shouldn't I?'

Taking his guttural grunt as agreement, I lifted the phone. The relief in his eyes faded when I dropped my hand, stepped back and sat on the bed. 'But if I do. If they come and take you off to hospital and you make a full recovery... well, you'd want to get rid of me when you come home, wouldn't you.' I leaned forward. 'What's that, you trying to tell me you'd forgive me? But what if you make a full recovery and change your mind? Even worse, what if you don't make a full recovery and are disabled, where will that leave us... me?'

I stood over him. 'Could you really see me as a selfless carer?' I laughed at the look in his eyes. 'No, I didn't think so.'

That wasn't the life I'd planned for myself. I'd great respect for nurses, but that didn't mean I wanted to be one. 'I think it's best if we let things run their course.' I tilted my ear towards him when he gurgled. 'What's that? You agree? Excellent!'

It would take time and I wasn't keen on sitting to watch as

he expired. Plus, I had to ensure I wasn't going to be held accountable. It was time to get clever.

Leaving Kasper where he was, I went back to the living room and picked up my phone. I debated whether it was better to ring and leave a voicemail or send a message and chose the latter for convenience. Either way, Tracy never switched her phone on until she woke.

Tracy, Kasper and I have had a big row, so I'm heading off to Broadway this morning to give him time to cool off.

Cool off... I suppose that was true at any rate.

I checked on my poor husband. He'd rolled onto his side and was still breathing with that hideous choking rattle. His one useable eye glared at me when I bent down. I smiled, patted his cheek, and got on with my preparations.

I pulled a suitcase from the top shelf of the wardrobe and opened it on the bed. The weather was to continue hot for the next week or so according to the forecast. Linen dress weather.

It only took a few minutes to pack what I needed. I dropped the case by the door and went over to Kasper. There was a phone on the bedside table only a few feet away. No point in taking risks, I unplugged it and shoved it onto the shelf in the wardrobe. 'We don't want you overdoing things trying to get to it, do we?' I was pleased to see he no longer had the energy to even grunt a reply. Crouching beside him, I looked at his twisted face. 'It won't be long, darling.'

I picked up my suitcase, grabbed my handbag and keys from the living room and left.

My plan was simple. Drive to a service station on the other side of Oxford, fill up with petrol then continue to Broadway. Once there, I'd park the car on the road outside the cottage, bring my case inside and turn on a couple of lights upstairs. It wasn't a long walk to the train station; I'd be back in London in a few hours.

It worked out exactly as I'd planned, the way the simplest plans often do. The journey to Broadway was straightforward and less than four hours after leaving the city, I was sitting on a train back to London sipping an appalling brew loosely referred to as coffee. Early afternoon I was back in the apartment, fingers crossed things were working in my favour here too.

They weren't, not quite.

When I opened the bedroom door, I was horrified to see Kasper still hanging on. I sat on the bed and watched his chest rise and fall slowly, taken aback at his determination to live. He opened one eye to look at me and I guess if looks could have killed, I'd have flopped back dead. Luckily, they didn't, and I simply smiled in return.

'Not shuffled off this mortal coil yet then. You should let go, pass over.'

I noticed the dark ring on the carpet around his hips before the acrid smell of body waste drifted towards me. I screwed up my nose but said nothing. He deserved some respect at this stage.

It seemed a good idea to make myself comfortable, it might be a long wait. I shuffled down the bed, swung my legs up and propped the pillows behind my back. 'You were wrong about my being with a man yesterday, you know. Since neither of us believe in the hereafter I suppose it would be kind to tell you the truth. Plus,' I shrugged, 'it will pass the time.

'I wasn't with another man, although since I'm baring my soul I have to admit to having had a few liaisons over the last year, but yesterday I was doing something far more important. I was checking to make sure the car that knocked Laurie down was safely locked away.'

I'm not sure if I imagined the look of horror on his face or not. It was hard to tell, his face was even more twisted than it had been earlier. Perhaps he'd had a further stroke, I believed it could happen that way.

I folded my arms across my chest. 'Let me tell you what happened to poor Laurie.'

CHAPTER FIFTY-THREE

I'd met Laurie at the gym. I wouldn't normally have paid any attention to one Lycra-clad blonde among so many, wouldn't have noticed her at all if I hadn't left at the same time after a Zumba class one evening and seen the man waiting for her outside.

A tall, handsome, blue-eyed super fit hunk of a man leaning casually against a Porsche. The arms of a white shirt rolled up, a Rolex on one wrist.

If I'd been the swooning sort, I'd have done so then, had a fit of the vapours and fallen at the man's feet. Or tripped over a crack in one of the shiny tiles and landed in a heap in front of him. I'd have done something if the woman hadn't come tripping down the stairs and straight into his arms. I recognised her then from the Zumba class.

And in that lightning second, I wanted him and hated her.

Having few morals and a heightened sense of entitlement, it was easy for me to come up with a plan to get what I wanted. It wouldn't have been the first time, and no doubt it wouldn't be my last. There was a lot of living still to do.

It had been so unbelievably easy to arrange. I monitored

Laurie's routine, noted which days she went to the gym, which classes she attended. I gave her a friendly wave, adding a brief hello and a smile the next time I saw her. After a few weeks we were bonding over the water cooler.

She wasn't particularly bright, was unbelievably gullible, and only too willing to share the secrets of her life and intimate details about her husband. I listened, encouraged her to talk and tried not to yawn when her inane chatter went on and on.

The more I got to know her, the more I was certain I was doing the right thing.

Kasper deserved better.

Finally, after a spinning class I thought would kill me, I decided it was time to get my plan rolling. Laurie and I stood together, panting, drinking from our reusable bottles, her in a Lycra outfit that probably cost more than the club membership, me in a cheaper version that was a little too tight and cut into my groin.

I wiped my face with the towel hanging around my neck. 'I can't come to Zumba tomorrow night, by the way. But, after-wards, if you're free why don't you drop around to mine. I'd love the company.' I pushed the corners of my mouth down. 'I tell everyone my divorce was amicable, sometimes I even manage to fool myself, but other days the pain is crippling.'

Quick sympathy flashed across her face. 'Of course I'll pop over. Kasper is away on business this week so it suits.'

Thanks to Laurie's blabbing, I already knew her husband was away. It was why I'd chosen that week to instigate my plan. 'I'm only a ten-minute walk from here, then you can get a taxi home, okay?' I opened my gym bag and scrabbled inside for a pen and scrap of paper, looking back at Laurie with a grin. 'Why is it you can never find paper when you need it.' I raised my hands in exasperation. 'Anyway, it's easier just to tell you.' And it left no evidence behind.

I waved to the exit. 'Outside, turn left, walk as far as the café, turn right, keep on that road till you get to a print shop, then turn left and that's my road, Marshall Street. I'm at number twenty-seven.'

'Right at the café, left at the print shop and you're at twenty-seven Marshall Street.' Laurie smiled. 'Easy. Right, I'll see you there. I'll go straight from Zumba so I should see you about seven fifteen.'

She didn't.

But I saw her.

The road I'd directed Laurie down... miles from where I lived... was a quiet residential road, the houses set well back behind long front gardens. The road was narrow, a pathway each side. No cars parked along its length.

It was exactly as I'd planned. I'd acquired a car earlier in the week. For cash. No questions asked. I parked the Citroën around the corner, slouched low in the driver's seat, lights out, waiting for Laurie to pass by.

At exactly seven fifteen, she crossed the road and turned into Marshall Street, her gym bag swinging from one hand, a bunch of flowers in the other. I waited for exactly a minute before starting the engine. With the headlights out, I turned onto the street, seeing Laurie on the footpath ahead.

There was no hesitation. No doubt. My plan was made. My future needed this.

I put my foot to the floor. The car jerked, bounced and slowed as it mounted the kerb, then shot ahead as I kept the accelerator pressed.

Even if Laurie had turned, if she'd seen the car and tried to get away, there was nowhere for her to go. No way for her to escape someone who was determined to get rid of her. She might have survived the blow that sent her flying forward onto the road. It had been the only weak part of my plan. How to ensure Laurie was dead, not injured. I looked to see where her body lay, several feet in front of me and drove, slowly this time, the wheels bumping over her battered body.

I didn't need to get out to know she'd never have survived such a catastrophic injury.

Laurie wouldn't be an obstacle anymore.

I saw a tear gather in the corner of Kasper's eye. 'I don't know why you're crying, you got over her quickly, didn't you? It was only a year later we were married. A year!'

Tiredness was beginning to hit me. 'I need to get some sleep. I think I'll take myself into the spare bedroom. Give you some privacy for your dying.'

There was no point in adding insult to injury by telling him he was starting to smell badly. Two or three hours' sleep would do me good. I needed to leave in a couple of hours and get back to Broadway, make my presence known around the town.

It would have made my life easy if Kasper had had the decency to pass away while I slept but when I went back two hours later, I was surprised to see he'd changed position and moved a little towards the bed. Perhaps he'd hoped to pull himself up or had been trying to get to the wardrobe for the phone. He was more determined than I'd given him credit for, but it wasn't going to do him any good. I was sorry to see he was still alive though, I didn't want him to suffer, he'd been good to me.

But his eye was shut, and when I nudged his leg with the toe of my shoe, he didn't stir. Maybe that last bit of effort he'd made had helped push him towards the finishing line. He was still hanging on by a tatty string of life but I didn't think it was going to be much longer. I'd go back to Broadway. Stay there a week or so, then return to find my dear departed.

Kasper's mobile phone was in my hand. I ensured the battery was flat and bent to slip it back into his inside pocket, annoyed to see his jacket had caught under him when he'd changed position. Did it matter where I put it? I shrugged and popped it into the outside pocket, my nose crinkling at the stink that emanated from him. Eau de death. It wasn't going to catch on.

Despite the noxious smell, I bent to press a kiss to his cheek. It was the odour that caused my eyes to water, not the sudden surge of regret.

Regrets are for fools. Whack.

I stood at the bedroom door and raised my hand in a final farewell.

I wasn't sure if it was the memory of that awful smell, the dust from the seat on the train, or maybe it was the dry heat that caused my eyes to water continuously on the journey back to Broadway.

CHAPTER FIFTY-FOUR

D I Cosgrave's eyes were assessing me. I hoped I was giving the right impression. Fragile, vulnerable, distraught. Livid at my husband's treachery. At least this last was sincere.

I glanced through my eyelashes at the detective wondering what he was thinking. Had I managed to convince him I was an innocent party to a man's final revenge? When Cosgrave continued to stare, I felt irritation bubble. 'Is that it?'

'For the moment, but we'll have more questions at a later date. You'll be staying here?'

'Yes, there'll be things to arrange.' I turned to look at Tracy and gulped. 'Kasper's dead, Trace, how am I going to cope?'

She slipped an arm around my shoulder as DI Cosgrave got to his feet.

'It will be a couple of weeks before your husband's body is released, Mrs Dexter. We'll keep you informed.'

I covered my face with my hands until I heard his footsteps recede. Tracy's arm was still around my shoulders. Hot and heavy. It was hard to resist the urge to shake it off. Her support had been invaluable, I needed it to continue for a little longer.

'I'll make us some more tea,' she said eventually, unable to resist a final hug before releasing me.

I'd have fancied a glass of champagne myself. One of those expensive bottles Kasper was keeping for the special occasion that had never come for him. As soon as they were all gone, Tracy too, I'd open a bottle and toast my new life.

It was three hours later before the door shut behind the last member of what I assumed were some sort of investigative team. I could have asked Tracy, I was sure she'd know, but then she might have told me, and I was weary listening to her, wanted her gone. Wanted that glass of champagne.

It was a further hour before I could convince her I'd be fine on my own.

'I can sit here and think of Kasper and the wonderful life we had, start the grieving process, it's the only way I can get through it.'

She threw her arms around me and dragged me into another bloody hug, then pulled back and looked into my eyes. 'You're being so brave, Jocelyn, but I really think I should stay.' She hugged me again, tighter, her scent choking me. 'Or a better idea… why don't you come back with me, stay for a few nights, just until you decide what to do?'

I pushed her away. 'Do?'

'Well, you can't stay here, not in the home where Kasper died.'

Was she crazy? 'He loved this place; I'll keep it in his memory.'

What did I need to do to get rid of her? Kill her off? 'How about you come back in the morning. We can have breakfast together.'

That did the business, tears welled in Tracy's eyes. 'Honestly, you're being amazing. I'll head off, if you're sure, but you just need to ring, and I'll be here, okay?'

'Okay, thank you.' When she still seemed reluctant to leave, I tucked my hand into the crook of her arm and urged her towards the door and down the stairs. 'Thank you, you were a lifesaver today.'

After she'd gone, my footsteps glided up the stairway. The bottle of Louis Roederer Cristal I coveted wasn't chilled, but I didn't care. With a loud pop it opened and foamed into the glass. 'Here's to you, Kasper. You thought you'd get me with that damn note, but you didn't!'

He hadn't, had he? I sipped the champagne. That detective, DI Cosgrave. He'd fooled me into thinking he was a Keystone Cop, but there was a sharp glint in his eyes. He'd not dismiss that note easily.

I had to rely on having covered my tracks.

I had, hadn't I?

The champagne, the very expensive Cristal, suddenly tasted like vinegar in my mouth. I was tempted to do what Kasper had done and throw it across the room. Instead, I sat on the sofa, looked out at the night and drank every damn bubble.

It would all work out. And I'd finally live happily ever after.

CHAPTER FIFTY-FIVE

Ruth Matheson looked at the message on her phone for the umpteenth time since it had pinged early that morning.

Returning to London. Permanently. But don't worry, I've cooked up a solution to your problem.

What could that very strange and rather scary woman have done?

Ruth had a busy day ahead of her. The town was running an open-gardens event the following weekend and she'd have upwards of a hundred people trawling through her garden. Admiring... criticising... lopping pieces off her plants when they thought she wasn't looking.

It was for a good cause, she tried to be charitable about it all.

Her plan for that day was to concentrate on the large rear garden. Flowers needed to be deadheaded, some would need staking and no doubt there would be plenty of sneaky weeds to pull up. She was convinced bindweed grew faster than any other plant in her garden and it was time-consuming if it wound itself around other plants.

The smaller front garden required little work, careful as she was to keep it pristine so townspeople and passers-by would stand and admire, maybe take notes for their own. Ruth would often look from an upstairs window and watch them with smug satisfaction.

The work in the back garden took longer than she'd planned, and it was late afternoon before she stepped out her front door. There was only some deadheading required. She had a basket over her arm, secateurs in one hand, clip, drop, clip, drop. Normally, it was a relaxing occupation. Not that day. She'd been wound tight since Jocelyn's message. What had that damn woman meant?

Ruth was doing a final tidy of the oleander bush when she stopped mid-chop, a horrifying thought crossing her mind. The secateurs dropped to the ground, the basket tumbling from her arm to spill its contents onto her velvety green patch of grass.

Jocelyn had gone back to London. Why then had she bothered taking a bunch of flowers the previous day? A few daisies, a sprig of alstroemeria and so much oleander that Ruth was about to remonstrate, saved from having to do so when Jocelyn stopped. *Oleander.* 'No!' Ruth gasped.

The basket and secateurs were abandoned as Ruth dashed back inside and picked up the house phone to ring a number she knew by heart.

'Hello?'

'Claire, it's Ruth. Are you okay?' The silence stretched. Ruth pressed the phone to her ear and tried again. 'Claire?'

'Why wouldn't I be okay?'

Ruth sank onto a chair behind. 'Listen, I need to talk to you. Is it okay if I come over?'

Claire's reply was less than friendly. 'Can't it wait till the craft night tomorrow?'

Maybe Ruth was being melodramatic. Perhaps the message from Jocelyn hadn't meant anything ominous. 'No, this won't wait.'

'Fine, come over then.'

It was a less-than-welcome invitation. Ruth didn't care. It might be that she was being stupid, but the memory of being a little afraid of Jocelyn the day before came back to her. Ruth wasn't a woman who scared easily but there was something not quite right about Jocelyn.

Less than thirty minutes later, Ruth was standing outside the manor house. Apart from the craft nights, she'd not been inside since before Covid had interrupted their lives. Her hand was trembling as she reached for the doorbell. If Jocelyn was correct, Claire and Teagan were planning something so awful it made her dizzy to contemplate. But if Ruth was right, Jocelyn was planning something even worse.

Ruth pressed the bell, leaning on it, listening to it sound within.

It was Teagan who answered, her surprise telling Ruth clearly that she wasn't expecting her. 'I need to see Claire.'

'I'll see if she's free.' Teagan looked as if she'd have liked to have shut the door and leave Ruth standing on the doorstep. Unable to ignore convention, she stood back in silent invitation. She didn't precisely point to a spot on the floor, but it was clear from her tone she'd have liked to. 'Wait here.'

Ruth felt weariness tug her down. She hoped Claire would invite her to sit, she wasn't sure she could go through all of it on her feet.

But Claire wore the mantle of lady of the manor easily and greeted Ruth with a polite invitation to come in and have a seat. 'Teagan is making tea for us,' Claire said, waving Ruth to a seat and taking the one opposite. 'I don't know why but tea always seems the perfect antidote to hot days.'

Had Ruth been in a different frame of mind she might have been amused at Claire's continuous stream of banalities as she waited for the housekeeper to bring the tea tray.

When it was brought in and placed on the table between them, Claire brushed off Teagan's offer to pour the tea with an abrupt, 'I'll see to it.' Only when the door shut behind the housekeeper did she reach for the teapot and fill two cups. 'Milk and no sugar, if I remember correctly.'

'Thank you.' Ruth accepted the tea, hoping the cup wouldn't rattle on the saucer.

'Have a muffin.' Claire held a plate towards her. 'They're lemon and if they taste as good as they smell they're delicious.'

Ruth didn't want one, but it was easier to accept. 'They do smell good.'

Claire took one and sat back on the sofa. 'Jocelyn came to say goodbye this morning, she made the muffins herself and brought them as a thank-you gift.' Claire broke a piece off with her fingers and popped it into her mouth.

I've cooked up a solution. 'Spit it out!' Ruth jumped to her feet, reached across, and grabbed the plate from Claire's hand. 'Quick, I think it's been poisoned!'

CHAPTER FIFTY-SIX

Claire spat the barely chewed morsel into her hand. 'Poisoned!'

Ruth dropped the plate on the table and sat back with a hand over her forehead. 'I think it might be.'

Claire laughed uncertainly. 'You think it might be? Why on earth would you think such a crazy thing?'

'Jocelyn called around to me yesterday.' Ruth's mouth was dry, she reached for the tea and took a sip. 'She told me about Alan.'

Claire's expression didn't change for a moment, then puzzlement crept across it. 'She told you what about Alan?'

'That he has dementia, that he's–' Ruth's voice cracked as she forced herself to say the word. '–dying.' Whatever response she'd expected, it wasn't for Claire to erupt in peals of laughter.

'Dementia! Don't let Dad hear you say that! And as for dying, that's simply nonsense. Granted, Covid hit him worse than we'd expected considering he'd had both vaccines, but he's coming through it and is almost completely recovered. Physically, anyway.' Claire sat back with her cup and saucer in her hand. 'I think it was your rejection of him that did most damage if I'm being honest.' She held the cup to her mouth and drank, keeping her eyes on Ruth's face. 'As far as I'm aware, Jocelyn has never met my father so why would she say such terrible things?'

'My rejection?' Ruth held a hand up, feeling as though she was being pummelled with contradictory ideas. 'I don't know what you mean.'

Claire sniffed loudly. 'Oh, come on, don't give me that innocent look. You ignored his letters. It devastated him when he was already being ravaged by Covid. You never even tried to see him until recently, it's why I said no when you asked, I wasn't putting him through that again.'

'You may not believe this, Claire, but I love your father.' Ruth had always been quick-witted and even as shock vied with relief that Alan wasn't dying, she was beginning to see her way through the thick fog. 'The last letter I got from Alan was months ago. I wrote several times since and he never replied. When I tried to speak to him by phone Teagan told me he wasn't well enough to take the call. And you're wrong, I did try to see him. Teagan said he was too unwell for visitors. And then you refused to let me come.'

Claire's eyes widened in horror. 'I thought... Teagan said...' She shook her head.

Ruth tilted her head towards the door. 'I bet that nasty piece of work does the post... Alan would have trusted her to deliver letters to me. I'd assumed he received the letters I pushed through your letter box. Obviously not.' Her mouth twisted. 'Teagan. She hated me for taking up with your father, I think she hoped he'd turn to her when your mother died.'

'Teagan hates everyone. I tolerate her because I must. Mother made Dad promise to look after her, and you know how much a man of his word he is.' Claire shook her head. 'I should have guessed there was something wrong, I'm so sorry.'

Ruth huffed. 'You wanted to believe the worst of me

because of Hannah.' She watched confusion flit across Claire's face and held up a hand. 'I'm not going to get into that, it's not why I'm here. When Jocelyn stayed here, she told me you locked her in her bedroom–'

'What?' Claire dropped her cup and saucer with such force the cup rattled and swayed before tipping over on its side and emptying the remnant of the contents over the table. She ignored the mess and leaned forward. 'That's the most ridiculous thing I've ever heard. Why on earth would I have locked her in?'

'She said it was to stop her finding out the truth about Alan.' Ruth sighed before running a hand through her hair. 'Let me tell you her theory.' When she'd finished her tale, she sat back.

Claire sat erect, glaring across at her. 'Let me get this right... Jocelyn snooped around my home after I offered her a safe haven. Unbelievable! And based on that, she believes I forced Dad to change the will in my favour, and I'm keeping him hidden away till he dies because dementia would invalidate a will. Have I got it right?'

Ruth nodded. 'It sounds crazy–'

'Because it is!' Claire tapped the plate holding the muffins. 'And you think she poisoned these to get rid of me so it would all come out. Then you could move in here and live happily ever after.'

Ruth held her hands up in defence. 'Someone broke into Jocelyn's cottage. Someone went into her bedroom the night she stayed here. She says her door was locked. What was I supposed to think?'

'I never locked her door! You know these old doorknobs, Ruth, and how often they get stuck and need a jiggle to open them.'

'But someone was in her room.'

Claire shut her eyes briefly. 'Teagan. It wouldn't be the first time. Mother caught her once coming out of a visitor's room. She doesn't take anything. Fundamentally nosy, that's all. I'd guess it was her who snooped around Jocelyn's cottage too, people often gave her keys to house-sit. I bet she got copies cut. God, I hate that damn woman. It was thanks to her I stayed away, you know.'

'Teagan?' Ruth shook her head. 'I thought it was because of Hannah.'

'No.' Claire frowned. 'Why would I have stayed away because of Hannah? We had a fling, it ended. I heard she'd married. Moved on. So did I. I don't talk about it because it's nobody's business, but I got married almost ten years ago. Abby and I have a place outside London.'

Ruth was taken aback. 'You've no intention of staying in Broadway?'

'Good grief, no, why on earth would I?' Claire looked appalled. 'I know you love it in Broadway.' She waved a hand around the room. 'You even love this draughty old mausoleum. But I don't, never have, and can't wait to return to my twenty-first-century house.'

'I thought–' Ruth shook her head. She'd had it all wrong. 'I thought you hated me, blamed me for splitting you and Hannah up.'

'Really?' Claire looked slightly bemused. 'Does Hannah still think I'm yearning after her? It was twenty years ago, for good-ness' sake.'

Ruth ignored her question. 'I never did try any conversion therapy, you know, despite what Hannah may have told you.'

'Hannah wanted to believe in it, I thought it was a load of old tosh. Our relationship was never going to last, we both wanted different things. Believing in the therapy, I think, made it easier for her to end it.' Claire sighed and smiled sadly. 'So, no, I don't hate you, Ruth. I did wonder why everyone was so reserved… unfriendly even… when I came back. Teagan said it was because you all blamed me for not coming home when mother was sick.'

'Teagan told us it was because you couldn't face seeing Hannah.'

Claire's eyes widened. 'That lying cow, it wasn't anything to do with Hannah. Abby, my wife, had cancer, she was going through chemotherapy at the time. Mum knew, she understood. I hadn't been home for years, but we did meet when she and Dad came to London, and they were at our wedding.'

'Teagan…' Ruth couldn't believe they'd been taken in by the lies the woman had spun all those years. 'You know she told everyone you wouldn't see them, and blamed Marcie's illness on the stress of it all.'

'She what?' Claire's voice went up several octaves. 'I knew she was a wicked cow, but that goes beyond everything. I tried to tell Mum, but she wouldn't hear a word against her. She knew I hated Teagan and would get rid of her if I could. That's why she made Dad promise to keep her on.'

'Teagan was clever, she whispered comments in the right ears and like Chinese whispers, these became distorted along the way.'

'But I guess I was always the villain of the piece.'

'Yes.' Ruth sighed. 'I'm afraid you were.'

'I never realised she hated me quite that much.' Claire got to her feet. 'Luckily for me, I'll soon be gone and she'll be your problem.'

CHAPTER FIFTY-SEVEN

R uth knew she was being dismissed but she couldn't go without knowing the truth. 'Jocelyn said Alan looked ghastly, that he was confused and called her Marcie. I need to know the truth.'

Claire dropped back on the sofa. 'For convenience, Dad is using the hospital bed they bought when Mum was sick. Perhaps it gives the wrong impression. And the night light he likes to keep on does make his skin a ghastly colour which wouldn't have helped.'

'She said he called her Marcie?'

Claire frowned in thought. 'I suppose...'

'What?'

'My mother's clothes were all disposed of to various charities etc, but I found a stack of cotton pyjamas in the airing cupboard under some sheets. I was going to give them away but didn't. When Jocelyn stayed, I gave her a pair to sleep in. Mum liked wildly-patterned pyjamas, if Dad had woken in the middle of the night and saw a woman wearing a pair, he may have imagined he was seeing his dead wife.'

Ruth's face cleared. 'That makes sense. Jocelyn is the type

of person who wants to see the worst in people.' Ruth desperately wanted to see for herself that Claire was telling her the truth, that Alan really was okay, and at the same time, afraid she would find him changed beyond recognition, Jocelyn's description of a cachectic man lingering in her head despite Claire's assurance. 'Can I see him?'

The hesitation was brief, but it was there. 'Dad has been through so much. He would hate the idea of Jocelyn coming into his room in the middle of the night, staring at him when he was at his most vulnerable. You know what a private man he is better than anyone, Ruth. Give me a day to explain to him about her, you, and that nasty devious Teagan. Come back tomorrow. I'll leave you together to sort things out then, I promise.'

'Okay, it'll give me time to get my head around things too.' Ruth pointed towards the muffins. 'I know someone in the West Mercia Police to talk to about those. He can tell us if we're right. Would that be okay?'

'Sure, but I think you've probably let Jocelyn's tall tales and downright lies get to you.' Claire got to her feet again, crossed to a sideboard and pulled open a drawer. A moment later she returned with a plastic bag and emptied the contents of the plate inside. 'You may as well take the lot,' she said, tying a knot in the top and handing it over.

Ruth got to her feet. 'This is all of them?' When Claire nodded, Ruth held them up. 'They look so innocent, maybe I'm simply seeing too much into what she said, but–' She looked closer at the muffins through the plastic. '–she said she'd cooked up a solution so if it wasn't this, what could it be?'

'She was probably winding you up. Best to ignore people like her.'

'Yes... but there was something about her, you know, I remember feeling a little scared at one stage and I don't scare easily.'

'Forget about her.' Claire tapped the bag. 'I'd forget about them too. Give them back to me and I'll dump them in the bin to be on the safe side.'

But Ruth hung on tight and shook her head. 'I'd be happier making sure.'

'Fine, whatever you think's right.' Claire tilted her head to the door. 'I'll see you out. Come back tomorrow, around the same time.'

Ruth turned on the front doorstep with a smile that lit her face. 'Tomorrow. Thank you.'

Later she couldn't remember the walk home but she'd a feeling she might have floated. Everything was going to be okay. Alan wanted her; she was going to have a chance at that happy ever after.

CHAPTER FIFTY-EIGHT

Claire stood staring out the door for several minutes after Ruth left. Such a strange tale she'd told. How much was exaggeration, a tortuous version of the truth, and how much was plain lying, she'd probably never know. Three months in a small town had turned Claire's brain cells to mush, or maybe it was simply that she missed Abby so much. So many years together, sparking off one another, challenging each other's thinking. Two sides of one whole, Claire was diminished without her.

When Claire had decided to come to Broadway, she'd never expected to have to stay for so long, but Covid had had that effect on life – it turned it upside down. Abby hadn't wanted her to come but Claire had missed being with her mother in the final days, she didn't want to miss being with her father. To be with him at the end, she'd put up with that evil monster, Teagan.

Evil. She'd not forgotten Teagan's sly pinches on her skinny child's arm when nobody was looking. Or the bemused expression on her mother's face when she found yet another of her precious ornaments broken. Teagan would swear she'd no idea who did it while making an obvious effort not to look in Claire's direction. A child's innocence was no defence against an evil woman determined on a course of action Claire could never understand.

Later, she wondered if, even then, Teagan had seen her as a deviant or whether she simply hated having a child in her precious manor house. Claire often wondered if that was one of the reasons she disliked the house herself.

She went back to the living room, wiped the spilt tea from the table with one of the serviettes and picked up the tray. Teagan would look at the empty plate and smirk at their indulgence.

Claire remembered the tin Jocelyn had given her. She'd put it in the kitchen without opening it. Had there only been four inside or had Teagan helped herself?

Carrying the tray, Claire pushed open the kitchen door with the toe of her shoe. The housekeeper was sitting where she often was, at the big pine kitchen table with a book open before her. She was a prolific reader, one book after the other, Mills and Boon romances, every single time.

Claire put the tray down on the other end of the table. It was as much as she intended to do, clearing it away was what Teagan was paid for. She did little else. 'I have to admit, those muffins were absolutely delicious, we devoured each one. I'm sorry I didn't think to ask Jocelyn for the recipe.'

'Humph.' Teagan turned down the corner of her page and got to her feet.

'I must get you a bookmark some time.' Claire shook her head at the book sacrilege and without another word left the kitchen. She stayed outside the door, listening as she heard Teagan filling the kettle. A creature of regimented habit, it was time for her tea break.

And she never had tea without something sweet to go with it.

Claire waited until she was sure Teagan would be sitting at the table, her head buried in her book, the mug of tea close by and whatever indulgence she'd chosen on a plate beside her, then she pushed through the door with a puzzled expression on her face. 'Did I leave my mobile here?' She looked around blankly. 'No? Where on earth did I leave it?'

Back outside, she leaned against the door and smiled. She hoped Teagan would enjoy the two muffins she'd taken. Hoped she ate every single crumb.

And more, she hoped Ruth was right and they were poisoned.

CHAPTER FIFTY-NINE

Two days following the discovery of my late husband's body, I was sitting in the living room of the apartment, an A4 pad open on the table in front of me. The end of the pen I was using was well chewed as I sought for inspiration. I wanted the décor to be totally different to the bland minimalist scheme Kasper and his first wife had chosen.

In the year I'd lived there, I'd added colour and interest where I could – a painting, fabulous cushion covers, a piece of artwork by a sculptor I admired. But the fabric of the apartment remained as it was – dull and bland. I planned to change it completely so when friends came to visit they'd *oooh* when they saw the view and *aaah* when they noticed the décor.

Thanks to Kasper's generous pensions I didn't need to work, but I'd thought about using the apartment to launch myself as an interior designer to a select few recommended clients. As I chewed the end of the pen and looked out the window, I was picturing clients fighting to hire me. It was a heady thought.

The doorbell interrupted my daydream of fame and celebrity and I almost regretted telling Tracy I needed time alone to absorb my loss. Truth was she was driving me nuts, but

I had to admit, she took her role of supportive friend seriously. Had she been there, she'd have rushed to deal with whoever was calling.

Expecting to see one of my friends on the small security screen, I drew a sharp breath to see DI Cosgrave staring into the camera as if he were looking directly at me. The sensation was so strong it had me stumble a few steps backward. My gaze shifted to my mobile and I wondered if I had time to contact Tracy, get her to rush over to be with me. *Stupid, calm down.* The detective had said he might have more questions. I'd nothing to be afraid of. My tracks were well hidden.

I took a deep breath and pressed the button beside the screen to speak. 'Hello?' One word, cool, slightly puzzled as if I really didn't recognise the sharp-eyed detective.

'It's DI Cosgrave, Mrs Dexter, may I come up?'

'Of course.' As I pressed the button to release the front door, I glanced down at what I was wearing. The black skinny jeans were okay but since I'd not bothered with a bra, the black silk tank top didn't leave much to the imagination.

I hurried downstairs. I'd been sleeping in the spare bedroom. To my surprise, the stain on the floor of the main bedroom made me feel squeamish, until I had the carpet replaced I couldn't call it mine. But the wardrobes were. After Tracy had finally left me in peace the day before, I'd spent an hour bagging up all Kasper's clothes. I'd shoved them into his precious office until I could organise having them taken away.

There wasn't time to be fussy. I grabbed a dark print shirt and pulled it on. Buttoned almost to the neck, it made me look drab but suitably funereal. With my plan for the day being to lounge around I hadn't bothered with having a shower or washing my hair that morning, nor had I applied any make-up. It would help paint a perfect picture of a grieving widow.

I stood in the hallway until the apartment doorbell rang,

waiting a full minute before crossing to answer it. 'I'm sorry,' I said, pulling the door open. 'It seems to take me so much longer to do things these days.'

He wasn't alone. Behind him stood a stocky grim-featured woman. 'Detective Inspector Cosgrave and...?' I raised an eyebrow, trying to keep my face carefully neutral while my insides squirmed. Two of them. Did that indicate something more than simply questions to tick off a list?

'Detective Sergeant Burke.' The woman's voice was rough, unpleasant. It was a surprising match for her face.

'Do come in.' I stood back and waved them inside with a lady-of-the-manor air I knew I was copying from Claire. It almost made me smile to think of her. I shut the door and turned to lead the way up the stairs. In the living room, I hesitated. The three sofas, positioned to make the most of the view, were a comfortable convivial place to sit for a chat. It would show I wasn't in any way worried.

The dining table, on the other hand, was more formal and official. Businesslike. Plus, there was something in the female detective's eyes I didn't like. Perhaps she looked at every person they questioned as if the guillotine was their next stop. Sitting at the table would allow me to keep my trembling hands from sight.

I took a seat at the end of the table. From there I could look out at the view. It would calm me if things became difficult. 'Would you like some tea or coffee?'

'No, thanks.' Cosgrave spoke for both. 'Just to keep everything official, DS Burke is going to read you your rights, Mrs Dexter. Okay?'

Pressing my hands together tightly, painfully, allowed me to keep my expression from changing as the detective, in her ugly gravelly voice, read me my rights.

CHAPTER SIXTY

D S Burke rested her spade-like hands on the table, her fingernails short and not particularly clean. 'Do you understand your rights as I have informed you?'

I was fixated on her hands, and it wasn't until she repeated herself that I looked up and met her eyes. 'Yes. They're hardly complex.' Ignoring her, I turned to Cosgrave. 'Do I need to get a solicitor?'

'You have the right, and we'll be happy to wait until one arrives but that does require you coming back to the station.'

Was that a threat? Maybe reading me my rights was simply a precaution, something that was done as a routine. I regretted not having watched more crime shows. Maybe if I had, I'd know what I was supposed to do.

I smiled as if it was all one big joke. 'No, it's okay. Let's get on with it.'

Cosgrave nodded as if it was what he'd expected me to say. 'There's a few things we need to clear up.' He reached into an inside pocket, drew out a folded sheet of paper, unfolded it and slid it across the table. 'This is a copy of the note found under your husband's body. A handwriting expert compared the writing to something we know your husband wrote so we know it to be genuine.' He tapped it. 'You asserted that he wrote this in revenge for your affair, is that correct?'

'Yes. He was very angry about it.'

'And there's no truth in his claim that you left him to die, and you were responsible for his first wife's death?'

'Of course not!' I glared at him. 'That would make me a monster, detective.'

'Indeed.' His voice remained calm. 'I spoke to the team investigating Laurie Dexter's death. There is no CCTV on the road where she was killed. As a result, they weren't able to identify the car or the driver, and despite extensive investigating they were no further towards making an arrest. It was being looked at as a hit and run. When I put it to them that it may have been murder, they started looking at it from a different angle.' He reached into his pocket for a second time and took out another folded sheet of paper. 'It's a relatively quiet area at night and all traffic accessing and exiting needs to pass one of two junctions. The team had already looked at this, but only at a time frame immediately prior to and after Laurie Dexter was killed. I asked them to widen the time frame to an hour before and after, and guess what?' He unfolded the page he held and pushed it across the table.

'This car–' He tapped the sheet. '–was seen at the junction a little over an hour before, and the same car slightly over an hour later.'

I forced my lips to move in some semblance of a smile. 'It seems a stretch to me, but then I'm not a detective. It would be wonderful to find out who killed Laurie, a shame Kasper didn't live to know.'

'Mr Dexter also wrote that the car used to kill his wife was in a lock-up.' His eyes flicked to the woman sitting to his right. 'DS Burke is incredibly tenacious.'

I looked at the smirk on her face. She was enjoying watching me squirm.

'Really.'

'Yes, she spent several hours on the phone ringing every lock-up in the city but as is often the way, success is its own reward.'

Burke grunted. 'It was one of the more low-end ones. No on-site security. One large clearly-marked CCTV camera at the entrance.' The smirk grew into a wide smile. 'The owner is a bit of a thug, but not a stupid one. As well as the obvious camera, there's a barely visible one further inside.' She nodded at Cosgrave who, again, reached into his inside pocket.

I wondered how many more sheets of paper were going to be taken out and which one was going to seal my future. I looked at the one he pushed towards me and almost laughed. 'That could be anyone!'

'It could, but we think it's you, Mrs Dexter.' He pulled the sheet back, folded it and put it away. 'We've applied for a warrant for the lock-up owner's files. We'll have it tomorrow.'

I hid my smile. I paid cash, using a fake name. The files wouldn't get them anything.

'We've also applied for a warrant for your fingerprints, Mrs Dexter.'

They wouldn't have missed my body going suddenly rigid. They were detectives, after all, they'd know the signs. My fingerprints would be on the damn handle of the lock-up. I was so sure they'd never find it, I'd not bothered using gloves or cleaning it before I left. Why hadn't I? What an idiot I was!

You were always a fool. Whack!

I stood so abruptly I startled both detectives, Burke rising, her fists coming up pugnaciously. When I laughed and waved to the kitchen, she sank back onto the chair, a slightly embarrassed look on her face. 'I need a drink. Are you sure I can't get you anything?'

When they shook their heads, I went to the kitchen and made a pot of tea.

You're a bad'un, always were, always will be. You'll end up behind bars, mark my words. Whack!

'That's not going to happen.'

'What?' Cosgrave sat forward, a frown creasing his brow.

I hadn't realised I'd said the words aloud and shook my head. 'Nothing, sorry, I was thinking of my mother.' I reached into the cupboard for the cakes I'd put there earlier and stayed at the breakfast bar. Eating cake. Washing it down with cup after cup of tea. Staring out at the view I loved. I'd almost had it all.

'It's lock-up number seven,' I said around a mouthful of cake. 'My fingerprints will be on it so there's no point in putting off the inevitable, is there?'

I smiled at the startled expression on Cosgrave's face. Perhaps he wasn't used to things falling into place quite so easily. I decided to make his day and confess everything. 'I met Laurie in the gym. She was a nice woman but an airhead. Honestly, she barely knew me and was telling me everything about her wonderful life, the fabulous apartment she lived in, the jewellery her doting husband bought her. Then I saw him. He was such a handsome man. I wanted him, the lifestyle, the happy ever after they seemed to have found, and I set out to get it.' I almost choked when I saw their horrified expressions, a paroxysm of coughing sending crumbs flying from my mouth.

'What about your husband, did you kill him?' Cosgrave had taken out his notebook and was frantically scribbling.

I cleared my throat noisily. 'He had a massive stroke.' Another swallow of tea, another bite of cake. 'Granted, he might have survived had I rung for an ambulance straight away, but I had to face facts, I wasn't born to be anyone's nursemaid.'

'So you left him to die?'

'To be precise, I waited for him to die. When he didn't oblige, I went away and came back a few hours later. He still wasn't dead, but it was only a matter of time, so I returned to Broadway and stayed there for several days. To make sure.'

Cosgrave stopped writing and looked at me. 'To make sure?'

'That he was dead.' I swallowed another piece of cake. 'You sound shocked, I can't believe this is the worst you've come across, detective.'

Cosgrave shook his head. 'Not a lot shocks me anymore, but do you really need to keep eating while you're telling us all this?'

I smiled sweetly. 'Oh yes, I think so.' I picked up the last lemon muffin and bit into it. 'After all, it might be the last chance I have, to eat something so good.'

CHAPTER SIXTY-ONE

D I Cosgrave sat behind his desk, his hands clasped behind his head. He was alone. DS Burke had gone out to get them both some decent coffee. Caffeine might clear his head. Something needed to because it was buzzing with conflicting thoughts... satisfaction with the perfect outcome to their case, the added bonus of solving a hit and run which hadn't precisely become a cold case but was certainly getting a bit chilly... and the irritating sensation that he'd missed something crucial. That he'd somehow been manipulated.

Jocelyn Dexter... there was something about her that made him uneasy. It wasn't simply the way she'd caved in so easily and confessed to everything... it was something more than that... as if she was one step ahead of him and looking back with a smile at his tardiness.

Burke would call it a flight of fancy. He dropped his hands to the desk. Maybe she was right. He should simply be content with a job well done.

There was still no sign of coffee ten minutes later when his desk phone rang. He picked it up absently. 'DI Cosgrave.'

'Hello. It's DI Ollie Fearon, West Mercia Police.'

'Okay. What can I do for you?' Cosgrave hoped he didn't sound unhelpful. He firmly believed in inter-force co-operation, but did it have to be that day when his brain was already scrambled? When there was no response, he tried to put more enthusiasm into his voice and rephrased his question. 'How can I help you?'

'I'm based in Evesham. We've had a bit of a weird one and it may be that you can help us.'

The sound of a drink being slurped reminded Cosgrave he was still waiting for his and he looked hopefully towards the door. There was no sign of Burke.

'Two days ago,' Fearon said, 'the housekeeper of Broadway Manor, Teagan Parsons, was found dead.'

The mention of Broadway pushed thoughts of coffee from Cosgrave's head. Broadway, where Jocelyn Dexter had spent several days. He didn't believe in coincidence. 'Okay, go on.'

A loud sigh came down the line. 'It's the strangest case. The doctor attending the scene couldn't see any cause for the woman's death and initially indicated it might have been a massive heart attack or stroke but then...'

Cosgrave pressed the phone to his ear and waited.

'The woman who found her, Claire Brandon, said the housekeeper might've been poisoned. We've had the results of the post-mortem, and it seems she was right.'

'Poisoned!'

'Yes. But you haven't heard the best bit yet. From interviews with all involved, it appears the motive was to get rid of both the victim and Claire Brandon to facilitate romantic relationships between two other women and their partners. How about that for a weird motive for murder?'

'Odd all right.' It could be someone else. Not Jocelyn Dexter. Cosgrave couldn't picture her killing for such an altruistic, if not downright bizarre reason.

But he was wrong.

'Our prime suspect, Jocelyn Dexter, left Broadway the same day. I contacted the Met to arrange to have her taken into custody and imagine my surprise to discover she was already under arrest.'

'Yes. Shit.' Cosgrave was finding himself unusually stuck for words.

'No, oleander.' Fearon cackled. 'Sorry, I'd better explain... Dexter poisoned Teagan Parsons using oleander from a neighbour's garden.'

'What!' Cosgrave was fascinated by poisons, especially ones easily found. 'That's a new one on me.'

'Me too, but according to the experts, every part of the plant is poisonous. We've had a warrant issued to search Dexter's cottage. We'll find the proof there.' He belched, hastily coughing loudly to cover it. 'So does our murder trump whatever you have her for?'

'No.' Cosgrave was almost amused. 'Dream on, she's confessed to two here.'

'Two!' Fearon whistled loudly enough to make Cosgrave move the phone away from his ear. 'I suppose we were lucky. Claire Brandon had started to eat the poisoned cakes the Dexter woman had brought as a gift. If she'd finished them, both she and Teagan Parsons would have been found dead and no one the wiser. It was a visiting neighbour who warned Brandon, but neither were aware the housekeeper had taken two of them for herself.' Another slurp drifted down the line but this time Cosgrave wasn't distracted by thoughts of coffee.

The clear image of Jocelyn munching through cakes as she spoke to them only hours before hit Cosgrave with the clarity he'd been looking for. That was what was so wrong about the whole interview with her. The damn cakes.

'Listen, Fearon, I'm going to have to ring you back, something urgent has come up.' He cut the connection and redialled the custody suite. 'Come on... come on,' he muttered as it rang. When it was answered he didn't waste time with preliminaries. 'It's DI Cosgrave. Have you checked the new woman recently... Jocelyn Dexter?'

There was a crackle of paper on the line before the custody sergeant answered. 'A routine check was done almost an hour ago. No problems reported.'

'Check on her again. I'm on my way.'

Cosgrave bumped into Burke who was coming in, a take-away coffee in each hand. 'Drop them, come on, there's something...'

Burke wasn't one who needed to be told twice. She didn't precisely drop the coffees but rammed them into the chest of a passing constable without explanation and followed Cosgrave at a run.

The custody sergeant was leaning against the desk carelessly tossing a bunch of keys from hand to hand and speaking to another officer.

'Have you checked her?' Cosgrave asked, looking down the corridor towards the cells.

'I checked the CCTV, she's asleep, same as she was an hour ago.' The sergeant held up the keys he was holding. 'I was on my way to check in person.' With a nod to the officer he'd been speaking to, he turned and headed down the corridor, stopping outside the third cell. He opened the viewing slot and checked before inserting the key in the lock.

The opening of the door didn't disturb the woman who lay curled up on the bunk, her hair loose around her face. Neither did Cosgrave's sharp, 'Mrs Dexter?' or Burke's loud gasp.

It was the custody sergeant who hurried across the cell. Cosgrave stood in the doorway, hands curled in frustration.

He'd known there was something amiss. 'The cakes she was eating, they were poisoned,' he said to Burke.

'Shit!'

'She's not breathing,' the custody sergeant said, reaching down to shake Jocelyn's shoulder. The response was instant and dramatic. Jocelyn groaned and jerked into a sitting position. Burke gave a startled yelp. The sergeant took a hasty step backward. It wasn't far enough, nor quick enough to avoid the orange-tinged yellow projectile that shot from Jocelyn's mouth. It hit him in the chest, splashing outward and upward, seemingly endless.

'Aaargh!' He stumbled away, wiping gunk from his face with his hand.

'If her head starts spinning around, I'm out of here,' Burke said, stepping into the corridor.

'She's not possessed, it's the poison. Go,' he said to her, 'ring for an ambulance, looks like we're not too late.'

The sergeant was bent over the small sink trying to scrub his face. There wasn't much of him that wasn't covered in gloop. Disgusting, and stinking. Cosgrave screwed up his nose. 'You'd better go, get cleaned up.'

Strangely, apart from her mouth, the projectile nature of the vomiting episode had left Jocelyn clean. Once the sergeant had gone, Cosgrave wet some toilet tissue and handed it to her.

'Thank you,' she said, taking it and wiping her face.

He wasn't sure she'd thank him for what he was going to say next. 'There's an ambulance on its way. You'll be okay.'

'That's what I was afraid of.'

———

I lay back and sighed. 'How did you know?' When he didn't immediately answer I turned to look at him. He was standing

275

VALERIE KEOGH

with a shoulder resting against the wall looking at me with a puzzled expression.

'I had a call from a colleague in the West Mercia Police. He wanted to talk to you about the death of a housekeeper in Broadway. As soon as he mentioned poisoned cake, I guessed.'

Teagan. My smile of satisfaction faded quickly as I realised he'd only mentioned one death. 'Just the housekeeper?'

'Yes.' He hesitated as if unsure how much to tell me. 'The other woman, she didn't eat any of them.'

A good outcome. Distance had given me a better perspective. I knew Teagan had been the one in my bedroom that night, I guessed it was she who'd searched my cottage. A devious, conniving woman, I'd have bet on it too that it was she who rang Hannah's husband, not Claire. Perhaps with Teagan out of the picture, the other women could find their way. 'For my first attempt at trying to do something for someone else, I suppose it wasn't bad.' I smiled at the detective's surprise. 'You're thinking I don't seem like the altruistic type?'

'Something like that.'

I folded the flat pillow in half and tucked it back under my head. My stomach was churning but there was nothing left inside to attempt an exit. 'I surprised myself too.' I remembered Hannah's sweet smile when she looked at her husband, and the photograph of Ruth with Alan Brandon. Remembered feeling envious. The stirrings of regret for things I had done. I shut my eyes to block the tears.

'You had to have been there.'

THE END

ACKNOWLEDGEMENTS

A huge thanks, as ever, to Bloodhound Books, especially Betsy Reavley, Tara Lyons, Heather Fitt, Morgen Bailey and Ian Skewis.

There would be no point at all in writing if I didn't have such wonderful readers – thank you to those who read and to those who review and blog – all much appreciated.

Writing would be a lonely business without writing buddies – as always, grateful thanks to the author Jenny O'Brien who reads an early version of my books to give me honest feedback and who generally ignores my 'this one is rubbish' cry. My US author friend, Leslie Bratspis, for her ongoing support, and to many others including: Jim Ody, Pam Lecky, Keri Beevis, Anita Waller, Judith Baker, Nathan Moss, Pat Gitt and Mary Karpin. These and many others make being an author much more fun.

Joyce Evans – I hope I did Stephen Melville Evans justice. It was a pleasure to write him in.

I'm a member of the Facebook group, The Paperback Writers. When I asked if anyone would like their name used in this book, I was inundated with offers – so a grateful thanks to all whose names I've borrowed.

And last, but never least, a big thank you to my amazing family and friends.

If you'd like to contact me – and I love to hear from readers – you can contact me here:

Facebook: www.facebook.com/valeriekeoghnovels
Twitter: @valeriekeogh1
Instagram: valeriekeogh2

A NOTE FROM THE PUBLISHER

Thank you for reading this book. If you enjoyed it please do consider leaving a review on Amazon to help others find it too.

We hate typos. All of our books have been rigorously edited and proofread, but sometimes mistakes do slip through. If you have spotted a typo, please do let us know and we can get it amended within hours.

info@bloodhoundbooks.com

Printed in Great Britain
by Amazon

48505780R00162